LONG
SLOW
BURN

LONG
SLOW
BURN

GRANT FOSTER

alyson books
los angeles | new york

MANUFACTURED IN THE UNITED STATES OF AMERICA.

THIS TRADE PAPERBACK ORIGINAL IS PUBLISHED BY ALYSON PUBLICATIONS,
P.O. BOX 4371, LOS ANGELES, CALIFORNIA 90078-4371.
DISTRIBUTION IN THE UNITED KINGDOM BY
TURNAROUND PUBLISHER SERVICES LTD.,
UNIT 3, OLYMPIA TRADING ESTATE, COBURG ROAD, WOOD GREEN,
LONDON N22 6TZ ENGLAND.

FIRST EDITION: AUGUST 2001

01 02 03 04 05 a 10 9 8 7 6 5 4 3 2 1

ISBN 1-55583-559-7

COVER DESIGN BY MATT SAMS.
COVER PHOTOGRAPHY BY PHILIP PIROLO.

CONTENTS

LONG SLOW BURN

I stood in the middle of the brick terrace at the rear of the house, scanning the horizon. The reports of doom I'd been hearing on an almost hourly basis were hard to credit. Nothing threatening loomed—no tongues of flame split the azure bowl of sky suspended above the parched, golden landscape; no smoky pall tainted the still, hot air. The radio continued broadcasting reports that the world was on fire, but the holocaust had yet to reach this quiet suburban enclave. And yet, while the nested wrens warbled softly in the oleanders,

birds sing   *poisonous evergreen*

another conflagration—one whose heat had already singed me—lurked in the wings, licking its chops, threatening to consume me utterly.

Three days! It had taken only three circuits of the earth on its axis to cast me adrift, to sever all the ties I thought had bound me to my time and place. I looked at the geraniums clustered at the edge of the pool, watching their scarlet petals fall and float like confetti on the water. The sun gilded the surface, obscuring the depths with an underlying silver shroud. I squinted, dazzled. It was a frighteningly apt metaphor for my former life.

When I drove out of the city on Friday evening, I had seen a hazy veil of smoke in the far distance. It was August, the season of wildfire, and the tinder-dry grass was aching to burn. Every radio station broadcast nonstop bulletins, warning of the approaching Armageddon. I tired of the babble and crammed a disc into the player, preferring to meet the end of the world with Ella and Count Basie.

When I turned off the highway and drove along the eucalyptus-shaded streets of Silverwood Estates, it was immediately obvious that the demon Chaos had been loosed on our bland little suburban world. The front doors of houses were thrown open, exposing the interiors, while the occupants filled all available vehicles with consumer goods of every description. Children were running back and forth across manicured lawns like miniature Noahs, frantically herding frazzled family pets toward the ark of the family car. By the time I pulled into the quiet cul-de-sac where I lived, I had been forced up onto sidewalks twice to avoid head-on collisions with drivers maddened by fear of some yet invisible threat.

"Jonas! Where the hell have you been?" Beth, my wife of almost 10 years, was standing in the middle of a bed of petunias, the suitcases she carried trailing the legs and arms of assorted garments through the dirt. Her blond hair, usually immaculately coiffed, was hanging in lank strings around her face. Sweat glistened on her forehead. "It's after 7 o'clock."

"I was at the gym. I always go to the gym on Friday. Remember?"

"Oh. The gym. Of course, Jonas. Mustn't neglect your perfect pectoral muscles. Or was it your deltoids today?" Her voice was pitched too high, and she was talking too fast. She was tightly wound.

"I didn't realize you expected me to be home early, Beth. You know I go to the gym because Dr. Lazarus told me I could either start to exercise or have a heart attack by the time I turned 40."

"I don't think he expected you to turn it into a lifestyle, Jonas." I shrugged. We'd had this discussion/argument a hundred times before. I had gone to the fitness center reluctantly at first, but then I quickly discovered that it offered all of the therapeutic benefits that my aptly named doctor had described. I found comfort from the dual stress of work and domesticity in the Zen-like repetitiveness of my routines. My blood pressure dropped, my heart muscle grew strong, and my body became a pleasure rather than a burden—to me, at least. For her part, Beth seemed to resent the fact that I had found something wherein I was complete, in and of myself.

"I didn't realize we were leaving town this weekend," I said, bringing the conversation back to the moment. Beth flashed me a baleful glance and lugged the suitcases to the back of her station wagon.

"It's the fire, Jonas. The goddamned fire." She turned to me, her arms rigid at her sides. "It's been on the news all day. Over a hundred homes were destroyed yesterday in Perrysville. There are three out-of-control brushfires in the county, and they're all headed this way."

"I didn't see signs of any trouble on my way out from the city," I said doubtfully. I had long ago stopped believing everything I heard on the news.

"I'm not going to take any chances with my life or Debbie's," Beth snapped, waving her hand at me dismissively. "If you're not too tired from your gym experience, I'd appreciate some help."

"Dadde-e-e!" Debbie, my 6-year-old daughter, came barreling out the front door, a copy of her mother in body and spirit. "Mr. Doodle won't come out from under the bed. He'll burn to death if you don't come get him!" Mr. Doodle was a Persian cat that had belonged to Beth before we married. Beth and Debbie loved him dearly. In my opinion, his only use was to provide a market for the producers of cat food and litter. Mr. Doodle returned my feelings of disdain, rarely acknowledging my existence except to sneer at me. "Daddy, don't let him die!"

"No one's going to die, honey."

"But mommy said…"

"I'm sure Mommy didn't mean whatever she may have said. Did you, Mommy?" Beth curled her lip and stalked back into the house.

I spent the next hour hauling whatever Beth pointed at out to the car. I was on my way back inside to inform her that the station wagon was full to overflowing when I noticed Harv, Rick, and a couple of other neighbors standing in the street not far from my driveway, deep in conversation. Harv looked up, saw me, and motioned me to join them.

"Evening, Jonas."

"Guys." I scanned their faces. They looked more exasperated than alarmed. "Are you all packing to leave?"

"The radio reports have been bad," Rick said.

"Houses are burning out of control on the outskirts of Bakersfield," another man added, his brow furrowed with worry. "The missus is completely freaked."

"Laura is hell-bent to get out of here too." Harv scuffed his toe through the gravel at the end of the drive. "I'm worried about vandals. All these houses sitting empty will be like a magnet for any asshole who wants to drive through and break in."

"I'm not going anywhere. I'll keep an eye on things." We all turned at the sound of an unfamiliar voice. I heard the confused mutterings, saw the looks of thinly veiled suspicion and dislike flicker across my neighbors' faces. I felt a little twitch in my gut as well, but it wasn't anything I could pinpoint as dislike.

"Kent Radke," the stranger said, stepping into the loose circle with outstretched hand. No one refused to shake with him, but eye contact was kept to a minimum. We were all aware of him, at least of his existence. He lived in a house on the far side of the cul-de-sac, with a woman whom I assumed to be his wife. There were no children, at least none that I had ever seen. "Don't get me wrong. I'm no hero. I'll leave when there's a need. I'm just not in any hurry."

Radke's offer was accepted with mumbled thanks, then the group quickly broke up and the men returned to their packing and other preparations. Radke stood watching them, then turned on his heel and strode back to his side of the cul-de-sac. I walked back towards the house, bemused by what I had just witnessed. No one had questioned Radke's ability to make good on his offer. No one had expressed any concern for his welfare or given any indication that they would offer to help him in any way. Then it came to me—they were afraid of him. Every last man. Afraid and intimidated.

It didn't make sense. There was nothing bellicose about the man. There was, however, something very physical. He was big and handsome, and he was shameless in his habit of displaying himself. He mowed his own lawn—something of an anomaly in the neighborhood—and compounded the crime by doing it shirtless, displaying a body that could have served as a model for a sculpture of one of the more muscular Greek gods. A gold hoop in his left ear, a matching bauble piercing his left tit, and a tattoo representing a strand of barbed wire encircling his right biceps added to the aura of danger surrounding him.

Harv had once confided that he thought Radke was just out trying to get our wives all stirred up. I had countered his ridiculous assertion by noting that the woman he lived with looked like a model. What I didn't mention was that Harv's wife hardly seemed the type that a man like Radke would go out of his way to inflame.

Two hours later I stood watching as a motorized caravan bearing the entire population of Silverwood Estates snaked beneath the eucalyptus trees in the gathering dusk. I had driven with Beth to the main road, where we waited while two neighbors who had tapped bumpers distractedly exchanged insurance information. Just as Beth was starting to ease into the traffic, I opened my door and got out.

"What are you doing?" she hissed, popping the station wagon back into park.

"I'm going to stay," I said, surprising no one more than myself. I hadn't known I was going to get out until I was standing there on the edge of the road, looking in through the window at my wife and daughter. "Nothing's going to happen. If the fire even gets close, I'll hop in my car and make a quick getaway." Beth gave me a look. The reference to my car had only raised her level of irritation. I'd bought the sleek Mercedes SL 600 for myself to celebrate my last promotion, and she had never forgiven me for it. It wasn't a suitable car for a man with a family, she had said.

"You can take your fucking car and drive it to hell." On that cheerful note, my wife drove away, spraying me with dust and small pebbles from the roadway.

I turned back to the house. There were no streetlights, and with everyone gone, the darkness was absolute. Or so I thought at first. Gradually, my eyes adjusted, and the stars, assisted by a sliver of moon, lit my way home.

The first thing I did was turn off the air-conditioning unit. With no other noises around, its mechanical hum disturbed the night. I opened the windows, grabbed a beer, and stepped out to the pool. I sat for a while and watched the moon on the water. I felt restless, unaccustomed to the solitude. It was as though I expected something to happen, but what?

I stood, stripped, dived into the pool. The chill of the water tightened my muscles, made me suddenly conscious of my body. For years I hadn't given my body much thought. I'd been too busy, first going to school, afterwards making my way up the corporate ladder. It was only after my body had rebelled against me that I had been forced to take notice of it—or else.

The gym had changed all that, made me think of myself as a complex, potentially well-maintained machine. My resentment at this new intrusion on my accustomed routine had faded, replaced by a narcissistic fascination with the way my body responded to my efforts. I had evolved from wincing whenever I caught a glimpse of my reflection, to standing purposely in front of full-length mirrors, watching my muscles swell and flex as I worked them.

I turned my head from side to side as I swam laps in the pool, watching the moon-gilt water slide over the swell of muscle in my arms and shoulders. As I touched the edge of the pool with my fingertips and somersaulted around underwater to begin the next lap, my thoughts flashed back to the gym that evening. I was working my arms, doing countless curls, using varying weights. I loved to watch the curve of muscle in my upper arm, innocuous at first, grow to almost frightening proportions as I pushed myself to the limit. The normally pale skin flushed with blood as the striations of muscle became increasingly visible beneath. Veins that normally ran like subterranean rivers swelled, finger-size, snaking across the tortured mass of quivering flesh.

I was on the verge of switching from my left arm to my right when I looked up. A man across from me was watching my arm intently, tracing the curve of his upper lip with the tip of his pink tongue. He was young, good-looking, his curly hair a ruddy blond, his face sprinkled with freckles. His eyes were a couple of shades lighter than his blue tank top, glittering like arctic ice. His body was impeccable. Our eyes locked briefly and he smiled at me. It was a warm smile, inviting intimacy. I dropped the weight I was holding with a resounding clang, then gripped it with my right hand and began relentlessly torturing my other arm.

Afterward, in the showers, the smiling man took his place opposite me in the steamy tiled enclosure. Seven of the 10 nozzles had been claimed, and the men were making desultory conversation while soaping away the sweat of their exertions. I nodded at the ones I recognized, exchanged greetings with a man who worked for the same firm as I, then concentrated on soaping my armpits.

"Great arms, man." I looked up. The smiling man's eyes flickered up and down my naked body. "You've really got great arms."

"Thanks," I replied, acknowledging his praise. The fingers of my right hand curled against my palm and I flexed, making my biceps jump, pumping veins back into sharp relief. It was a childish braggart's response, but it was so natural that it was automatic. His smile broadened and he slowly ran his hand down over his tight, nicely defined torso, from his throat to the pubes that curled around his prick.

I said nothing else to him, but I didn't look away. I stood there, shifting my stance, soaping my other armpit, flexing again. A man turned on the nozzle to my immediate left and stepped under the spray. I glanced at him, nodded at his grunted greeting, then looked back at my admirer.

His stance was unchanged, except for one salient detail: His cock now jutted out of his bush, angled high, the pink-ish-ivory shaft veined with blue, the knob on the end crimson. I looked at his face—it was as red as the head of his dick. He searched my face for something—confirmation?—and, not finding it, gathered up his soap and shampoo and left the showers.

"Damned queers," the man beside me muttered. "They're everywhere." I didn't answer him, but his words made me much more uncomfortable than the eyes of the smiling man.

I counted out the last three laps—98, 99, 100—then pulled myself up out of the water, arms and legs trembling with exertion. I rolled over onto my back, tucked my hands behind my head and looked up at the stars. The sky was ablaze with them, shimmering like dewdrops caught in a spider's web. I breathed deep, savoring the warm night air, fragrant with eucalyptus. *weak, listless*

I stretched languidly and ran my hands over my body. My fingertips bumped against the spongy head of my hard cock. I looked down. It was levitating an inch above my belly, bouncing up and down in time with my heartbeat. I looked around for a towel to cover myself, then realized that there was no need. I was alone with no chance of intrusion. For some reason, that knowledge triggered a wave of horniness edged with an almost teenage intensity. I curled my fingers around the swollen shaft and began to jerk off.

I probed my fantasy banks for an image to accompany my unaccustomed indulgence. My wife flashed on the screen of my eyelids briefly, but her parting remarks earlier hadn't

relating To body;
sensual

exactly encouraged <u>carnal</u> thoughts. Besides, that aspect of our lives had been in what could politely be described as a slump for almost a year. I next tried to visualize Linda, a coworker with whom I'd had a tepid affair last winter. She failed to come into focus, much as our supposed passion for one another had failed to materialize in any substantial way.

As I continued to stroke myself, a new image crept <u>unbidden</u> into my mind. It was the smiling man from the shower at the gym. His lean, sculpted physique resolved with perfect clarity on the Technicolor screen of my imagination. His pale skin flushed with pink; the coppery hairs on his legs and arms; the bellyward curve of his erection—every detail was as clear as day.

It was an image that should have disturbed me, but instead it inflamed, making my cock jerk against my palm. I fingered the knob, smeared leak along the veiny shaft. My mind's eye caressed the smiling man's body, the angular planes of his shoulders, the full, heavy curve of his pecs, the tender, nubbly texture of his tits. They were swollen, as though sucked to erection. A pale blue vein branched across his shoulder, pulsing beneath the skin. Downy hairs sprinkled the surface of his taut gut, glistening like gold.

His thick-stalked cock was throbbing, matching the rhythm of my own pounding heart. The arrow-shaped tip gleamed crimson, while weeping <u>viscous</u> goo drizzled down to his balls. His fingers skittered up and down the shaft, matching the pace of my own pumping fist. I sought out his ice-blue eyes, stared deep into them, saw fireworks as my orgasm ripped me out of the fantasy and back into the moment. I opened my eyes, stared down at my cock. It strained against the confines of my fingers, flexing wildly. My balls pulled up tight between my legs, and my muscles tensed. A final stroke, and I twitched with pleasure as warm, pungent sperm spewed out over my heaving chest and belly.

Fruitful
prolific

I smeared my seed across my chest, touched my fingers to my lips, tasting. It was salty, organic, dark, fecund. My muscles slowly relaxed, all the tension flowing out of them as I lay listening to the lapping water in the pool and the secret night sounds of insects.

* * *

I awoke early the next morning, ate a light breakfast, swam laps in the pool, then climbed out and sat on the tiled edge, letting the sun dry me. I felt electric, my limbs buzzing with pent-up energy, my skin tingling. I glanced down at my cock and saw that the unruly beast was beginning to swell again, less than eight hours since I'd serviced him last. The solitude definitely made me horny.

After weighing the merits of another orgasm, I opted for a more strenuous physical workout—at least for now. I braced my hands beneath me on the warm tiles and began to do push-ups, slow and steady, determined to reach 100. I bested my goal by 50, then collapsed, gasping for air.

"Bravo!"

"What?" I sprang up at the sound of the strange voice. "Who are…?" It was him. Radke. Kent. The man who had volunteered to stay behind and keep watch.

"Sorry to have startled you, but your front door was open. I promised to keep an eye out for vandals. Remember?" He shrugged his broad shoulders. "I thought I was the only one foolish enough to hang around waiting for the world to end."

"I, uh, changed my mind at the last minute. I don't know why." I touched my hand to my hip, then realized that I was naked. I looked around frantically for something to cover myself.

"Don't worry about it," he chuckled. "There. How's that?" He stepped out of his shorts and tossed them aside.

The equality of nakedness eased my discomfort. "I hate clothes myself. I only wore those this morning out of sheer habit. If I'd given any thought to being alone here, I would've beaten you to it. To tell you the truth, being under the watchful eye of the Silverwood Wives Club has made me a little shy." He smiled at me, a twinkle in his eyes. "I'm well aware of what the neighbors think of me, but I don't much care. I am who I am, nothing to be ashamed of, nothing to hide." He stood before me naked, hands at his sides, indeed hiding nothing.

"Uh, sure." I couldn't resist the urge to check him out. His dick, nestled beneath a glossy thatch of pubic hair, was roughly the same size as mine, which, for some strange reason, I found very comforting. Having satisfied my adolescent curiosity, I looked back at his face. I couldn't understand why my neighbors disliked him so. His expression was frank and open. He couldn't help it that he was so handsome, or that his body conformed so totally to the benchmarks that generally pass for perfection.

"Don't let me interrupt your workout, Jonas." He'd remembered my name after our hurried introductions the day before. I found myself warming to him even more.

"Oh, this isn't a serious workout, Kent." I'd remembered his name as well, not my standard behavior. It was a failing that annoyed Beth to no end. "I'm just restless."

"I know what you mean. I've run the perimeter of the subdivision twice this morning. Trouble is, I'm still a little jumpy. Must be something to do with all these empty houses." He sat down beside me on the tiles. "Do you like sit-ups?"

"Does anybody?" I looked at him and grimaced.

"Only those of us who are slightly less than sane," he replied.

"If that's the criterion, I guess I qualify."

"Want me to show you a really grueling type of sit-up?"
I nodded. He winked at me. "Watch this," he whispered con-spiratorially.

I watched. He braced his hands behind him and raised his legs in the air, toes pointed. He raised his hands and clasped them behind his head, making a very muscular V of himself, then proceeded to twist his torso from side to side, touching opposing elbows to knees. I watched the muscles in his arms and legs begin to bulge, saw the sweat begin to trickle down his sides, saw his abs rise in ridges.

"Now you try it." He had stopped, his chest rising and falling, his face flushed, his perfect body sheened with sweat.

"What the hell." I replied, bracing my hands behind me. Raising the legs was easy, but when I tucked my hands behind my head I kept tipping sideways. After several unsuc-cessful attempts, I gave up. "This doesn't seem to be happen-ing for me, at least not today."

"You just need some help." He moved closer to me. "Balance is the key with this one. Do you mind?" I shrugged, not quite sure exactly what he was planning to do that I might mind. "Brace your hands behind you." I did. "Now raise your legs." I obeyed again.

"Now for a little ballast." He straddled me, his cock and balls swinging back and forth like a pendulum. As he settled down on top of my hips, I felt the cheeks of his ass, hotter than the sun, pressing down against my flesh. His balls rolled against my belly, and the head of his cock plugged snugly into my navel. Every muscle in my body tensed.

"I, uh…" My tongue stuck to the roof of my mouth.

"Just put your hands behind your head and start hitting my tits with your elbows." I must have looked like an idiot, staring at him slack-jawed, but he just smiled and slapped his palms soundly against his pecs, leaving no doubt as to where I was supposed to aim.

"That's it, Jonas. Good." I twisted my torso to the right, bringing my left elbow into contact with his ringed nipple. I lowered my body and twisted to the left. About 20 reps into it, my legs started sinking towards the ground. He noticed and reached back, pressing his palms against the underside of my thighs, applying a slight upward pressure. "That's better, Jonas. Give me 10 more."

"Can't," I gasped, feeling the muscles in my legs begin to cramp.

"Ten more," he repeated. Our eyes locked. His were narrowed, willing me to continue. I did, focusing all of my efforts on bringing my elbows into contact with the thick, rubbery nubs of flesh capping his pecs. When I completed the last rep, I collapsed on the tiles, sucking air.

"It's a bitch, but it works wonders," he assured me, his palm pressed against my belly. "Like a rock."

"Thanks." I sat up, suddenly unnerved by the thought of a naked man straddling my equally naked body. Our chests smacked together, and suddenly we were literally face-to-face, so close my eyes couldn't focus. He put his hands on my shoulders but made no move to rise.

I was suddenly aware of every point of contact between us. His dick was mashed against my belly—mine was pressed against the tightly muscled curve of his ass cheek. He inhaled, and the ring through his tit brushed my skin. Whatever was going on here was no longer in the realm of man-to-man bonding through exercise.

"I, uh, Kent, I don't…"

"Shhh," he touched his fingers to my lips. Our eyes locked. His gaze was piercing, as though he could see right inside me, read my thoughts. It should have been disconcerting, but it was not. My panic subsided, overwhelmed by giddiness as I let control pass to Kent. I gripped his arms, my fingers closing over the ring of barbs binding his biceps.

Neither of us moved. And yet, we must have moved, because our mouths touched, and his tongue slipped between my lips, dislocating my entire world. It was a man's kiss, no doubt—the texture of his skin, the strength, the slight electric prickle of whisker on his upper lip. And then there was the body, on me, against me, beneath my groping hands. Nothing soft about it, nothing yielding. The texture of the skin, the smell, the musculature, all unmistakably male.

"Don't move," he whispered, pushing me down onto my back. "Put your hands behind your head." He remained astride me, his hands moving slowly over the terrain of my body. I closed my eyes, aware of the pressure of his hands, the heat of the sun, the weight of his cock and balls against my belly. His hands slid slow and easy up my sides, his thumbs counting ribs, then rubbing against my nipples. I groaned with the sheer pleasure of his touch.

Kent's hands moved on to my arms, massaging my biceps. I felt him shift, lean forward. He lifted his hips, and my cock, freed from its captivity, swung around and pointed up between the walls of our bellies. He braced his knees on either side of me and dragged his balls up along the shaft. The loose skin of his scrotum felt like hot silk.

He braced his elbows on either side of me and began rocking back and forth, the only points of contact between us his balls on my cock, his knob rubbing my belly, and the tip of his tongue flickering teasingly against my skin. I bore the sweet torture for as long as I could, then gripped his shoulders, scissored my legs around his narrow hips, and wrestled him onto his back.

I sat up and looked down at him. He was simply astonishing. His torso was covered with an almost invisible down that only resolved into hairs in a pencil-thin line from his navel to his pubes. I bent my head and licked his salty skin, tracing a line from mid-belly to his gold-hooped nipple. The metal was cool against my tongue, the flesh pliable and warm. When I licked the silky bud of flesh, his prick throbbed against my thigh.

I bit down on the hoop and tugged gently. His pec flexed, pressing hard against my lips. I looked up at him, saw him watching me through heavy-lidded eyes, saw his teeth through his parted lips. I grinned at him foolishly, then burrowed into the moist salty hollow of his armpit. I lapped the short hairs that curled there into spikes, then strayed back to his succulent tit. After nibbling that delicacy, I headed south, over the ridged landscape of his belly. As my tongue neared his navel, my nerve faltered and I hesitated.

Kent's fingers tangled in my hair. He pulled my head up and looked at me. "There are no limits other than the ones we set with each other, Jonas. My body is yours to explore."

"I'm sorry," I said, feeling the blood rush to my cheeks. "I'm not...I haven't...I don't know what I'm doing."

"You may never have done it before, Jonas. That's not the same as not knowing." He winked lasciviously. "I love your tongue," he whispered.

Encouraged by his words, I licked lower, past his navel to his groin. I avoided his rigid cock, although the hot shaft rubbed against my cheek as I slithered down his anatomy. At the point where his legs forked out, I had a choice—down to the toes, or up into his musky crotch?

I chose the crotch, heart pounding madly against my ribs. I had never nuzzled between a man's legs before. All the organs were exposed—the throbbing cock, the fat, heavy, pendulous balls, drooping down over his tightly puckered asshole. I pressed my nose against the sac his big balls were enclosed in, sniffing his musky, distinctly male smell. The chemistry of it drove me wild, made my own balls draw up tight between my legs, made my cock throb as it oozed hot, thick drool against his calf.

I pressed my lips against his ball sac first, then my tongue. I lifted the heavy orbs up, letting my tongue slip beneath, pressing against the thick ridge that ran back to his asshole. It was a part of my anatomy that I had explored only cursorily. Still, I felt drawn down, down to the musky center, the forbidden point, the point I had never allowed my thoughts to wander towards.

As I tentatively explored this region, Kent's knees began to draw up, exposing the furry crevasse between his tightly muscled ass cheeks. Without being forced to move, to make a decision, my tongue skittered through the dense moss and across the puckered lips of his hole. I touched the funky ring of muscle and it gaped for me. My tongue shot out instinctively, jamming into the bittersweet warmth of his body.

He bucked and so did I, cementing our mouth-to-ass union. I wiggled my tongue, and his hole contracted around it. I reached up and pinched his tits, and his hole squeezed tighter, spitting my tongue out into the open. I probed again and was welcomed back into him. I lapped hungrily at his soft innards and dared to run my fingertips up along the swollen shaft of his cock. I rubbed the fat, spongy head. Hot goo gushed out of him and pooled in his navel. I dipped my fingers in it, sniffed, then sucked my fingers dry. I dipped again, this time pushing my slick finger up into him beside my wriggling tongue. He moaned, and his fat balls rolled against the bridge of my nose.

"Yes!" The word burst from his lips, sharp in the still morning. I had risen up, hooked my arms under his knees and rolled him onto his broad shoulders, pushing against his springy asshole with my hard cock. I thrust my hips, met the resistance of muscle, then sank slowly into his tender bowels. His breath escaped in a low sigh as I pushed deeper into him.

As I sank into his ass up to my balls, he groaned as if in pain. I started to pull out but was stopped by the palms of his hands pressed tight against my ass. "Fuck me!" he growled, his voice raw with the urgency of desire.

I obeyed, thrusting my hips, driving back into the defenseless heat of him. I braced my hands on both sides of his head and looked down at him, our eyes locked as I began fucking my first man. It was incredible—the sense of power and control as I drove my cock into him, coupled with the knowledge of the power in his swollen biceps, his broad chest, the sleekly muscled thighs that pressed against my waist. He was mine to use, to fuck, yet he had the power in his fists to knock me unconscious. Instead, his knuckles rubbed against my jaw as he whimpered under my pounding assault.

I slowed myself, looked down at the point of union between us. My belly was tight against his ass, no light between us. Then I began to withdraw, watching the distended shaft of my cock emerge from his body, pulsing with my hot blood. His asshole grabbed at me, showing a rim of pink against my cock as I pulled back into the clear. I saw the opening slowly closing as his muscles squeezed down tight. The pucker appeared impenetrable, yet when I touched the swollen head of my dick to it, it gaped wide, beckoning me back inside.

I humped in a state of bliss, savoring every sensation that shot through me, overloading all my senses. I fought off the inevitable but couldn't succeed for very long. I felt the jism rise within me, felt it boiling up out of my balls, ready to explode into the open, carrying me along on its thick, creamy tide. "I'm coming," I cried.

"Let me see it!" Kent pulled his ass off my flexing cock. I pressed against him, spewing jism over his ridged abs and up over the swollen mass of his pecs. Sensing his need to join me, I ducked my head and swallowed his cock. I should have gagged on it, but I didn't. It slid down my throat, and I began to suck, determined to turn him inside out with the same pleasure that I had just experienced. He thrust up, bashing his balls against my chin, squeezing my head between his hard, sweaty thighs. I redoubled my efforts and he cried out, squirting his jizz deep down my throat. No gag reflex marred the occasion. I sucked him dry, savoring the hot, thick liquid issuing from him, rolling it over on my tongue, then swallowing.

When I finally spit his limp dick out onto his belly and raised my head, the azure sky was marred by streaks of charcoal. The scent of smoke was in the air. I looked down at Kent. His nostrils quivered. "Fire," he said.

* * *

Kent stood behind me, arms around my waist, sniffing at the air. There was no hint of trouble, aside from the unsettled chirping of the wrens in the oleander. I leaned back against him, sniffing anxiously at the air. "Do you think we're in danger?" I asked.

"It doesn't look good, Jonas. Unless that brings relief." I looked to the west. A bank of clouds was lined up off the coastline, dark as bruised flesh. Lightning flickered at the leading edge of the storm, seeming powerful enough to set the world on fire.

The clouds swept forward, across the wide, dry plains. Bolts of lightning shot down towards the earth, creating fireballs on the horizon. I shivered as the winds began to blow. It was clearly a race between the fire and the flood. The grasslands around us began to glow orange beneath the bruise-purple clouds.

We were surrounded with frightening speed by a shimmering wall of fire. Even at 200 yards' distance, I could feel the heat. Eucalyptus trees on the outskirts of the community began exploding into flame, spraying debris high in the air. More trees began to ignite, bringing the fire closer to the center. Flames began to dance along the cedar shakes of a roof about three blocks down the street. For the first time, I began to be afraid.

"What are we going to do?" I turned to Kent, saw my fear reflected in his eyes. Still he smiled, brushed his lips against my jaw.

"Pray for rain," he said finally, releasing his hold on me. "Until then, maybe we should think about getting in the pool."

Suddenly, there was a deafening crash. I looked up, expecting to see flames leaping from another house, much closer this time. Instead, my upturned face was splattered with rain. The drops fell thick and heavy out from a sky the color of pewter. Within seconds the skies opened, sending water down in torrents. The force of it collapsed the umbrella that shaded the table beside the pool and stripped the blossoms from the hibiscus and geraniums, littering them on the ground like bright confetti.

Water cascaded off the roof like a waterfall, overwhelming the gutters. The air, only moments before thick with smoke, now reeked of ozone and fresh, clean water. The burning grasses, shrubs, and trees quickly faded from orange to ash. Even the burning rooftops were overwhelmed by the fury of the rain. Kent and I watched as the pool filled to overflowing and began to lap around our ankles. I clasped his hand and pulled him back into the house, down the hall toward the bedroom.

* * *

After we had made love for the third time, the rain ceased. We walked outside, naked, watching the clouds pull back like a veil, revealing a night sky studded with a million stars. "This is perfect," I sighed, reaching out to Kent and pulling him close. "I don't ever want it to change."

"Everything changes, Jonas." His arms, warm and strong, slipped around me, enclosing me in a magic circle. "Everything."

"I don't want it to," I replied petulantly.

"It still changes." He kissed my forehead. "Don't think about that now. We still have tonight. Let's not lose that."

"Is that all we have?"

"I hope not, but I don't know the answer. It won't be the same, but what I feel won't change just because these houses are populated again." He stroked my ass. "I'm crazy about you, Jonas. You must realize that."

"I realize it all right," I sighed, pulling him closer. "I've got the same problem."

"It's not a problem, Jonas. OK?"

"What about your wife?" I asked.

"Jessica understands my…needs," he replied. "We allow each other the freedom to explore our sensual natures." He smiled at me. "That shocks you, doesn't it, Jonas?"

"Well, it sure as hell hasn't been my experience that Beth encourages much in the way of independent exploration. Certainly not sensual exploration."

"I'm sorry for that, Jonas, although it has definitely made you an enthusiastic and exciting lover."

"I don't know what I would've done if you hadn't come along, Kent."

"Then someone else would have been bowled over by you." I started to protest, but he shook his head. "You were ready to explode, buddy. Beyond ready. It was inevitable." My thoughts strayed briefly to the smiling man, but I said nothing. "I just happened to be in the right place at the right time. Lucky for me, I'd like to add."

"What's that?" I heard a low thrumming, too loud and steady to be the drone of insects.

"Cars," Kent said. Then I saw the lights, snaking across

the horizon. "Civilization."

"Shit," I muttered, feeling suddenly cold.

"Want to go for a quick one?" Kent asked, slipping his hand between my legs. The thrill of his touch against my balls sent a shock of pleasure through me.

"Do we have time?" I asked.

"There's always time, Jonas. Always." He pulled me down onto the cool, damp grass. His warm lips sparked vital heat through me once again.

The Unwelcome Guest

"Rick!"

"Yes, ma'am." I stepped out of my bedroom and went to the head of the stairs. My mother was standing directly below me, beside the telephone table in the downstairs hall.

"I was just talking to your Aunt Estelle."

"Oh?" I felt a knot in the center of my gut. "You don't say." Aunt Estelle was my mother's eldest sister. I hated it when she called. It tended to ruin my life for long stretches of time. "Nothing wrong, is there?" I should be so lucky.

"No, dear. Nothing wrong at all. We had a lovely chat. You'll be glad to hear we're going to have some company for the next few weeks."

"Mother, how could you?" I howled. Company from that quarter could mean only one thing—my geek cousin, Harry Creighton.

"Now, Rick, Harry's a very nice young man. He's quiet and well-mannered—and he won a scholarship to the university." She didn't mention the fact that I was given a blank piece of paper at my graduation exercises and was currently attending summer school in hopes of earning a valid diploma. She also failed to bring up the fact that the only job I'd been able to snare was parking cars three afternoons a week at the country club where my old man was a member. She didn't have to—it was all there in the tone of her voice.

"Harry Creighton's a freaking dweeb!" I snarled, figuring I owed it to myself to make my feelings known. "His face looks like a cheap pizza, and you could start a fire with the lenses in his glasses. He…uh, he picks his nose." I was improvising now. "He…he smells bad. The last time he was here, we didn't get along at all. He hates me!"

"I'm sure he doesn't hate you, Rick," she retorted. "Harry's much too mature for that sort of nonsense. He'll be here this afternoon, so you'd better get your room cleaned up."

"But I won't be able to survive if he's here. I have to study. He snores like a buzz saw, he—"

"He's coming, and you'll be civil to him. This isn't a discussion, Rick, it's an announcement." She had assumed what I refer to as "'the tone,'" which meant that I was on really thin ice. I decided to shut up before I had to clean out the basement or something even worse. Harry was coming, and the fact that my summer was now completely fucked was of no consequence to my mother. I stalked back into my room, slammed the door, and flopped down on the bed.

Actually, I couldn't blame Harry for the fact that my life was coming apart at the seams. The summer school gig was bad, but I wasn't alone—several of my buddies were facing the same prospect. The valet parking job had flexible hours and tips had been pretty good so far. No, the real problem was the fact that something was wrong with me. It wasn't just something like not knowing what to do with your life or hating your parents—this was serious.

To put it right on the line for you, my dick didn't work. Well, that's not entirely true. I beat off every chance I got, and my whanger always worked just fine for me. Hell, it looked OK—about six inches long, crimson-capped, fat enough to make a handful—and it snapped to attention every time I touched it, ready to tingle and spit. The trouble was that every time I got around a girl, the damned thing shut down and refused to do what dicks are supposed to do around girls.

I didn't even know anything was wrong till a couple of my buddies from the swim team set me up with Sally Mitford for a blind date. Sally goes down like a drawbridge and she's got huge tits, so the guys figured she'd be the ideal first piece for me. Well, I took her to a movie where we necked all the way through to the final credits, then drove her up to Lovers' Lane. I had a couple of shots of bourbon under my belt and a condom in my pocket and thought I was all ready to go, but when she stripped, my peter shriveled up and refused to do anything. She tried sucking and jerking and rubbing it between her tits, but we got no action. My dick was dead. I finally told her I'd been injured playing tennis. She cried on my shoulder and promised she'd carry my secret to the grave.

I lied to the guys about what a great fuck she was, then I set my sights on Vicki Keller. She was a virgin and very religious. I figured I just couldn't make it with a girl like Sally, who'd been spending most of her senior year in the backseats of cars with her dress up over her head. Well, I spent four months bringing Vicki up to the point of giving it a try, but the same damned thing happened. Which is to say that nothing happened. This time I cried on Vicki's shoulder and told her I respected her too much to steal her virginity just to add another conquest to my list. She held my hand and told me what a wonderful man I was.

That was the end of dating—I was running out of excuses. I didn't know what was wrong, but it had to be pretty bad if I couldn't get a hard-on when I was in the same room with a woman.

Then there had been that business with Larry Dumont. All we were doing that afternoon was wrestling. Larry's a cool guy—quiet and a good student but with a hell of a build on him. Funny, you wouldn't figure a guy who liked music and art would also be into wrestling, but there you go. Anyhow, we were in the gym after school, and Larry and I decided to go a few rounds. The locker room was all shut down, so we didn't even think twice about stripping down to our shorts. That didn't leave much fabric between us, but we were just a couple of guys horsing around. You know?

Well, Larry took me down fast and kept me down for the better part of half an hour. He outweighed me by about 20 pounds, so I wasn't all that surprised. I wasn't quitting, though, just because he was stronger than me. I squirmed, bucked, snorted, and grunted, doing my best to flip Larry over onto his back, all to no avail. He just held on, his big muscles bulging, smiling this goofy smile at me.

By the time I realized that his hips were pumping, I guess mine had started doing the same. I'm pretty sure it was all a matter of blood pressure, due to the strain of the wrestling. Why else would two normal guys get hard-ons in a clench with each other? I sure as hell didn't want to have sex with Larry, and I'm sure he felt the same, but what could we do? His belly was so hard and warm, and the hairs on his chest were tickling me, and it was late and we were all alone. Bottom line, we humped each other's bellies until we both spit big jizz wads. After it was all over, neither one of us said anything about it. What could you say? Just one of the hazards of being horny. We tried wrestling a couple more times, but the same thing kept happening, and I was starting to get worried. I hadn't said anything about it to Larry because I didn't want to hurt his feelings. No point in that. I just decided that the next time he called me up and wanted to schedule a wrestling session, I wouldn't go. Or maybe I'd go, but I'd make damned sure I didn't get a hard-on again. Whatever, I sure wouldn't get suckered into humping his hard, hairy belly again, no matter how good it felt.

Now, to top it all off, Harry was coming and I wouldn't even be able to beat off in my own damned bedroom. Since there's no lock on the bathroom door and I have two younger sisters, my style was definitely going to be cramped.

I figured I'd have one more go at beating my meat in privacy before Harry got here to put an end to my favorite pastime. He was so frigging perfect, he probably didn't even jerk off! The very thought of old four-eyes pounding his pud was just about enough to gag a maggot! I pushed thoughts of Harry out of my mind, put a heavy barbell in front of my door to deter unexpected visitors, and stripped for action.

I've got this mirror on the door of my closet, right at the end of my bed, so I can watch myself beat off. I really get off on standing there, posing and pounding my dick. I don't want to brag, but I've got a good bod. I was on the swim team for three years running, played varsity soccer, and went out for gymnastics my senior year—until my chemistry grades went through the floor and I got suspended from competition, that is. I don't have much bulk, but my definition is excellent, and I've got a belly that's ridged like a washboard. Hell, even my buddy Larry had mentioned it more than once.

By the time I'd kicked off my shorts, my dick was already rising up to take a look around, leaving my big nuts hanging down low and loose between my thighs. Once again, I'm not bragging, but I've got the biggest balls I've ever seen. Each one is about the size of an extra-large egg—I've checked this out, just to make sure I had my facts straight. The guys tease me about it in the locker room sometimes, but you can tell from the way they talk that they're just jealous. My buddy Larry had been so amazed by them that he'd spent about half an hour one night checking them out.

A few months ago, I was at a newsstand in the city and picked up this magazine that had pictures of a dude who shaved his balls and had 'em all tied up with a leather thong. I thought it was all too weird at the time, but that night after I got home and started jerking off, I tried tying a shoelace around my bag. I liked the pressure on my nuts and the way it made them look even bigger. Then I started wondering how they'd feel if they were shaved. I went into the bathroom, got out the shaving cream, smeared it on my nuts and carefully peeled them bald. They were so sensitive afterwards that I came all over myself just rubbing them. So, naturally, the next day I went out and bought a long, rawhide thong.

My big balls brew jism by the quart. No matter how often I go after it, I can churn a shot that arcs high in the air, higher than my head. Hell, I can hit the mirror from a distance of 10 feet. When I'm ready to blow, my whole body knots up, and the come just blasts out all over the place. Sometimes after I'm done, it looks like I've hosted a circle jerk right in my bedroom. After the first time we accidentally got each other off, Larry went so far as to claim that I was trying to drown him.

I grabbed my dick and started pumping. I turned at an angle, checking out my bod from the side. I'd been doing double duty on the bench presses, and my pecs were showing the results. They jutted out like a polished marble shelf, capped by the fat knobs of my tits. My belly was a convex arc, and my butt was sticking out, full and round, pale as milk. I rose up on my toes and watched the muscles in my long legs flex. Soccer had done wonders for my thighs and calves.

When I spun around to face the mirror, my balls banged against my hard thighs like the clapper in a bell. The dull ache registered deep in my belly and out at the tip of my dick. I stood staring at my reflection in the mirror, watching my hand as it began to pump.

Dicks are cool—I mean the way they change while you're jacking off. They don't just get hard and spit, after all. First they stiffen up and get kind of tingly when you touch 'em. It's only after you really get into it that they start to show their true character. Mine started out straight as an arrow, the shaft ivory, the head a ruddy pink. Larry's honker arced down just a little bit, which was kind of wild because sometimes the head would get caught in my navel. Anyhow, once I got into jacking, the shaft thickened and started popping red and purple veins. The head grew too, getting darker, going from crimson to an angry purple.

By the time I was getting close, my dick was so hard, the shaft arced, pointing the head up. The crown rim flared out, the slit in the tip gaped open, and no matter where I touched it, it felt like I had a finger jammed in an electric socket cranked up to 220 volts. I kept on pumping, watching as my balls started doing pull-ups, fighting to climb on top of my meat.

I rubbed my belly and pinched my tits, flexing my muscles till the blood pounded in my eardrums. My belly churned as my fist kicked into overdrive. I took a deep breath, rose up on my toes and pounded my fist frantically against my groin. Three. Two. One. I was off and spurting, the jism gushing out, spraying the mirror, the walls, the floor around me. I stroked till the last spasm rocked me, then stood there, grinning at myself in the mirror. My body was rosy pink, the skin glowing, my muscles still pumped, pulsing with blood. It had felt so damned good, I wanted to go for another round. What can I say? Jerking off makes me horny.

* * *

I was just about 10 strokes away from getting that rush that starts in your toes and shoots sparks up to your gut for the third time in a row, when my mother started calling up the stairs. "Rick, come on down. Our company is here."

"Shit," I muttered, stopping in mid stroke, leaving my balls bouncing and my dick vibrating in the air. I grabbed my underwear, slipped it on, and tried to stuff my aching stiffer back inside. That didn't work, so I trapped it up against my belly with the elastic and pulled on a baggy T-shirt, careful to leave it untucked. As long as I kept my shoulders hunched forward, you'd never know I had a raging boner.

"Rick!" Mother didn't sound quite as pleasant this time. "What are you doing?"

"Just straightening my room for my guest," I said sweetly, trying to paste a smile on my face as I walked down the stairs. "Hey, Harry," I said, my voice phony as hell. "Glad to see you."

"Thanks for letting me stay," Harry said, stepping across the hall to shake my hand. At least his acne had cleared up, even though his glasses still made him look like he was staring at me through a magnifying glass. It was the middle of summer and he was wearing heavy wool trousers and had his shirt buttoned up all the way to the neck. Aunt Estelle hovered around him like a worried hen.

"Where's your suitcase?" I asked, figuring I'd better haul it upstairs for him so he wouldn't collapse under the weight.

He gestured to a small bag by the front door. I grabbed it, and my mom smiled approvingly. "Come on up." I led the way to my room, Harry trudging along behind.

"Don't forget your vitamins, dear," Aunt Estelle trilled after us. "Three times a day for the red ones, once for the blue and green."

"Yes, Mother," he muttered, a tone creeping into his voice that I hadn't expected. My mom and Aunt Estelle disappeared into the living room, and I was on my own with Harry. I thought about sneaking into the bathroom to finish off my hand job, but I didn't even have the heart for that. There was very little doubt in my mind that my life was on a downhill slide.

✱ ✱ ✱

I successfully managed to avoid Harry for most of the next three days. I had classes in the morning and my valet job in the afternoons. I even went so far as going to the library after work and staying there till dinnertime. Then the weekend came, and I was stuck. The school library was closed, and I wasn't scheduled at the country club till the following Monday. To make matters even worse, my grandmother fell and broke her wrist, so my folks had to drive over to Centervale for a few days to take care of her. They piled my sisters into the car and left me on my own with the last great geek of the Western world. My mother made it crystal clear that I was to spend the weekend entertaining my guest. I had no doubt that Harry would squeal on me if I didn't.

After the folks drove off, I stomped up the stairs to my room. Harry was sprawled out on the rollaway bed, probably ready for his precious little afternoon nap. I slammed the door irritably.

"What's with you?" he asked, sitting up and looking over

at me. I glared at him—funny, but without his glasses and with his hair all mussed up, Harry didn't look so bad. I put that unsettling thought out of my mind and sat down at my desk. "You don't like me, do you?" he continued, evidently determined to make me talk to him.

"No, I don't, now that you ask," I snapped, all my restraint deserting me when I thought of the long weekend ahead of us. "My summer was already shit, and now I'm saddled with the world's biggest geek." There, I'd said it and I'd just have to live with it.

"It isn't my fault you were too damned lazy to make a passing grade in chemistry," he shot back at me, jumping up off the bed. "You played around all semester and then figured you'd pass on your good looks. It just doesn't work that way, Rick."

"I'd rather flunk out of school than be like you," I retorted, losing my temper. "Who asked you anyway, you stinking turd?"

He closed the gap between us and grabbed the front of my T-shirt, ripping the neck. I was so shocked that I just stood there like a dummy, gaping at him. "I'm tired of your mouth, Rick. I don't like being called a geek, and I'm sure as hell not going to take it from a spoiled little prick like you."

That was the final straw. First, he'd fucked up my life, and now he'd fucked up my favorite shirt. I calmly reached up, grabbed the front of his baggy old shirt and ripped it open, sending buttons flying all over the place. I expected that to send him scurrying over to the closet, looking for another shirt to cover his skinny wimp's body, but he just stood there, staring daggers at me.

I was doing some staring of my own, believe me. Instead of the bony rib cage and soft gut I had expected, I was looking at a serious torso. His pecs swelled out full and tight, capped with big brown nipples. His gut was as well defined as mine—you could see the ridges clearly through the mat of dark hair growing on it. As I continued to stare, Harry shrugged the torn shirt off his broad shoulders, and I got a look at a pair of biceps that resembled veiny cannonballs. Even his damned forearms put mine to shame. I couldn't fucking believe it—not only was the asshole as smart as he'd ever been, now all of a sudden he was built as well!

My thoughts were interrupted when Harry growled at me. I mean really growled. I looked up and saw that his face was all red, his brown eyes flashing danger. I took a step back, but it was too late. His hands shot out, and next thing I knew, I was bouncing off the wall hard enough to jar the books off the shelf above my desk. Instinctively, I lowered my head and butted him in the gut, knocking him onto the bed. Then I made for the door, figuring I'd better give him some time to cool off. He was up in a flash, though, flying off the bed and tackling me before I'd gone two steps. I hit the floor, face down. Harry reached out with one hand and shoved my heavy chest of drawers against the door, trapping me in the small room with him.

He moved fast. Before I could catch a breath, he was kneeling at my head. He shifted his body forward and his knees pinned my arms to the floor. I struggled and squirmed under him, but I wasn't going anywhere. "You need to be taken down a peg or two," he snarled.

"Fuck you!" I howled, nose buried in the carpet, still struggling to get away from him. He yanked on the waistband of my running shorts and the next sound I heard was fabric ripping. "What the hell are you doing?" I gasped.

"I figure you need a good spanking," he replied, his voice suddenly about an octave deeper than usual. The next thing to go was my briefs. He ripped them off me, then reached around and jammed them in my mouth! That done, his hands cupped my ass cheeks, gripping them hard.

I let out a briefs-muffled squeal the first time he hit me, his hand coming down solidly on my butt. The skin tingled and burned, getting hotter as he continued waling away, his big hand scorching the skin on my poor ass. He'd smack me with both hands, then grab my cheeks and pull them wide apart, exposing my asshole. I was squirming under him, not knowing what the crazy fucker was going to do. He was breathing hard, his knees on my upper arms, his thighs pressed tight against my ears.

"I'm going to beat your ass till it glows in the dark," he muttered, the blows coming thick and fast. It was right about then that I realized I was getting off on what he was doing to me. I couldn't fucking believe it, but it was true. I could feel my prick getting hard, swelling between the carpet and my gut. I raised my ass to give it some room, and he grabbed the insides of my thighs, pulling them wide apart, forcing my ass even higher in the air. My dick was getting stiff as a board. First wrestling, now spanking! I was seriously demented.

"That's it, Rick," he grunted, "show me that pretty pink hole." I tried to pull my legs back together, but Harry wouldn't let me.

The closest I came to bucking him off me was when his fingers touched my asshole the very first time. My whole body spasmed and jerked, almost unseating him, but not quite. He fingered my hole while he spanked me, pushing against the tight ring of muscle, doing his damndest to force his way in. I stopped struggling when he breached my defenses, my eyes filling with tears of rage and humiliation.

The worst part was realizing how damned good his finger felt, sending shocks of heat along to my belly. He kept it deep in me, and I started humping the floor. I didn't want to do it, but it was like when I wrestled with Larry. My cock throbbed every time his damned digit twitched inside of me. Almost before I realized it, the son of a bitch was finger-fucking my asshole.

"You like that, don't you, Rick," he chuckled, thrusting his thick digit in and out, faster and faster. His fingertip grazed something up inside of me, and I shuddered violently, pushing my ass up, hoping he'd hit the same spot again. "I guess I punched the magic button, huh?" His finger poked deep, and my body was racked with another wave of pleasure. "You'll like it a whole lot more before I'm done with you."

"I...unh!" I was about to say something, but he hit that spot again, and my mind went blank.

He kept working his finger in my hole, stirring and poking and prodding around in the tight channel. Then he let out a long whistle, scooped my balls up in his other hand, and pulled them back between my legs. "Hot balls, man," he muttered. "Is this so you don't lose track of them?" He tugged the thong which I wore almost all the time, then hawked a wad of spit on the tingling globes and rubbed it in with his thumb.

"A-a-a-h!" I groaned. I couldn't believe it! The person I hated most in the world had me pinned to the floor with a finger rammed up my asshole—and I was laying there with a hard-on that wouldn't quit, hoping he'd keep on pumping his hand till I passed out from the sheer pleasure of it. Oh, man, this was really fucked!

All of a sudden, Harry wasn't sitting on me anymore. I started to scramble to my feet, but he yanked hard on the thong tethering my balls, and I changed my mind real quick. "Get up nice and slow, Rick. I'm holding the reins, dude." He pulled the cord again, and a dull ache shot up my asshole. I fought the urge to rise on my toes and increase the pressure further. "Don't you forget it." I nodded, then stood and waited for further instructions.

He coiled the thong around the index finger of his left hand while he looked me up and down. His face was flushed, and beads of sweat had formed on his forehead. His tongue flickered out over the pinkish curve of his upper lip, moving very slowly, left to right. "You are one hot-looking fucker," he muttered, more to himself than me. He raised the finger he'd been plugging me with to his nose and sniffed at it. His nostrils quivered.

"Take off my pants, Rick. Do it nice and slow. Don't try anything funny." He gave the thong a warning tug, then tickled my sagging balls with the tip of his bound finger.

I fumbled with his belt and the zipper of his trousers. When they fell to the floor, he kicked them aside. There was a huge bulge in his underwear, running over to his right hip. His dick head was marked by a big wet spot, clear evidence that I wasn't the only one who had been turned on by the spanking and the ass play.

"On your knees," he growled, his voice a husky rumble. I sank to the floor, watching the thong slowly uncoil its length from around his thick finger. He gripped my shoulders fiercely. "You're going to suck my cock, Rick. You're going to suck it nice and sweet. All tongue and lips. No teeth." He pressed the toe of his shoe against my nuts, pushing them up and back, letting them roll against my asshole. "I like your balls, Rick. I like them almost as much as you do. I want to kiss them and fondle them. Don't make me have to cram them up your pretty ass, man." He brushed my lower lip with his fingers. Without thinking, I licked them. I could taste myself! "Think you can remember that, Rick?" I nodded. Harry smiled.

When he shucked his briefs down over his hips, the biggest dick I'd ever seen swung over and smacked me on the cheek. I mean, it was way bigger than even Larry's piece of meat. I crouched down, looking up at it. His huge, hairy balls hung low, suspended from a shaft as thick as my wrist. The underside of the immense organ was pale, bisected by the thick, swollen juice tube that ran from his piss hole back between his legs to his asshole. The head resembled a big purple helmet, glistening with dick drool.

"You can start by licking that mess off the end," he growled, thrusting his hips forward and poking me in the mouth with the fat, spongy glans. I stuck out my tongue and made contact. The slippery goo leaking out of him smeared my lips and coated my tongue. It was hot and salty, and it turned me on totally. I lapped again, and he spurted another glob onto my lips.

"Polish the knob, Rick," he purred, his balls swinging back and forth between his hairy thighs. Harry's eyes fluttered shut, his long lashes fanning out over his cheekbones. His hands lay slack on my shoulders now, and his thighs pressed lightly against my chest. I probably could have slammed a fist into his nuts and ended the whole thing right there, but I no longer wanted to. Hell, this was a lot more interesting than a hand job! I'd never really figured myself for a queer, but maybe I was. Shit, Larry'd freak if he ever figured that one out! I stroked the hair on the backs of Harry's muscular thighs, opened wide and initiated myself into the joys of sucking dick.

Harry's piece had a life of its own. It pulsed and throbbed, the fat head puffing out tight when I licked around the rim of it. I tongued the trigger of nerves just beneath his piss hole, and the hairs on his body bristled. I started bobbing my head back and forth, swallowing just a little more dick each time. The skin was soft as silk, the swollen veins that twined around the shaft rolling away from the pressure of my tongue. My own hard-on was hugging my belly, honey bubbling out the tip, running down the shaft, coating my balls.

"On your feet," Harry said, grabbing me by the ears and pulling me forcibly off his hot, throbbing root. I stood so close, the hairs on his belly tickled my aching cock shaft. He put a hand on my shoulder and spun me around to face the big mirror on my closet door. He ran his hand down my

back, over my ass, and on down into my crack. Then his finger was back in my hole, poking at that spot up in me that
made my knees weak when he hit it. "You like that finger up
your butt, don't you, Rick? Tell me you like it."

"I like it, Harry. I like it a lot." I groaned and started
humping my hips, pushing back against his hand.

"You like my big cock too, don't you?" I glanced in the
mirror and saw it bouncing up and down in front of him, a
dense mass of dark pubes curling around the thick base.

"I like it, Harry," I nodded, my attention focused on the
incredible rushes I was getting from his finger.

"If this feels good," he punched the magic spot another
time, "just imagine how this is going to feel." He fisted his
prick with his free hand, squeezing tight. It swelled to frightening proportions.

"I don't think so," I whimpered, panic starting to set in.
"There's no way in hell I could survive having that thing
shoved up my ass. I'd split open right down the middle."

"Don't be stupid, Rick. Your ass was made for fucking.
You're a natural for it. Look at yourself in the mirror." I
looked. My dick was spurting juice, and my fat balls were
hugging my shaft. I was flushed pink all over and panting like
a damned dog. Hell, my asshole was squeezing his finger like
I wanted to pop the bone right out of it. Maybe he was
right—maybe I couldn't fuck a girl because I wanted to get
fucked myself. It was all a total mindblower!

"Grab that chair." I pulled my desk chair over in front of
us. "Spread your legs and lean forward." His finger popped
out of my ass, leaving me sucking air. He clamped a hand on
my neck and folded me over the back of the chair. I grabbed
the seat of it and held on tight. He smacked my cheeks
soundly with his huge hard-on, then began probing my
crack. I felt the heat against my hole, then the relentless pressure as he began battering at me.

"O-o-oh..." I damn near jumped over the chair when he pushed the head up into me. "Jesus Christ! You're killing me! Stop it!" If he heard me, he didn't pay any attention. He humped my ass frantically, every thrust pounding another inch of his monster meat up my chute. Once he was wedged firmly inside me, he stopped pushing and started rubbing my back and sides, his fingertips caressing my knotted muscles soothingly.

The pain quickly subsided, and the burning in my asshole was overwhelmed by the fire in my belly. I started grinding my hips around his throbbing spike, moving slow and easy, gradually getting used to the idea that I was getting fucked. When I sucked my belly back tight, I was jolted by a stab of pleasure—similar to what I'd felt when he'd had his finger up in me, only better. Much better.

"Stand up, Rick," Harry directed, pulling me back against him. I leaned into him, the hair on his chest and belly tickling my back. He rubbed his torso against me, his hips pumping as he worked his way in deeper and deeper. By the time his pubes finally began to tickle against my smooth ass, I felt like I had a second spine. I breathed a huge sigh of relief.

"You OK?" he whispered, his breath tickling my ear.

"Fuck me!" I growled. He wrapped his arms around my chest and did as I asked. I was way too hot to stand still for long, so I started fucking him right back—pushing and twisting and squirming against him. The stuffy room echoed with our snorts and groans, and the wet sounds his dick was making as it plunged in and out of my asshole.

He started rubbing my belly, his fingers tracing lower and lower till he had his hand on my dick. My ass pipe clamped down like a vise, making him fight to pull out for his next thrust. I reached back and gripped his hairy butt to steady myself. He kept on jacking my meat, driving in and out of my hole like a man in a hurry.

"I'm coming," I howled, gasping for air as my nuts exploded in a white, sticky flood. My first shot got the mirror on the door, as usual. Then he really started pounding me, battering the spot up in my ass that felt so frigging good. I grunted and shot again, this time hitting the ceiling.

"Oh man," Harry groaned. "Shoot it, Rick. Damn, that's hot!" I tensed and blew another blast on my horn, this time hitting myself under the chin. Harry kept on pumping my dick, his teeth digging into my shoulder as he started filling my quivering chute with his hot load. I could feel him blowing it up into me, the heat flooding my gut. His steady humping lost all its rhythm, degenerating into a series of spastic jabs that curled my toes.

After we'd shot our wads, we both hit the floor like a ton of bricks. Harry's body was hot on top of me. "I hope you've learned your lesson, you frigging pervert." His tongue wriggled in the curves of my ear. "I figure you won't call me names again, will you?"

"And if I do?" I teased, flexing my ass ring around his pecker.

"You know what'll happen to you. I'll beat your ass, then I'll fuck you bowlegged. And you'll love every frigging minute of it."

"Any chance you'll help me with my chemistry?" I asked, twisting my head around and grinning at him. He grinned back. All of a sudden, I had the feeling that this might turn out to be the best summer of my life. Hell, maybe I'd even introduce old Harry to my buddy Larry. If the three of us got together and then got to wrestling, who could tell what might happen?

On Sutter's Cove

"Over there," the old man said gruffly, nodding his head in the direction of the shore. "He'll row you across. Name's Davey." The old man spat on the ground at my feet and went back to mending his nets. I picked up my suitcase and my sketchbooks and set out across the crunchy shale to a solitary blue-and-white dinghy pulled up near a cluster of rocks. I scanned the area but saw no sign of life beyond a solitary gull preening on the boat's prow. Then I saw a foot—bare, long-toed, the callused sole black with dirt.

I stopped, ready to call out, not sure I remembered the name. Davey? Danny? Then, I looked into the face of the sleeping man and for a moment felt incapable of speech. I've looked at many men. Some move me, some don't. I couldn't tell you why this one affected me—I saw no eyes as deep as pools or ivory teeth exposed by a dazzling smile. It was just an impression, gained from the curve of his lips, the line of his jaw, the shadow his curly hair cast on his broad forehead. He was a man, plain and unadorned. He moved me.

I guessed him at about my age, somewhere in his mid 20s. I also guessed—because he had a boat—that he was a fisherman or in some way connected with the sea. The old trousers and stained shirt gave no indication of rank or wealth. His hands were tucked behind his head, a pose that pulled his shirt up, baring a two-inch band of belly. It was a nice belly—flat, punctuated by a deep navel, tufted with a narrow vertical band of fur.

A wide, worn belt interrupted the view. It cinched a badly faded pair of trousers, bunched up in the crotch, molded around a three-part lump that seemed to stir slightly as I watched. As the seconds ticked by, I could tell for a fact that the lump was moving, one portion growing away from the other two, resolving itself into a burgeoning erection. I watched as it stretched out to full length and pushed up urgently against the fabric, outlining a long, thick, arrow-straight shaft. I licked my lips nervously, repressing a strong urge to reach out and stroke it.

"You'll be wanting me?" I jumped back, flinching as though I'd been struck. The man rose from the boat, stretching, his cock still hard, pulsing against his faded trousers.

"What?"

"To row you across."

"Yes. I…I'm sorry," I stammered. "I didn't mean to startle you."

"I'm not startled," he retorted. He jumped out onto the shale, picked up my suitcase and tossed it in the bottom of the boat. He pushed the craft down to the surf and stood waiting, the water lapping around his ankles. "Come on, then," he commanded. I grabbed my sketchbooks and approached, my face scarlet, my heart pounding. I felt a fool. I took his outstretched hand and steadied myself as I clambered aboard. His palm was rough with callus, his fingers strong and warm.

He pushed off, gripped the oars and began rowing us rapidly across the water. He sat facing me, his hard-on unabated, stretched along the inside of his left thigh. I tried not to look, but my eyes were drawn to it like a magnet. Every time I looked from his groin to his face, he was watching me. The journey took an eternity.

I jumped up the instant the boat touched the shore on the other side, anxious to disembark. I misjudged my distance and abruptly measured my height in the mud and sand. I scrambled to my feet, spitting brine and grit.

"Damn," I muttered, crouching down to feel around in the muck for my glasses. The fevers that had almost killed me the previous winter had weakened my eyes. The doctors assured me that it was only temporary, but I wasn't sure I believed them.

"Found them," Davey said. I held my hand out towards the sound of his voice. "Wait a minute. You're hurt."

"I..." His shadowy form came closer, and I felt his hand on my cheek. My heart fluttered against my ribs like a frightened bird. He dabbed at my cut with a wet rag. The salt stung, but I welcomed the pain as long as it kept him touching me. When he was done, he gently wiped my face and settled my glasses back onto my nose. As his face came back into focus, I saw that he was smiling. What a clumsy fool he must have thought me.

"Don't worry. We'll have you scampering over these

rocks in no time. The house is there, just above high tide line. Makes you think you're on board ship."

"Thank you," I muttered. I took a step forward and almost went sprawling again.

"Here you go," Davey said, gripping my elbow firmly.

"I've been ill," I said, anxious to excuse my clumsiness.

"The sea air and sun will fix that," he assured me, half-carrying me to the cottage. He eased me into a chair on the front porch, then dashed back to the boat to gather my belongings. "You'll be all right by yourself, then?"

"Yes. I'm fine. Just a bit tired. Thank you."

"The Widow Renfrew will be cooking for you. The woman conjures magic with a spoon and a black iron kettle." He walked back to his boat and pushed away from shore. Before he picked up the oars, he raised his hand to me. "Welcome to Sutter's Cove," he called. I watched him until his boat disappeared on the horizon.

* * *

The days lengthened as spring metamorphosed into full summer. Davey had been right about the Widow's cooking—the woman was a genius. My bony frame began to fill out under an onslaught of her incredible seafood stews and homemade breads. Days spent walking on the shore and over the headlands observing the seabirds I was drawing brought pain and fatigue at first, then increasing vigor.

With the vigor came unsettling thoughts. It would be unfair to blame Davey for them, although they certainly centered around his person. Before my illness, at home and later at the university, I had focused all my energies on my studies, leaving no time for any thoughts of a physical nature. I had always hidden behind my natural shyness and a scholarly reputation, avoiding romantic entanglements without losing my access to the better homes of the city. Now I was rested, relaxed, alarmingly healthy—and very confused about sex.

As a youth, I had never gone in for the sort of nonsense practiced by some of my fellow students at boarding school. Their nighttime antics in the dormitories struck me as sordid and vaguely repulsive. Unfortunately, this unwillingness to join in had left me woefully ignorant of matters sexual. All I knew was that when I saw or thought of Davey, my intellect took a backseat to the demands of my body.

He came to the cove frequently, bringing supplies and mail. He was always pleasant, but I was too shy to talk to him beyond the barest civilities. After he had made his deliveries, Davey often anchored his dinghy in an uninhabited inlet about two miles distant, a secluded spot that was invisible from the village across the bay. There he would strip naked and swim in the cobalt water, then sprawl on the sandy beach to dry. On most of the occasions when I saw him, the exercise, sunshine, and warmth aroused him. Then, thinking himself all alone, he would do what nature intended in order to relieve himself. I discovered this entirely by accident. I regret to admit that I wasn't man enough to turn away from the spot and leave him to his privacy.

I had rounded the point that day and was struck breathless by the sight of him. He was naked, knee-deep in the surf, his head thrown back, his arms stretched high above his head. I had woven countless fantasies around the narrow strip of belly I had seen that first day, coupling it with imaginings of his swollen, almost-visible cock.

That day, nothing was left to be imagined. His chest and shoulders were taut with the muscle of a man who rowed miles every day. His sinewy arms were thick with crisp dark hairs that curled from his wrists to his elbows. His belly was flat, his hips narrow. His legs were long and pale and furry. His heavy sex hung down between his thighs, arcing out slightly over his pendulous testicles.

I sank onto my knees in the high grass and watched. Davey turned away from me and ran along the shore, kicking up sparkling plumes of water in his wake. His back was tanned by the sun, V-shaped and strong. His pale, firmly rounded ass was so beautifully made that I ached to touch it. The cheeks flexed and dimpled as he loped along, giving meaning to erotic references that had been nothing but abstract concepts to me before. As I watched him run, my cock stiffened within the confines of my trousers.

Davey turned before he was out of sight and retraced his steps. I feared that he would see me, but he stopped just a few feet below my hiding place and sprawled back onto the sand. He was so close I could hear him breathing, could smell the acrid perfume of his sweat. He tucked his hands beneath his head and closed his eyes. I watched his chest rise and fall, waiting for him to go to sleep so that I could effect my retreat unseen.

But then I saw what was beginning, and I could not bring myself to move. Davey's cock swelled, rolled over the curve of his right thigh, then swung around and hovered above the narrow band of hair that connected his navel to his groin. I had imagined it many times in many ways, but the reality outstripped all my fantasies. It was darker than the rest of his olive skin, dusky brown, cabled with thick blue and crimson veins. The head of it strained against the crinkled skin that shrouded all but a tiny pink circle and a gaping slit, moist with piss.

He slowly lowered one arm, grasped the base of the rigid stalk that jutted up out of the salt-crusted tangle of his pubic hairs and squeezed it. The head grew and grew, purpling as it emerged from its cowl. And then there was no more extra skin, just a fat knob capping a long, thick shaft of rigid flesh. My hand reached out, gripping the empty, salt-laden air.

He began to pleasure himself, pumping his clenched fist slowly up and down the length of his cock. I watched, hardly daring to breathe for fear that I would be discovered. He was beautiful, so strong and uninhibited, his back arched, his hips thrust up, his toes buried in the golden sand. And perhaps most fascinating of all, he was utterly without shame.

He licked the fingers of his other hand and swiped them against the head of his cock. The crimson bulb swelled, the slit in the tip gaping like a tiny mouth. He slowly trailed his fingers up the center of his body from his cock to his lips, licked his fingers, then swiped them against his cock again.

After several repetitions of this circuit, his cock began weeping thick clear liquid that he smeared in glittering trails across his body. And then he abandoned the throbbing organ, leaving it to leak and levitate above his convex gut while he began making slow, gentle love to the rest of his body. He stroked arms, belly, thighs, and chest, paying special attention to the thick, hard points of his nipples. The slightest touch to them registered visibly in his cock, making it swell and rise higher into the air.

His balls were drawn up tight between his legs now, two fuzzy brown orbs that jiggled slightly as he went back to stroking himself. It was clear that he was nearing the moment of crisis—his sweat-streaked torso was flushed pink, the veins in his strong arms throbbed beneath his skin, his mouth gaped open, and a low-pitched moan rose on the breeze.

His hips jerked high, and a ribbon of white shot out of him and splattered in the sand around his head. He pumped his fist, and another thick burst gushed out and pooled on his heaving belly. He continued stroking and shooting for a long time, then all the tension drained out of him, and he lay motionless, save for the rise and fall of his chest.

A few moments later he rose from the sand and loped over to his boat. He washed himself, retrieved the bundle of his clothing, dressed, and rowed out into the bay. I watched until he was out of sight, then walked across the sand. I looked down at the impression left by his body, scanned the shore, stripped out of my clothes, and lay where he had so recently lain. I ran my fingers through sand made clumpy by his sperm, crumbled the bits across my belly and chest and daydreamed of him as I worked my own rigid cock to climax. The universe exploded in sun-dazzled bolts of color behind my clenched lids as my hot life sprayed out onto my skin. I sat bolt upright, startled by the sound of my own echoed voice, calling "Davey!" to the boulders on the shore.

❋ ❋ ❋

"Mr. Billingsly?"

"Who's there?"

"It's Davey." I am such a liar. I knew he was on my porch. I had been watching for his boat, following its progress across the bay and into the cove beneath my windows. I stepped out onto the porch, an expression of what I hoped might be disinterested surprise on my face. He returned my look with a frank, open, honest smile. "Good day to you, sir."

"Please call me Edmond." I felt my cheeks go hot as I spoke. I was like a blushing maiden whose courtship had reached the stage of first names. Davey's smiled broadened.

"Good day, Edmond." My name on his tongue was a delight to all my senses. "You've received a package from Boston."

"The illustrations for my book," I said, accepting the parcel from his hands. His knuckles brushed my wrist during the transfer, and a shiver shot up my spine.

"May I see them, Edmond?"

"Of course you may, Davey." He stood beside me at the table in the hall while I fumbled with the knotted twine. It resisted all of my efforts.

"Let me do it, Edmond." He produced a knife from his pocket, flicked open the blade, and severed the string in an instant. I had not stepped aside, so our arms touched from shoulder to elbow. The heat of him burned through the fabric of my shirt. I removed the wrapping and opened the portfolio.

"You drew these?" I nodded. They were the publisher's lithographs of the birds that I had sketched on my walks and then drawn at night. The plates were beautifully wrought, the colors of the birds' plumage truer to life than my original watercolors. "You've got them to the life, Edmond." He held one up to the light and examined it critically. "You love them, don't you?"

"Yes," I replied, surprised into the recognition that I did, indeed, love the graceful creatures I had watched for so long.

"I do too, Edmond. I do too."

✳ ✳ ✳

As time went by, Davey and I became friends. This would, of course, have been impossible in the class-ridden confines of the city, but out here, far from friends and family, it was as natural as breathing. Davey took a real interest in my work and often rowed me to uninhabited islands along the coast in search of new species of birds.

As our bond of friendship grew, so did my guilt. Although I had often sworn that I would never again go to that deserted stretch of beach where Davey took his solitary pleasure, I could not stay away. If I skipped a day, then I would lay awake at night, sick that I had missed a chance to observe, even from a distance, his delectable body. Then I would go and wait and watch, and the guilt would gnaw at me, spoiling my peace.

On a glorious day in mid August, I was in my usual spot, crouching behind a stand of grass, spying on Davey. I had watched him strip, watched the muscles shift under his skin as he raised his arms up towards the cloudless expanse of summer sky. He stood now, weight on one leg, the other crooked slightly, a hand on one hip, looking out over the water at a gull skimming the surface of the waves. The sight of him almost caused me pain, he was so beautiful. Everything about him was perfect—the swell of muscle in his arms and chest, the slight outward curve of his belly in repose, the dark hairs clustering around the base of his heavy-hanging prick. I wanted to reach out, to touch him, rather than crouch back here like a thief, stealing glances at something I could never have.

He turned towards the shore and began to walk to his accustomed hollow in the sand. He reached the spot but did not stop. Instead, he began to climb the dune towards my hiding place. I looked around in a panic, seeking fruitlessly for escape. What would he think of me? How could I ever look him in the eye again? How could I survive without him for a friend?

"Edmond." My heart lurched. This couldn't be happening. It was a nightmare. And yet—it was his voice, borne by the sea breeze. It was undoubtedly my name. "Edmond. Come here. I know you're there. Come to me."

I wanted to run, to jump into the sea, but I didn't. His eyes were fixed on me, his hand reaching out to me. Looking down along his torso to his crotch, it was easy to imagine that his cock was reaching out to me as well. I stood up and approached until I was standing directly in front of him.

Davey stood before me, smiling. I smiled back stupidly, unable to speak. I watched as he began to unbutton my shirt.

I shivered as he pushed the suspenders off my shoulders, but any protest I had thought of making died in my throat when he leaned forward and kissed the center of my chest. I felt it like a hot knife through my heart.

When he unbuttoned my trousers and pushed my underwear down around my thighs, I staggered back and would have fallen if he hadn't caught me around the waist. While he held me, I kicked free of the folds of fabric and stood before him, as naked as he was.

"You're delightful to look at, Edmond," he said, his voice soft and husky.

"I...I'm not," I protested. "I'm..." He pressed his fingers against my lips, silencing me. He began kissing my body again, my nipples, my shoulders, my Adam's apple. His hands were on me, stroking, squeezing, kneading my flesh. I began to touch him as well, to feel the hard muscle beneath the furry, sun-warmed skin. I ran my fingers down along the ridge of his spine. When my hand grazed against his ass cheek, he made a sound like an animal growling. I quickly moved my hand away.

"Touch me wherever you like, Edmond," he said, grasping my wrist and pushing my hand hard against the swell of his left buttock. "Touch me." I let my fingers curl against the firm flesh, squeezing it. The muscle flexed against my grip. My fingertips slipped into the moist, furry warmth of his crack. The feel of the damp, short hairs curling against my fingers and the knowledge of where I was touching him made my aching cock throb. He pushed his leg against me and raised it, causing my hand to slide further around his backside. My fingers trailed down, bumped over his bung hole, prodded his fat, heavy balls. He growled again, only this time I continued to stroke the fuzzy orbs, wise as I was now to his ways of expression.

Suddenly, without warning, he pushed me away. I started to speak, to ask what I had done wrong, but I froze when I realized his intention. He dropped to his knees and began licking the scarlet tip of my prick. His tongue lashed the tender bulb, then curled around the shaft, shooting sparks of incredible pleasure up and down my spine. He sniffed at my balls, licked them, then looked up at me and winked.

I gasped when he opened his mouth and lunged forward. The head of my cock hit the roof of his mouth and plunged deep into his throat. Then, his forehead tight against my belly, his hands clenching my thighs, he began to suck me. I gripped his shoulders, hard with muscle, hot from the sun. My knees buckled and pressed against his chest. Warm spittle trickled from the corners of his mouth onto my balls.

My cock slid out of his mouth. I looked down at the glistening crimson prong, standing high, straining to hug my belly. Davey kissed the tingling tip, then spun around and crouched in the sand, his head down, his ass thrust high. Lust and instinct brought me to my knees. My cock slapped against his tailbone, and his beautiful ass cheeks tipped higher. I saw the slot at the base of his crack, pale pink, gaping slightly. I rubbed my cock against the moist heat, desperate for more, unsure how to proceed.

"Fuck me, then," he said gruffly, grabbing my cock and pressing it against his hot asshole. My hips thrust forward, driving me into his body.

He groaned, and his fingers dug into the warm sand. I watched the muscles in his back knot, watched the wedge of my cock pry him open as I sank into him, inch by inch. I thrust again, driving deeper. He groaned again, and I fell forward, pumping my hips until my belly slapped against his ass.

I lay against his body, my prick pistoning in and out of him. He was rocking under me, raising his ass to meet my driving thrusts. I wrapped my arms around him and pulled him upright. I looked over his shoulder and saw his hard cock pulled up tight against his belly, pulsing, spitting clear juice. When it flexed, his ass muscles flexed as well, tightening the warm channel I was buried in. I nuzzled his neck, one hand flat against his belly, the other wrapped around his flexing cock.

I was trembling, my breath coming in ragged gasps. I bit my tongue, fought to hold back, to make this magic last. Davey lost control first, bucking against me, squirming like an excited puppy in my embrace. I was helpless, trapped in the hot, soft confines of his body. I grabbed his cock, felt it flex against my palm, felt the hot sperm gush out and drip down onto my knuckles. I pumped my fist, pounding his cock as I pounded his ass, spewing my hot seed up into him.

Afterward, he melted back against me, chest heaving, his head lolling against my shoulder. I nuzzled his neck and stroked his slippery belly, dazzled by what had just taken place. My cock remained hard, buried deep inside of him. He felt it and squeezed his ass around it, a throaty growl escaping him as he kissed the soft skin of my throat. My hips began to pump, rocking both of us as a breeze rose off the waters of the cove, blowing his soft hair against my lips.

Scenes From Life

6:37 A.M.

I wake as morning's first light lays tracks of pink and apricot across the clouded horizon. The coolness of night still holds sway, but that will quickly pass. Fine by me—heat makes me horny. So does the chill of winter, for all that. Hell, he does it. Makes me horny. I open my sleep-heavy eyes, and my heart jerks at its moorings. The faint light silhouettes his prone form, the curve of shoulder, the point of the fingertip-thick nipple, the riot of silky black hairs that feather his sculpted chest. I reach across and touch, stroke the short fluff on his slightly convex gut, push low and lower, to his groin.

The hairs there grow longer, coarser, catch at my fingers, twine around them, struggle to hold them captive. I touch the root of him, moist and hot, soft now, easily stroked to steel; move down the veiny length of him to the puckered silk of the cowl. Once at the end, my finger teases its way into the piss-and-sex funky warmth, snuggles against the velvet glans.

He moans softly, rises on one shoulder, rolls towards me. His heavy hand slips up my thigh, coming to rest on the firm, smooth curve of my ass. I shift my body closer, let my cheek come into contact with the mat of fur on his broad chest. My breath ruffles it like summer wind across dark wheat. His balls, fat, come-heavy, roll over my knuckles, droop hot against my wrist. My cock touches the furred curve of his thigh. He snorts in his sleep, breathes deep, swells his chest, pushes the hard, warm muscle tight against my lips. I inhale, suck in the scent of him, feel my cock stretch against his leg.

I look at his sleeping face, the long sweep of lashes, the hairs at the bridge of his nose that threaten to knit his thick brows into one, the scar on his right cheek, livid brand of some long-forgotten brawl. His nostrils quiver, his upper lip twitches, pulls away from strong, white teeth. He swallows and his Adam's apple jumps in his throat. I feel a rush of lust so intense I...

November 15, 1980

This is, I swear, my earliest memory. Proto-memory perhaps, dating from a time when I was able only to discern light, darkness, vague shapes. I lay at the bottom of a cage, surrounded by a warm softness, staring up into white.

There is a sound. I turn my head. Through the bars a dark shape looms. Huge blue lights pierce the shape, glow between the bars. A thing, long and menacing, separates itself from the shape, slides across the top of the fluffy warmth, coming for me. Closer and closer it approaches. Two appendages separate from the long, shadowy thing, touch my leg, clamp tight, biting my flesh. I gasp and gurgle, fill my tiny lungs, open my mouth, and scream, scream, SCREAM!

The blue lights blink rapidly, a seam splits beneath them and white fangs appear, guarding the entrance to a midnight black cavern. A demonic laugh rises out of the gaping maw, growing louder and louder, drowning out my scream. A voice—familiar, warm, and safe-edged now with anxiety, cuts through the cacophony. The wiggling, painful thing releases me, withdraws. The blue lights recede into the shadows. The warm, safe voice scoops me up and cuddles me against life-giving warmth. I blink and watch the shadow of the monster disappear.

6:38 A.M.

…am unable to resist. His left arm is drawn up, tucked under his head, baring his pale armpit. My face fits neatly in the mossy hollow, acrid with the scent of him. I sniff my fill, lick the salt bitterness, suck the taste of him into me. I shift my head on the pillow, bring my tongue within range of the browny-pink nub crowning his left pec. I touch the point, make contact, see the aureole prickle with bumps, see the nipple push up, tighten, thicken, reach for my tongue. I lap it once and then again, licking the short hairs around it flat. He groans, a sound deep in his chest that resonates in my groin. I press closer, part my lips, bite the hot, hard nub, and sink my teeth into it. His growl rumbles on as he breathes deep, the wall of his body pushing hot against me.

My cowled finger is gradually pushed out of its sanctuary by his expanding cock; every hard, throbbing inch memorized by my hands, tongue, throat, and asshole. Thick, long and hard, probing deep into me at will, pumping, thrusting, stretching, plowing my yielding body until he spills his thick, hot, copious seed into me, onto me, drenching me, floating me on a sea of spermy bliss.

I peel back loose skin, capture the knob as it emerges, press fingertips against the spongy rim, tickle the piss hole with a callused fingertip. Another groan, his fingers on my ass cheek flex, dig into the muscle. His thigh shifts against my cock, tickling the stalk, urging it to stretch across the hard, hairy expanse of flesh. I raise my leg, crook it over his, opening myself to his anticipated caress. I…

August 10, 1983

I am 3 years old; my brother Joey, 5. It is hot, a Midwest August—hot that twines around arms and legs like sodden cotton batting, sapping away all life. Our father is at work, our mother lying down with a headache. Our mother has lots of headaches. They require bed rest for her in darkened rooms, absolute silence from us, and outdoor play.

Joey and I are in the backyard, fenced and shadeless, hot, dry, desolate. I sit in my sandbox, shoveling buckets of sand and twigs. Joey stands tall outside his tent. It looms behind him, green and mysterious, filled with treasure, off-limits to me. He looks my way, sneers, turns, and steps inside. The flap comes down, shutting me out into the sun-scorched void.

"Joey!" I'm standing in the shadow of the tent, my hand hovering near the flap. "Joey!"

"Shut up, creep."

"Joey! Please let me in. Please. Please. Please!"

"Go away." Dismissed, I sneak into the house, open the big refrigerator, pull up a chair, grasp the pitcher of lemonade, haul it outside with me, fitting tribute for the god of the tent.

"Joey, I got lemonade. Mmmmm, it's nice and cold, Joey. Tastes real good. Let me in and you can have some." I put my lips to the

rim of the pitcher and tip it up. The cool liquid gushes down my throat, trickles off my chin, makes tiny pockmarks in the dust outside the tent. "Sure is good, Joey. Mmmmm!"

"Gimme." His face, square-jawed, lower lip puckered, appears in the gap between the tent flaps. His blue eyes drill through me, challenging me to disobey. His hand shoots out, intent on relieving me of my treasure, my sole bargaining chip. I clutch it closer. It sloshes, cool and sticky, down my bare and scrawny chest.

"No, Joey. Let me bring it in the tent. Please. I'll be good."

"Well…" He eyes the lemonade. I take another gulp, roll my eyes ecstatically. "Come on, then. Just don't touch anything." He stands aside and lifts the flap. I crouch and scurry in before he changes his mind. The flap zips shut behind me. Darker than outside. Hotter, too. Still, I'm inside the sacred enclosure.

We sit on opposite sides of the tent, drinking from opposite sides of the lemonade pitcher. Every time Joey swigs, I swig. Like a contest. At last the pitcher is empty—and I am more than full.

Gotta pee but don't want to leave. Joey'll never let me back in. What to do? Ignore it. Watch him sit there, sweating, studiously ignoring me, intent on tying multiple knots in a length of twine.

Minutes tick by. I really gotta go and pee. Don't dare to move, to bother Joey. Concentrate on his fingers instead, watch them wriggle, creating ever more complex lumps along the twine. If I don't let myself think about it, maybe I won't have to go anymore. Maybe it'll just pass by. Maybe…

Uh-oh. Too late to go anyplace. First, the feel of wet heat between my legs, my shorts going all dark in the crotch. Squeeze it. Make it stop. No stopping, the dark spot extends beyond my shorts, onto the blanket I'm sitting on, spreading wider and wider, to the edge of the blanket and beyond. A narrow stream forms on the nylon floor of the tent, approaches Joey's bare feet, closer and closer. I watch, mesmerized, terrified, horrified, paralyzed. This is it. The end of the world.

"What the…?" Joey looks down in disbelief as the yellow

stream engulfs his bare foot. He immediately tosses the twine aside, glares at me, takes in my stricken expression, the moisture still oozing from between the dirty fingers that clutch at my crotch. "Robbie! You pig. You...you...you asshole!"

I'm not really sure exactly what an asshole is, but his tone makes it clear that it is a horrible thing. He jumps up, grabs my arm, hauls me out of the tent, throws me down in the dirt, begins pounding on my head with the plastic lemonade pitcher.

"Stop it, Joey. I'm sorry. I'm so sorry." He stares down at me, his face distorted with contempt and anger. He throws the pitcher on the ground, returns to the tent. The flap closes, then opens again. He throws the pee-soaked blanket out on top of me, and I lay under its soggy mass, sniffling, my world irrevocably damaged.

6:39 A.M.

...tug at his ball hairs, feel his hard-on begin, feel the blood flood in, swelling the stalk. The bulbous knob escapes my fingers, pushes up the length of my wrist and forearm, planting warm, piss-salty kisses on my skin. I suck his nipple harder, feel his dick respond, growing, stretching, thickening, going from pale worm to dark, hard, dusky, thick-veined weapon.

A final bite against the nubbly texture of his tit, a final glancing lick, a brush of lips. I hunker down, kick at the thin, rumpled sheet, free my legs and feet. I press my face against the musky moist maleness of his torso, the hairs tickling my cheek. I lick shiny trails down his sternum, over the furry, hard arc of his belly, through the forest of his pubes, to the place where his manhood emerges from his body.

My tongue touches him, his fingers tangle in my hair, pushing me down, pulling me closer. He strokes my neck, my cheek, my shoulder, shifting his body, spreading his legs wide. I wrap my arms around one strong thigh. My legs curl around his calf, crushing my own hard-on against the furry bulge of muscle. The hairs tickle me, make me wriggle and flop on the bed like a grounded fish.

I kiss the tip of his prick, taste him on my lips and tongue. I pull away, fist his hard-on, squeeze it tight, watch the blood pulse in, swelling veins, making the knob grow until it's shiny, smooth, and crimson. The spongy flesh is hard now against my lips. I part them, cap him, suck greedily, my fist tightening, my tongue and teeth tormenting him, making him gasp, buck, groan, dig his fingers hard into my shoulders. He grunts, his mouth begs me to stop while his cock begs for more. I believe what his cock says, suck harder, dig my tongue into the gaping jizz hole gouged in the tip.

I come up off him, press my thumb tight against the base of his dick and push up, milking him. I see the thick, crystal liquid bubble out of him, quiver, drool down. My tongue shoots out to catch the heavy flow. It drizzles across my lips, slides down my throat, sets every nerve on fire. I hump my cock against his leg, feel my own stickiness pump out, smell the heady perfume of the two of us, mingling with the encroaching heat of morning.

After sucking him dry—for the moment—I take away my hands, put them on his belly, begin rocking, pumping my head back and forth, lips on the rigid shaft. His fingers lace behind my head, his muscles flex, his hips shoot forward. I feel him spear me, push his manhood down my throat, the girth of it cutting off my air, the length and power of it unleashing floods of pent-up lust that wash over my limbs, making me weak with hunger for him.

I swallow him whole, feel his balls bounce off my chin, feel his knob swell deep in my throat. I push my head back, paw at his hard, sweaty torso, my body language begging him to use me, take me, master me, fuck me, fuck my body, fuck my body with his body. I...

July 3, 1986

I remember the darkness, warm and soft, laced with night sounds that send icy prickles scooting up and down my spine. Cowboys and Indians. I have been the Indian, set up against the cowboys of Joey and his friends. I am outmanned, outgunned, outrun and overpowered. They catch me, tie me to this tree and then go off to tell the settlers that they have prevailed.

That was hours earlier, when the sun was still high. Now it is dark, and I am tired and hungry and beginning to be afraid. I shift my eyes from side to side, see only gradations of darkness. There is a rustling in the leaves—a footfall? the slithering of a snake?—that freezes my blood.

"Joey!" My voice destroys the tapestry of the night, shatters it to total silence. For what seems hours, all I can hear is the steady, rapid thumping of my heart. Then the night gradually begins again—full of insects, night creatures, and the uneasy cries of roosting birds.

More hours pass, bringing fresh horrors, creaking branches, snapping twigs, a feral cry to freeze the blood. I'm thirsty. My nose itches. A mosquito buzzes in my ear. I strain against my bonds to no avail. The ropes are tight, biting my flesh at wrist and chest and ankle. I don't like being an Indian, even if I did get to wear the feathers in my hair and paint stripes on my face. Why be an Indian when the cowboys always win?

Contemplating that when a new horror jolts me. There, in the distance, glowing bright, a single, malevolent eye. I dance a little tarantella of terror against my bonds—still to no avail. It is a demon. A demon, come to fetch me. Joey has told me about demons lurking in the woods. Then, at home, safe in my room, I had discounted his stories. Now, alone, tied ready for sacrifice, I see and I believe. It is out there, that demon, bloody-fanged, sharp-clawed and evil-eyed, winking through the trees, coming, coming fast, coming closer, coming for me.

"Don't take me," I squeal, frantic to make a bargain, to gain time. I'm so very young and small to die. "Don't take me. Don't eat *me. Please. I'll be good."* I have a vague notion that demons don't like good little boys. *"Please, please, please, please! I won't..."*

"Shut up!" The demon sounds familiar.

"Joey?" My voice quavers. I hiccup with relief. *"Joey, you came back to save me."*

"Shut up, Robbie." He shines the light directly in my eyes, blinding me. *"Mom made me come get you. I would've let you rot."* He fiddles with the knots and the rope that binds me goes slack. I stagger away from the tree, toes and fingers tingling, legs rubbery. I reach for my rescuer, throw my arms around him, try to hug his warm, familiar body next to me.

"Ugh! Keep your grubby hands to yourself, you turd." He shoves me hard and I fall on my ass in the dirt. By the time I scramble to my feet, the light is rapidly disappearing through the trees and I have to run to catch up.

6:40 A.M.

...rub my chest against his thighs, feel his balls nestling against my neck. I swallow, squeezing his cock tight. He groans and bucks, his hard-on trapped deep inside of me.

He sits up abruptly, pulls my body around, his dick still wedged in my throat. I feel my thighs on his shoulders, my balls against his chest. His stubbled chin rakes my inner thighs, scrapes along the swollen perineal ridge between my legs. That bristling chin rakes on, grinds across my tender, puckered hole, makes me buck, grunt, grab at his strong legs. He reaches under me, rubs my belly, tweaks my tits. My asshole spasms, gapes. He takes advantage, drilling his long hot tongue through the fluttering ring of muscle.

I flex my arms, push up, dislodge him from my throat, lash at his swollen organ with my tongue. He retaliates, stabs at my ass, licks my balls, tugs roughly on my sex-bloated tits. I buck and writhe, start doing push-ups on his prick. I...

February 7, 1990

Two am: I can't sleep. I'm hungry—and I failed another math test today. Dad isn't going to like that when he finds out. After staring out the window for a long time, watching the snowflakes crash against the frozen panes, I climb out of bed. The floor is cold, colder than the snow, I'll bet. I dig my fleece-lined slippers out from under my bed, wrap my flannel robe around me. I tuck my favorite Spider-Man comic in my pocket, just in case I need a companion in the kitchen to share my milk and cookies.

Out my door, careful to close it firmly behind me. Don't want Mom checking on me if she gets up to go to the bathroom. Down the hall, tiptoeing, careful to avoid the squeaky boards. Almost to the landing when I stop. There, under my brother's door, a strip of light. I'm curious. Joey always sleeps at night. He never flunks tests or gets called names by other boys. He has no reason to lie awake, plotting ways to become invisible in gym class.

I creep up to the door, press my ear against the cool, white-painted panel beside the knob, listen. Nothing for the longest time, then a groan. I hold my breath, press harder against the door. There it is again. Definitely a groan: drawn-out, deep-throated, agonized. Joey must be sick, bad sick, to moan like this.

I lower my head, squint, peer through the keyhole of his door. I can see his bed, covers rumpled, kicked back. I strain to see more, focus on the pennants above the bed, the ultra-cool scale model of an Air Force bomber hanging from the ceiling that I can never touch on pain of broken arms. I see his pillows, piled against the wall, but I can't yet see my suffering brother.

I turn the knob, slowly, quietly, hardly daring to believe my own boldness. This room is so off-limits, it isn't funny. Still, Joey is sick. Maybe I can help him. The knob turns, the door glides silently inward. I take a deep breath and step inside.

I see him, sprawled naked across the bed, see the source of his agony. Something has happened to his pee thing. It is stiff and swollen, flushed a dark, angry crimson. He is gripping it with both hands, his shoulders hunched off the mattress, his face contorted in anguish. His mouth is wide in a silent scream, as though unable to bear the pain an instant longer. What has happened to him? Is it some disease? Has he slammed it in the door? Was he 'playing' with it? I've been warned about such play but can't imagine why anyone would do such a stupid thing. The warning must have been meant for boys without toys to play with.

"Joey!" My whisper rings out like a shot in the silent room. My brother's eyes fly open and he glares at me, teeth bared.

"What the fuck?" He releases his pee thing and pulls the blanket across his middle. The injured flesh continues to twitch and throb uneasily beneath the thick fabric. "What are you doing here?"

"I heard you groaning. I thought you hurt yourself." My eyes stray to the twitching blanket. "What happened to your thing?"

"Jesus, man. Don't you know anything?" He shakes his head with disgust. "Come over here, Robbie." He smiles, but he doesn't look very happy. "Come on, guy. I'm not gonna hurt you." I approach him cautiously, ready to retreat at the first sign of trouble. As usual, I'm not quite quick enough about it.

"You miserable, scab-picking, booger-eating, shit-for-brains faggot!" He grabs me by the arm and wrenches it around behind my back until my hand is practically touching my neck.

"Ow!" I squeal. "Stop it, Joey. I'll…I'll tell!" Thud! I see stars a split second after my head makes contact with Joey's closet door. He has one hand on the back of my head, the other pulling my arm up so hard I'm on tiptoe. "Stop it!" Thud! Another constellation-inducing blow.

"Shut the fuck up, you dumb fuck." Thud! "You tell anybody anything and you're dead." Thud! "You understand?" Thud!

"You're hurting me!" Thud! My voice rises to a panicked whine. Joey eases up on my arm a little but maintains his grip on my neck. "Please, Joey. Please. I won't tell. I…I thought you were hurt. Please."

"You don't know nothing," he hisses, his voice harsh in my ear.

His voice has changed recently, the clear, reedy tenor replaced by an uncertain baritone that sometimes cracks. It isn't cracking now. "You're so stupid, I'm ashamed to be your brother. You just keep your damned mouth shut and stay the fuck out of my fucking room. You understand?" The pressure on my neck increases.

"Sure, Joey. I…I understand. I'm sorry. I…"

"Shut up!" Thud! "And don't call me Joey. That's for babies. My name is Joe." Thud! "Got it?" Thud! "Joe."

"Sure…Joe." The name is unfamiliar on my tongue. A stranger's name. "Sure."

"Now get out of here and be quiet about it." He releases me and I almost fall. I wipe my arm across my face, smearing tears and snot, then dart into the hall and stumble back to my room, no longer hungry.

6:41 A.M.

…feel his big hands on my ass, spreading my cheeks wider. He nips at my ass lips. Sparks race along my spine, flooding the pleasure centers of my brain. I feel his teeth and tongue, his hot breath. His fingers are in me, stretching me, making my chute gape. I suck him harder, still pumping up and down on him, priming him.

He hawks, spits, pushes it up into me with his tongue. I buck and shake as his heat drools into me. A final lick, from him, from me, and I am flipped again. This time I'm seated on the bed, facing him, chest to chest, cock to cock. I look deep into his eyes, study their familiar azure depths. I lean closer, drawn powerfully to him. Our chests touch, heart beating against heart. Our lips touch, our tongues. Our breath mingles, becoming one breath as a long kiss begins.

I touch his strong neck, trace the high-arced curve of muscle in his shoulders, fingers trembling as the dusky fuzz that dusts him tickles against their tips. His big, strong hands slide down my back, cup my ass, lift me slightly. I feel the head of his dick directly under me, the heat of it against my ass lips making me squirm with desire. He pulls me up and close, his fingertips massaging the aching slot behind my balls. I hump his belly, frantic to feel him breach me, slide up into me, fuck me till I come.

His muscles tighten, his biceps swell against my sides, his chest presses hard against me. He shifts on the bed, breathes deep, thrusts his tongue deep…

November 12, 1998

"Go Bulldogs!" I run down the sidelines with a pail of water and a towel. A time-out is called, and the players lumber over towards me, thirsty, sweating, their exhaled breath explosive like the snorting of young bulls.

"Over here, Robbie." I trot towards Gunnar Svensen, the beefy, blond fullback. He takes the ladle I give to him, swishes water around in his mouth, spits it at my feet. Then he roughly grabs the towel draped across my shoulders and wipes his face. He leaves, giving me a look, his lips curled in a sneer, his eyes flickering up and down my frame. I turn from him to serve another player.

Matthew Benson, quarterback, he of the muscle-corded, hairy forearms. He is not handsome, but his body is achingly beautiful, every muscle sculpted, honed, perfectly proportioned. He takes the ladle, his fingers brushing my wrist. I feel it through my body, up my spine, and in my crotch. He smiles. I smile back, then realize that he is looking beyond me, into the stands. I look back, see Rebecca Jackson waving, see Kevin Reston behind her, his model-handsome face wreathed in smiles. Which one is Matthew smiling at? I choose Kevin, because it suits my fantasy that the most beautiful man in the senior class should have the most perfectly muscled athlete in his thrall.

The referee's whistle blows, and the ball is back in play. Our team wins, cinching a place in the state playoffs. I am elated, because my time among these strutting male animals will be extended for a few more weeks. Soon school will end, and I will graduate, banished forever from this inner circle.

"A-a-argh!" I am jerked back to the present. Matthew Benson is bearing down on me, his helmet off, his eyes wild. I stand in abject terror as he approaches, mighty arms outstretched. He grabs me, flips me around, lifts me high in the air. Then I am on his padded shoulders, headed for the center of the field. Someone hands me the school flag and I hoist it high as Matthew takes me on a victory lap, accompanied by the team, the cheerleaders, and a ragtag band of boisterous fans. I smile, dazzled by the attention, by the pressure of his huge hands against my thighs, his sweaty head pressed tight against my belly, my tingling cock pressed hard against his brawny neck.

I look around for someone I know among the crowd to share my small triumph, but there is no one. No one from my family is here, of course. Mother is too delicate, dad is out of town, and Joe, two years graduated, now works nights. Classmates who deign to speak to me don't attend football games, don't understand my obsession with the sport. Undaunted, I wave the flag. It's the only time I have ever been the center of attention among these men, and I am happy.

After the lap, I am unceremoniously dumped, left to deal with the equipment. I trudge from storage room to locker room and back again, gathering, cleaning, shelving. I make a final circuit, lock the storage room door, prepare to go. Halfway up the stairs, I stop and turn around, drawn by the ghostly male camaraderie of the showers. I go back down, deluding myself that I only wish to wash the sweat from my body.

I strip and step into the shower room. It is still steamy. The football players are gone, headed to the victory dance, giddy with the promise of getting laid, yet the smell of male sweat lingers in the air. This proximity to even the memory of strong male flesh excites me. I watch them on the playing field and in the locker room, and my cock swells. My heart beats faster when I see a muscled forearm feathered with hair, or a bulging calf, or the triple lump in a sweat-soaked jock. I dream about men at night. My fantasy man even has a face, though one I hardly dare imagine, much less name.

I adjust the taps, step under the cascade of steaming water, and begin to bathe. I squirt liquid soap into my palm, lather my chest, and belly. I like touching myself, like feeling the hard curve of muscle in my smooth chest, the ridges that crease my flat belly. I stroke lower, tangling my fingers in my pubes. I graze the base of my dick and feel a little thrill of warmth shoot down the shaft. My balls tingle and draw up tight between my legs for an instant, then sag back down against my thighs.

I reach for more soap, lather my legs and arms, my neck and face. Then I step under the water, let the pulsing jets rinse me clean. I turn off the water, shake my head, run my hands down over my taut nakedness. I am horny, so very, very horny that it claws at my belly like a beast trapped within me. I look down, watch my cock begin to grow, lengthen, thicken, swell with blood, rise up.

I walk through the locker room, grab a white towel, begin to dry myself. The pressure of my hand, even through the rough cloth, is torture to my tingling skin, a sexual assault, stabbing me straight to the groin. I toss the towel aside and walk to the narrow bench bolted to the floor in the middle of the double row of lockers. I straddle the bench, brace my feet, lean forward and grip the sides. The room is silent except for the distant knocking of a steam pipe and the sound of my own heavy breathing. I lower my hips, arch my back, drag my balls against the worn wood, suck the smell of stale sweat deep into my lungs. My cock knob touches the surface, and I prickle with gooseflesh.

I slowly pump my hips, dragging my dick along the cool, smooth wood. My eyes flutter shut, and I see Joe, my fantasy, no longer to be denied. He lays beneath me, his muscles taut, smiling up at me as I hump his cool, hard belly. I caress the bench, slip my hands beneath, press my chest down against it, against Joe. The muscles in my legs flex as I push down, crush cock and balls against the unyielding surface. I rise slowly, slip my hand between my legs. I finger my hole, humping my forearm now, lips against the bench, conjuring Joe's mouth from the unresponsive wood. "Joe," I murmur. "I want you. I need you." My flanks quiver, my cock throbs, and my voice dissolves into a groan.

I hear the groan echoed in a voice familiar, not my own. I look over my shoulder at my brother. He has appeared out of nowhere, naked, fully aroused. I blink, but the vision doesn't disappear. He rocks back, and the overhead light gleams on his hard-on. It throbs, the head swelling with his blood. He is eyeing my ass, licking his full lips. He hasn't shaved, and the charcoal stubble on his cheeks lends a rough, slightly dangerous air to his appearance. I swallow noisily. This vision can't be true, yet it fails to disappear. The high cheekbones, swarthy skin, chiseled jaw, azure eyes, curly black hair— it is my brother or some otherworldly twin sent to haunt my lust.

He smiles, his long, thick fingers flexing against his furry thighs. I blink again. Joe never smiles at me, even though we continue to inhabit the same room in our parents' house. We have always been at odds, words and deeds at cross-purposes. I worship Joe, love him, lust for him, dream of him, masturbate daily with his image before my eyes. My great fear is the day he will earn enough money to pay off his truck and move out of my life. His feet shift and his cock sways heavily. I have always thought Joe oblivious to my efforts—the efforts of his younger sissy brother—to replicate him somehow, to mirror his swarthy, hairy, thick-muscled perfection in my own pale hairless flesh. I look away, look back. The image remains.

"Robbie," Joe says quietly, stepping towards me.

"How did you find me?" I had thought myself invisible to him, beneath the register of his consciousness.

"I know your habits, Robbie. I've always known them."

"You've seen me here before?" I croak.

He smiles again. "Since the first night. The others left, but you never came out. I was afraid that something bad had happened to you. I came. I saw. I stayed to watch."

"You've seen?" His smile broadens. The body I have dreamed of in secret for so long is here for me, with me, by me, soon to be part of me. I long to reach out, touch him, neck, shoulders, chest, and arms. Eyes trace the throbbing veins that cord from elbow to wrist, trace the fine black line that splits his gut from navel to hard-on. I look down at his cock, watch it rise towards his belly, cowled head swelling, jizz-hole gaping. A single glittering drop fills the slit, trembles, drools down to the floor. I look along the bloated ridge along the underside, see his fat balls draw up tight, then sink down, defeated by their own seed-heavy weight.

I long to leap at him, throw myself on him, but being a younger brother has provided too many long years of conditioning for me to take the lead. Instead, I remain motionless, hard-on jutting, heart pounding, swaying slightly, drawn to him by a tide force in my blood. My cheeks burn scarlet. I start to move, to change my wanton pose.

"No!" Joe, expression stern, steps over to the bench, braces a hand against my shoulder. He leans forward, his face coming close to my face, his lips close to my lips. He touches me, his hands hard on my belly and my ass. I jerk against his hands, cry out, my scream stifled by his strong, hot mouth. I feel the stabbing thrusts of pleasure as though I am being murdered by my lust. His fingers, work-roughened, grind against my tender flesh, stirring a heat that threatens to ignite me. My body stiffens, my muscles swell, my fingers clench convulsive on the bench, my knuckles whiten.

"Robbie." I open my eyes at the sound of my whispered name. My brother is looking at me, his eyes glistening, a furrow deep as pain between his brows. He swallows. I see his Adam's apple bobbing in his throat, see his lips move, fail to speak.

He kneels behind me, pries my prick away from my belly, pulls it back between my legs. It throbs, hot against his thick forearm. I feel his breath on my skin, and then his tongue, hot and wet, lapping from my cock head, up the shaft, across my balls to my asshole. He licks me, pushes into me, insistent. I cry out, claw at the bench, the shock of sheer physical pleasure as he eats my hole almost more than I can bear. He caresses the curve of muscle in my thigh, strokes my crack, tongues me again. I feel him behind me, his body heat, his *breath, his hands, his ramrod cock prodding insistently at my ass.*

One thick arm wraps around me, fingers splay on my belly, holding me as though I might think of flight. His jabbing prick pokes closer to its goal, the tip sticky, burning hot. I hear him hawk and spit, then he holds his cupped palm before me and I spit too. He groans as he anoints his hard-on with our mingled juice. From that moment the world is forever changed. His...

6:42 A.M.

...fingers tighten against my back and I cry out, my scream celebrating the searing pain of penetration. I am raw from the repeated couplings of the night before. It is almost as though we both are struggling to make up for the years of deprivation. Joe's chin presses my flesh, his snorted breath bursting hot upon my skin. His thick prick plows into me, sinks deep, deeper, deepest, until his balls bounce off of mine.

I grip his thick forearms, tangle my fingers in the coarse black hairs. He groans, his broad chest swelling as he gasps with pleasure. I feel his cock swell and flex as he thrusts deep into me. He kisses me, and all the pain in me burns away. My swollen cock begins to twitch against his sweat-wet belly.

I wrap my arms around his strong neck, bucking up and down on him, riding hard, my asshole grabbing frantically at his pistoning hard-on. It seems to grow inside of me as he continues to hump, stretching my hole, opening my guts wide. Joe is sweating now; fat oily drops of liquid roll off him, tickling against my body, soaking my skin, making me slippery in his encircling arms.

He grabs my cock, flogs it, pumps it, coaxing the come out of me. My head rolls back, my mouth gapes, my chest heaves, my hard-on flexes against his palm. He begins to snort, bull-like, loud and louder, every agonized groan accompanied by a gut-wrenching thrust of cock, stabbing me harder, deeper, marking me as his with every stroke.

And then all movement stops, except the flexing link that joins us, man to brother, brother to man. I feel my own nerves tingling, feel my balls knot between my legs. His fist squeezes my prick, my hips twitch, my asshole clenches. I peek at him through slitted lids, watch his eyes droop, his mouth gape, the veins in his neck stand high. His nipples thicken, jut out; the hairs on his chest begin to rise. He cries out, and I am suddenly flooded by a gushing geyser of thick heat. I grab at my belly, feel it begin to cramp as his scalding jism fills me full to overflowing. I erupt as well, spewing my sticky leak out onto his heaving belly. His breathing slows, his grip on me eases, his lips flutter against my sweat-streaked neck. I find his lips, suck his tongue into my mouth. He falls forward, presses me against the bed. Morning floods the room, and another day begins.

Without a Clue

Maybe I'm just dumb or something, but I didn't have a clue about what was going on between Drew and me. I mean, he was the line foreman of my section, so we naturally spent a lot of time together. Hell, I didn't know shit when I first started out, so he stuck right by my side almost every minute of the day, looking over my shoulder, constantly watching me so I didn't hit the wrong lever or push the wrong button. Never once did the man yell at me, no matter how many dumb moves I made. Matter of fact, he was usually whispering, leaning in next to me, his lips practically brushing against my ear, his hard body pressing against my back.

Drew got a real kick out of teasing me, and he embarrassed the hell out of me more than once. First time it happened, I was in the break room listening to the guys brag about who was the most buffed-out dude on the shift. Everybody was vying for top honors, and the shit was piling up deep.

Right in the middle of it all, Drew came walking in and got an earful. "Bullshit!" he snorted. "I'll show you the best damn build in the whole factory." Next thing I knew, I was looking through the fabric of my T-shirt as Drew yanked it off over my head. "Check this out." He leaned over me and draped his brawny arms over my shoulders, splaying his big hands against my naked torso. The long hairs on his forearms tickled my smooth skin like a bird feathers. I tried to wriggle out of his grasp, but he had me pinned.

"Check this out, men." He smacked my belly hard, making me tense up. Then he traced the ridges of my abs with his thick, callused forefinger. "None of you beer-guts could hold a candle to old Randy here. Get a load of this dude's pecs." Drew's thick fingers curved against the swell of muscle in my chest.

"He's got bigger tits than my old lady," one guy blurted out to general laughter.

"Hey, Drew, check and see if you can get some milk out of those pretty pink titties."

"Maybe I will," Drew retorted, pinching my left nipple. I squirmed, skewered by a bolt of heat that shot through me, right out to the tip of my rapidly stiffening cock.

"Drew!" I yelped. "Stop it."

"Just kidding, buddy," he replied, picking up my shirt and holding it for me. I stuck out my arms, and he pulled it on over my head, just like my mother had done when I was a little kid. Afterwards, I had to run the gauntlet of all the guys in the break room. They were giving me shit, grabbing at me like I was some big-titted cheerleader caught in the locker room after a game. I fended them all off and made my escape, my face red as a beet.

On the way back to the shop floor, I ducked into the can to take a piss. I had just let loose when someone sidled up next to me at the long trough. I glanced over. It was Drew.

"You thinking about clubbing someone?" he asked, staring pointedly at my dick. I was still about half-hard from having my tit pinched, and it was taking all my concentration just to keep the piss flowing.

"Yeah," I retorted. "You."

"Is that so?" he shot back at me. "I'll keep that in mind." He shook, packed away his piece, zipped up and walked off, leaving me staring down at what had now become a full-fledged hard-on.

* * *

"I'll be right back, Randy. Make yourself at home." Drew disappeared down the hall. It was Friday night and we'd been out drinking after work. I'd given him a ride to his place because he claimed he didn't feel safe to drive, although I never saw him take even a swig of the brew he'd been nursing. Still, I didn't want him to get arrested for driving drunk.

"Oh yeah, that's much better." I turned to look at Drew, and my jaw damn near bounced off my shoes. He had stripped down to his briefs. He must've ordered the skimpy scarlet shorts from a mail-order catalog because he sure as hell hadn't got them anywhere in this hick town. They were cut real high on the sides and in the back, leaving nothing to the imagination.

I couldn't keep from gawking. The man had the prettiest butt I'd ever seen. His muscular legs were dense with long, dark hairs, but his cakes were smooth as a baby's. Only no baby would've had muscles like Drew. Believe me, you could've bounced quarters off those meaty hemispheres of flesh.

It was clear that he'd been lying the other day in the break room when he'd claimed I had the best build in the place. I mean, I'm no slouch, but he made me look like a piker. His bod was competition quality—broad shoulders that tapered to a tiny waist, pecs that jutted out like a furry shelf, awesome arms and a gut ridged like a washboard. He somehow seemed too big to be contained by the small room we were standing in.

"Too hot for clothes," he said, flashing a big grin at me. "Why don't you go ahead and get comfortable?"

"Uh…sure, Drew." I took off my work boots and my socks, then jettisoned my T-shirt.

"Aren't you still hot, buddy?" he asked softly, ruffling the line of hairs that split him down the middle. I was feeling warm, but I didn't think taking off my jeans was gonna help. I did it anyway, tossing them into a corner. My own shorts were strictly from K-Mart and couldn't hold a candle to Drew's. His eyes flickered from my face to my crotch and back again, making me very conscious of the fact that my dick wasn't getting any smaller. Then he folded out the hide-a-bed, turning his tiny living room into an equally tiny bedroom. He sprawled on his belly in the middle of the bed and flipped on the TV. A baseball game swam into focus. "Sit down, buddy."

I eased onto the edge of the bed and tried to concentrate on the game. Trouble was, I couldn't get past Drew's backside. His muscle-knotted calves and thick thighs didn't faze me. Even the incredible musculature of his broad back and massive shoulders didn't bother me all that much. What stopped my eyes dead every time were the perfectly sculpted, perfectly hairless twin globes of his ass. It didn't help that every time he moved, his muscles would flex and cause dimples to appear in his cheeks. I bit my lip and forced my eyes to the screen.

"Damn!" I looked down. Drew was squirming around on the bed, clawing at the back of his right thigh. "Got an itch, man," he groaned. "Help me out?"

"Sure," I replied, putting my hand tentatively on his thigh.

"Higher." My fingers scrambled over the furry terrain. "Up a little more." I obeyed, getting dangerously close to those succulent mounds of muscle that had captured my undivided attention. "There. Right there." As I scratched, my fingers nudged the thin band of scarlet that threaded between his legs. Long, moist hairs curled around my fingers. His body heat damn near seared the skin on my knuckles.

"That feels good, buddy. Don't stop." I raked my nails up and down, pressing hard against his firm flesh. Occasionally, my fingertips would graze the swollen ridge that ran between his balls and his asshole. It was an area I had explored enough on my own body to know that it was as much a part of a man's dick as the part that jutted out front and center. Every time I made contact, his long legs seemed to spread a little farther apart.

A few minutes later, somebody hit a home run, but Drew didn't move. He was out, snoring softly, his head pillowed on his thick forearms. I was still pretending to scratch his leg, but the truth was I just didn't want to stop touching him. Drew shifted on the bed and his calf pressed against my thigh. He sighed softly, and his ass muscles flexed.

Believe me, his ass wasn't the only flexing body part in the room. I tried to ignore it, but every time I thought I might have things under control, Drew's succulent ass would jiggle, and then boom—my dick would start doing push-ups on my belly, oozing thick, clear goo.

I guess that was when it finally dawned on me why I couldn't keep my hands or eyes off of Drew's succulent ass.

OK, so I'm a little bit slow. The good news is, I was bright enough to know that what I was thinking about was next to impossible. The bad news is, it didn't make my dick any softer.

Whatever. Within minutes, my poor brain was overwhelmed by a tidal wave of testosterone, and I found myself on my knees between Drew's outspread legs, my cock throbbing while I felt up his muscular butt. A couple of minutes later, I was beating my meat like mad, freckling his butt cheeks with my cock honey. Drew groaned and bucked a couple of times, but he didn't wake up.

I touched the head of my dick against his skin, rubbing my hot, swollen knob against his cool ass flesh. I traced the full, hard curve of muscle, then skidded down into his crack. My knob brushed over the thin red strap between his cheeks. I gently pulled the strap aside and stared longingly at his asshole. It was pale pink, ringed with short dark hairs. My hand trembled as I drew closer and closer. Then I made contact.

The second I touched that warm, moist slot, Drew bucked, impaling himself on my stiff finger. I knelt there, paralyzed with fear, waiting for him to jump up and deck me. He snorted, and the tight ring of his sphincter muscle grabbed at my finger, but he still didn't wake up.

I wiggled my finger and sank deeper into him. His butt flexed as he rose off the bed. I looked between his legs and saw that his cock and balls had fallen out of his skimpy shorts. His prick was pointing straight down, as hard as my own. I pried my dick away from my belly and pointed it at him. When I thrust my hips forward, the head of my meat skidded against his butt, across his balls, and down the shaft of his cock.

Drew bucked again and my finger totally disappeared. His ass was high in the air now, his knees drawn up under him, his thighs splayed wide. I slowly pulled my finger out of him, watching the pink lips surrounding his pucker suck at my knuckle. When I pushed it back in deep, Drew's balls drew up into a tight, furry knot.

I was jacking like mad. Long strings of goo were hanging off my cock, glistening on Drew's pale skin and staining his sheets. There was going to be no hiding what was coming, but I didn't care. I rubbed my dick head against his ass one last time and let loose with a flood of jizz. I swear it was the biggest load I'd ever shot in my life. The first blast gushed down Drew's crack, and his asshole snapped at me so hard, it damn near broke my finger. I just kept on blowing jizzballs all over his sweat-slicked backside, pumping my prick while his ass tube massaged my finger.

When I came back to my senses, I was slumped between Drew's legs, my finger still crammed up his butt. There was come everywhere, all over him and all over the sheets underneath him. Jism was oozing out of his piss hole, so I knew he'd come as well. In his sleep, no less! I started to mop it up, then got an inspiration. I leaned down and began licking the thick, creamy mess off his smooth buns. The splooge I'd spewed went down real easy. Afterwards, I fell asleep, still watching Drew's ass while he snoozed away.

* * *

"Old Drew was pretty hammered last Friday," I told a coworker over coffee on Monday morning. I had to drive him home."

"Drew? Drunk?" The man shook his head. "You've got that all wrong, Randy. Drew doesn't drink."

"He told me he didn't feel safe to drive," I protested.

"He buys a beer so the guys won't razz him too much, but he doesn't drink. His old man was a drunk. Drew's always treated it like poison. He must've been pulling your leg."

"Yeah." I sat there staring at my cup. I hadn't told the man about the fact that he'd been pretty hammered on Saturday and Sunday night as well—or about the fact that the events of Friday night were repeated almost blow for blow, except for me using more fingers every time. Hell, I was scheduled to meet with Drew tonight after work for a beer, and I knew I'd have to drive him home again—not that I was complaining, you understand. Maybe I'd talk to him and see if he could help me get this thing all figured out. I mean, hell, I was damn close to running out of fingers to stuff up that hot hole of his, and I only had one thing on me that was thicker. On the other hand, if I brought all this up, I could embarrass the man, and I sure as hell didn't want to do that. I just didn't have a clue what to do. Not a one.

Mark of the Dragon

"Hey, guy! Congratulations!"

"Thanks, Jay."

"Wow, Grant. Way to go!"

"Thanks for your vote, Geena."

"Very well done, Mr. Foster."

"I couldn't have done it without your help on my campaign speeches, Mrs. Freeman. I really appreciate all you've done for me."

Christ, wouldn't they ever go away and leave me alone?

I'd only run for senior class president because it was expected of me. That's the way it had always been—as the son of Martin Foster and the younger brother of Clayton, certain things were expected of me: academic excellence, athletic achievement, social skills, and becoming president of the senior class at Atherton High. I had always known exactly what was expected of me every step along the way—and I had always marched to meet my fate like a good soldier.

At least I had until very recently, when something had begun to happen that I couldn't explain—or ignore. I could pinpoint the exact moment that it all began, and I knew what the agent of the disruption was, but there was no acceptable, logical reason for the reaction. All I knew was that it scared me, knotting my stomach by day and haunting my dreams by night. I knew in my gut that I had to be constantly on guard, or it would destroy everything that gave my life structure and meaning.

If I hadn't been there that particular day, at that exact time, then none of this would be happening—or could it be that simple? Was that the lie—or was it the rest of my life? Was this one thing so true, there could be no other truth to substitute? Could one steamy August night contain the only truth the universe held for me? No! Impossible! I was terrified by the thought, yet I came back to it again and again, haunting it like an unquiet spirit.

It had been late and hot. Sweat was soaking my shorts and shirt, squishing in my shoes, dripping on the tennis court as I perfected my backhand. By the time I finished, I was alone except for the hard-shelled brown bugs that crashed against the court lights and crunched underfoot like some nightmare cereal.

I sprinted back to the gym, gasping the humid air, unable to stir even the memory of a breeze with my flailing limbs. The locker room was empty, row after row of closed steel boxes secured by padlocks. Fluorescent tubes flickered over-head, adding their buzz to the oppressive heat. I stripped out of my clothes—shirt, shoes, socks, jock—all splattering salt drops as they hit the concrete floor beside the bench.

Into the showers, lights glaring off the white tiles, even the cold water tepid, heated by the baked earth it flowed through. I stood there, all alone, letting the water pour along my body, feeling the blood pulse along veins that twined like pale blue ribbons from my shoulders to my wrists. I curled my fingers into fists, watching my forearms tense, thicken, my biceps curve up, quivering against my hairless skin. I took a deep breath, stretching my ribs under the layered muscle of my chest, watching the rise of pectorals, capped by tits like big pink gumdrops. I was teetering on the verge of horny, so close that all I'd need to tip the balance would be the touch of fingers against my belly, sending an ache of pleasure through my groin, an ache to curl my toes and bring my prick to throbbing, sticky life.

Then I saw him, and my hand was frozen to my side. Him. The Punk. He had no name—at least none that I knew then. He was of the background—one of those who fill the back rows of classrooms, crowd the periphery of student assemblies and other school events, adding bulk and color to the scene, but nothing of substance or importance. Nothing of importance. No. Not at all.

Tall—he was tall. And thick. Yes, thick all over—shoulders, chest, arms. Especially the arms. Triceps, biceps—big, separate knots all bound together by prominent veins. Veins like cables. On the left arm, dancing across all that knotted power, was a dragon, black and scarlet, back arched, claws extended, breathing fire across the pale skin of his shoulder. His powerful chest jutted out over his belly like a shelf, sprinkled with short brown hairs that grew in concentric rings around his meaty tits, the left one hooped with a gold ring that gleamed in the harsh light.

Him. The Punk. He wasn't quite handsome—his face all planes and angles, features too big, his stubbled jaw too heavy for perfection. But his eyes! His eyes were blue as neon, wide-set, bristled with long dark lashes. They were intense, hot eyes that burned my skin wherever he looked. And he was look-ing, looking all over me, searching for something. Was it some weakness he sought, some flaw? The pressure of his gaze made me go hot, made my bare skin prickle.

I wanted to move, to turn away but was rooted to the spot, skewered by his bold stare. He kept looking at me, his lips curling in a smile—or rather, a baring of teeth. His hand trailed slowly down over the arc of his belly, traced a branch-ing vein across that wall of flesh, through the clustered curls of his bush, onto the shaft of his cock, down, down to the hooded tip. I swear, I felt it in my belly when he flicked his finger against the shaft, felt the sensation that made it twitch, the skin shift, retract, expose a tiny point of moist, pale pink. Felt it again when he rubbed the spot, then pulled his hand away, trailing a tiny, crystal string that stretched towards me as he raised his hand. He sniffed his finger, licked it, then let it drop back to his groin.

Why couldn't I move? Why couldn't I turn away, take my soap, wash myself, rinse myself, and leave him standing there, leering vacantly at the place where I had stood? Instead, I remained motionless as he reached down between his legs, powerless to move when he gripped the loose skin on his dick between thumb and forefinger and began shak-ing himself awake.

It grew quickly, thick and strong like the rest of him, stretching, rising through the air till it pointed at my belly, alive and dangerous. And then he stood there, lips pursed, eyelids heavy, balls swaying as he began stroking, pulling, beating off.

I watched, stared, couldn't tear my eyes away from him. It was so long, so thick, so powerful, the skin pulling up over the tip, puffy and wrinkled, then stretching back, baring the shiny purple glans. Back and forth his hand went, fingers clenched tight as he pumped and pumped. The muscles in his chest twitched and danced as his fist flew faster. His biceps flexed, his belly ridged, the tendons in his forearm strained beneath his skin like cables.

No sound in the room but the water splashing and his breathing—our breathing—rough and ragged, chests heaving, balls drawing up tight. Once, in mid stroke, he lifted his hand to his mouth to lick it. His cock slapped up against his belly, the head rising inches above his puckered navel. He lapped his tongue across his palm, gripped his prick and pointed it back again, aiming it at me.

Still I watched, saw his balls roll along the shaft, his piss hole gape, the rim around his crown flare out like the head of a cobra, poised to strike. And then, suddenly, he stopped. His eyes flew open wide, his thighs bulged, his nostrils flared. His only movement now was a flicking of a fingernail against the trigger of his cock.

There was a moment of held breath for both of us. His prick swelled so tight, the shaft flexed like a bow, the head drew back, and a drop of white quivered in the deep-cut slit. It splattered on the floor, pushed out by a blast of his jism that arced across the room and exploded across my belly, branding me. I cried out, the heat of him burning into me, making my blood boil, shooting through my veins like fireworks. He shook, his hand trembled, and another molten shot arced across the room, hit my aching balls, frosting them with white.

I felt a churning in my belly, looked down, saw my own prick, a steel bar, jerking and flexing in the air. There was a feeling, like a fist in my gut, then I was shooting, coming, erupting. Never touched, never touching myself, I was spilling my load all over the floor.

I stood there, dizzy but afraid to move, feet planted, chest heaving, as the man—Him, the Punk—stalked across the room to me. He touched my belly with his finger, scooped his jism off me, then reached down and caught the creamy drool from my own cock. He held up his white-washed digit between us. Two bands around the callused, oil-stained finger, one white as cream, the other the color of old ivory—slowly dripping down to the webbing, catching in the coarse hairs on his knuckle. His tongue, long and pink, flickered out, lapped half the band away. The finger moved closer to my lips, making my eyes cross as I struggled to focus. The smell hit me, reeking, pungent, male. My tongue, out of my control, snaked out, made contact—and I took my first communion with a sigh.

* * *

"Grant! Good job."

"Yes!" I jumped, startled back to now. A booster scurried by, ducked through a door. The hall empty, clock showing class time. I clenched my book sack, began striding down the hall. I sensed before I saw him, felt his eyes on me, drawing me. I sniffed the air, smelled him, felt the heat of him radiating out into the hall around me.

I glanced and he was there, expressionless, blue eyes wide, scalp freshly shaved except for the bristling strip down the center of his rounded skull, and the tail, long and sleek, hanging down his broad back to tickle his meaty ass. Not a move—more a flicker of the pupils as he stared at me—drawing me over, deflecting me from my course. I wanted to go away from him, fought to go, then turned and walked his way.

His first real touch on me was like standing in a puddle

and grabbing a high-voltage line. I couldn't breathe as he began to unbutton my shirt—why?—one, two, three buttons, then folding the flap of fabric back. His eyes fluttered shut, his head sank down low, his lips brushed my chest, the curve of my pec, fastening on my nipple, sucking greedily like a hungry baby. I felt a tingling sensation, then every nerve in my body began to sing along with the rhythmic sucking of his hot, wet mouth. My prick jerked and stiffened in my pants, as I felt a hot string of saliva trickle down my belly, inside my shirt.

About the time I felt my heart would burst, he raised his head and licked his lips. "My vote," he rasped, his voice coarse, chipped around the edges. I glanced down and saw a livid purple aura hovering around my tingling nipple. The point stood out from the curve of muscle, still reaching for the warmth of his mouth and the silken motion of his tongue. He winked and stepped aside, slipped through a door to the outside, and was gone. Him. The Punk. Nemesis. My man of dreams.

As I turned back to my class, I heard a locker slam farther down the hall, a muffled chuckle, footsteps tapping the floor. I tensed, snapped my head around, saw nothing. Still, I pressed my hand against my chest and felt a chill around my heart.

* * *

"Christ, man, what happened to you?"

"Nothing," I muttered, my hand flying to cover the livid mark on my belly. "Ran into my dresser in the dark."

"Looks like the dresser gave you a hickey, man."

"Right." It had happened again. Him. The Punk. He'd been at me again, followed me, trailed me, caught me, stopped me on an evening in the woods. He'd dropped to his knees, tugged out my shirttail with his teeth, pressed his forehead against my gut. I shivered as I felt his lips against the skin, the gentle steady pressure of his sucking leech's mouth. I felt the tingling in my balls, the throbbing in my cock, the curling of my toes against the soles of my shoes. I put my hand against the column of his neck—pushing? pulling?—holding him there against me?

My fingers twined in the coarse tail of his hair, looped it around his neck, pulled it tight, like a noose. His eyelids fluttered, lashes so close they tickled against my skin like bugs. I shuddered and he looked up at me, eyes full of...something. He stood, began tucking my shirt in, knuckles against my skin, fingers wedged into my pants, their tips caught in my kinky pubes.

"Remember me," he rasped. Him. The Punk. And walked away, leaving me standing in the dark woods, all alone.

Remember? Yes. That was simple. I only needed to see the expressions in the eyes of those around me. Hands raised to mouths, sly whispers, bits of paper in my locker scrawled with crude words. Remember? Only sporadic applause now at my accomplishments on the playfield and in the classrooms. Averted eyes now. Heads shaken sadly. Looks of hostility where admiration had once been the norm.

And still, I couldn't stop. No way to resist. Drawn to him, to the Punk, just as a porch light draws a poor, demented bug inexorably toward destruction. I knew he knew my haunts, my routes, my pathway through those woods. Knew he waited for me there, once a week at first, then nightly, secure in the gut-born knowledge that I would return.

Naked now he stood in a hidden grove, ringed with trees and rocks, difficult to reach, far enough from my path to assure him that I came for him. Him The Punk. Tall and thick and pale, moon gleaming off his bare skin, muscles etched in warm marble. I pushed through the barrier shrubs, he sniffed the air, nostrils flaring, cock twitching, already beginning to swell from just the scent of me.

Tonight. It was time. Confrontation. Naked, stripped of all distinction—as I had been stripped bare at the school. *Sorry. Too bad. Not a good example. Rumors have come to us. Can you explain?* Explain! Not yet. Not yet, but soon. Tonight.

I tore off my clothes, casting them aside until I, too, was naked. Naked as him. The Punk. Tonight I would know what, if not why.

We stood together, two naked animals, sniffing the air as we circled around one another. So big, so perfect, self-contained, his muscles twitching, shifting, flexing as he moved around me, cautious, tensed, almost delicate. And, oh, God—the smell of him! The heady scent rising from him, from his cock and balls and ass that made the flames rise to lick my belly and my groin.

"Why?" I screamed, raising my hand, letting it fly in a wide arc towards him. It made contact with his cheek, snapped his head to one side, brought that glossy tail of hair forward, fanning across his shoulder, cascading over his torso like a curtain of dark silk. His thick chest rose and fell, the muscles in his belly tensed, but he made no sound beyond a sharp intake of breath.

"What are you doing to me?" My hand rose again, fingers curling to a fist. It drew back, slammed against him, into the sculpted perfection of his chest. A faint sigh rose from his lips, his arm shot out, his fingers encircled my wrist, manacled me. I tensed, waiting for the blow to knock me down, break me in half. Instead, he drew me to him, pulled me in the circle of his heat, a heat that radiated through the coolness of the moon-silvered autumn night.

"Touch me," he whispered. Fingers drawn in low against his belly, the skin like heated silk where it curved down to his groin. I swallowed, licked my lips, trembled as my hand was drawn up over the ridged gut, my fingers tickling against the fine line of hairs splitting him in half. Up my hand was drawn, over the rise of chest, the hollow of the throat, the sharp line of the jaw to his lips. "Touch me." Lips moving against me now without a sound.

Once touched, I had my answer. I wanted him with all my being, drawn to him, the lack of him a physical pain. Wanted him. Wanted to dig my fingers into his gut, rip him open and crawl inside, wrapping him back around myself, becoming him, melting into him. Barring this, what then?

A twist of my wrist snapped the circlet of fingers. His big hand dropped back to his side. I stood before him, our hard chests touching, the ring through his tit ringing the nipple on my own chest. My hand slipped from his mouth back again to his neck, tangling in his mane, pulling his face to mine.

Touch me? The kiss, first contact of mouth on mouth, lips, then tongues twining, thrusting, parrying. His saliva sweet on my tongue, coating it like honey, breath streaming down across my face and neck, warming my skin, sheening my chest with lustful sweat. More contact, feet unmoving, drawn like opposing magnetic poles—first thighs, then bellies, then cock to cock, pelvis joined to pelvis, front to front, cemented from knees to shoulders. We stood there, siamesed, sharing breath, nerve endings knit together, his skin to mine and back. Touch me!

I touched. Hands slipped from his chest, down his sides, around his waist, feeling, exploring, touching the curve of his ass. The long tail of his hair trailed down along his spine, tendrils reaching into his crack. I followed the hairs down into the sweaty crevice between the hard mounds of his cheeks. He shivered against me, shifted his feet wider apart, arched his back, let my hand curve lower on the full, hard roundness of him.

"Yes." My fingers worked down to the other channel, other opening into him. Soft, moist, springy muscle puckered like the lips already probed by my thrusting tongue. I rubbed the spot, felt him tremble, saw his eyelids flutter, heard a sound, like a sob caught in his throat. I pushed, slow and gentle but relentless, up into him, hard and harder until I breached the ring and slid up into his hot insides. I wiggled my finger around in him, poking, probing, savoring the sensations as he spasmed and shook in my arms.

"Fuck me." Felt more as a vibration in my own throat than heard as a sound from his. My body, galvanized, jolted at the sound. He stepped back, dropped to his knees, rolled facedown, arms spread-eagled, ass thrust up, knees wide apart. I looked down along his body, split into two perfect halves by the valley of his spine, saw the sweat beading on the cheeks of his ass, the pucker of his hole, the dangling balls, all bathed by the silver moon.

Led by no skill but instinct, I dropped down, sniffed him like a dog, shivering at the rich funk of his smell. I licked him, stuck my tongue up into him, wiggled it around. The chemistry at work between us made me hard, drew my nipples into points, yanked my balls tight against my body, forced me up on my knees, cock dripping, pointing. I clamped my hands onto his hips, thrust forward, speared him with all my strength.

A howl escaped him. His muscles knotted, made him a warm rock except for the tender, squirming softness of his bowels. I took the thick tail of his hair, twisted it, wrapped it across his mouth, like a bridle, drew his body up, pulled him against me, forced his head back. I pulled back and then, with all my might, stabbed my cock into him, driving it deep, twisting it in him like a knife. My other hand stroked his taut belly, teased the stiffness between his legs, pinched the skin puckering over the head of his thick cock, caught the ring threaded through his tit, pulled it, twisted it, testing him to the limits of his endurance.

"Now!" He screamed it—or I—our bodies bucking, writhing, spasming in the throes of absolute pleasure. I felt him coming before I came myself, felt the quaking, rocking, spasming waves that shook him, threw him to the ground to writhe and squirm beneath my weight, pumping his ooze out over the ground. I threw myself down on him, held him, wrapped my arms around his body, buried my face against his neck, sobbed in great gasping breaths as my virginity pumped out of me and into his hard body.

"Why?" My question, whispered after, as we stood there in the grove, his big head bent. I could feel him, feel his lips, the sweet erotic pressure as he began to suck his mark onto the smooth curve near the center of my chest. I filled my lungs with air, pressing the flesh up against him, driving my leg between his thighs, pressing his cock hard against his gut. "Why?" My fingers tightened in his long tail of hair, pulling but not pulling him away, not breaking the steady, gentle sucking of his full lips.

"Dragon's mark." His voice low, lazy, full of sex. "Dragon's desire." His muscles tensed, biceps swelling like big veined balls, quivering with power. His knuckles whispered against my jaw. "Dragon's man."

* * *

"Jesus, man! Far out! Can I touch it?"

"No problem, Jay." Fingers touch, tentative, the gelled spikes of my crudely chopped blond locks.

"Shit, does it hurt?" I shake my head from side to side, puff my chest out, display my nipple, newly pierced. It still throbs from the needle plunged through the tender flesh the previous night by Dragon as he pinned my arms to my sides, his hips churning around the axis of my prick, piercing me as I was piercing him.

"Radical, dude." Another awed expression, taking in the Doc Martens, the faded jeans, tight as a second skin, displaying more than they hid.

"Chemical, man. Chain reaction." I turned, leaned, lapped a trickle of sweat from the Dragon's muscled side. He groaned, flexed, inclined his head to me.

"Outta control!" A shocked voice from the periphery.

I smiled and nodded as my Dragon slipped a thick arm around my naked chest. "Soon, man. Almost. Not yet. Not quite."

Clean Living

"Good morning, Joel. Your uniform is in the back. You may hang your street clothes on one of those hooks behind the door. You did remember to bring a pair of white tennis shoes, didn't you?" I nodded. "Good. Now, then, get changed and we'll get our day started."

"Sure thing, Mr. Jeffers." I took one more look at the ramrod straight, white-clad figure, then scurried through the pharmacy and into the back of the store. I felt positively scruffy by contrast, even though I was freshly shaven and my hair was still damp from the shower. With his slicked-back helmet of blond hair, his glittering steel-rimmed glasses, and his spotless uniform, Mr. Jeffers looked like he'd just stepped out of sterile packaging.

That shouldn't have surprised me, I thought, as I sat down and untied my shoes. Mr. Jeffers was famous—in Hutterville at least. He was one of the founders of the "Clean Living" movement, headquartered in an office above the hardware store down on Main Street. The way I looked at it, this was a bunch of people who had just a little too much time on their hands. They were dedicated to healthy food and exercise—which was OK—and to celibacy, which I thought was OK till Mary Beth Hicks told me what it meant. Not having sex was what it meant, and I honestly couldn't say I approved of that at all. I hadn't exactly had any sex—unless you count all those times in the bathroom with the door locked—but I sure wanted to have some, and the sooner the better.

Still, Mr. Jeffers was offering good money for doing what was basically janitorial work. I wasn't quite sure I understood exactly what was going on, because when Mary Beth had applied, he had only offered her five bucks an hour. I never told Mary Beth because I didn't want to hurt her feelings, but he offered me seven bucks an hour and free uniforms. I would've thought he'd want a pretty girl with big knockers working for him, but he didn't. Probably would've been too much of a temptation for the head of the local celibacy movement.

"Wait!" I spun around, pants in one hand, shirt in the other. Mr. Jeffers was standing in the doorway, looking at me intently.

"I…I'm not quite ready yet," I said, which was pretty obvious, unless I was planning on wandering around the store in my jockey shorts.

"I can see that, Joel," Mr. Jeffers retorted, his gaze flickering from my face to my feet and back again. The tip of his tongue skidded across his upper lip. "Before you get started, I just wanted to spend a few minutes talking about hygiene. I know that young people sometimes aren't as careful as they should be about keeping clean."

"I'm 20 years old, Mr. Jeffers," I replied, somewhat defensively. He licked his upper lip again. "I took a shower this morning and brushed my teeth."

"Excellent." He took two steps forward, and I took one step back. I bumped up against the wall. He kept coming. When he finally stopped, there wasn't more than a foot between us. I had to crane my neck to look him in the eye now. Mr. Jeffers was tall. Next thing I knew, his big hands had encircled my wrists, and my arms were raised high in the air. I rose up onto my toes. Mr. Jeffers was also strong.

He ducked his head and sniffed, his breath ruffling the hairs in my armpit. I giggled, then my face grew hot. "That tickles," I said, squirming in his grip.

"You don't use an antiperspirant, do you?" he asked. I shook my head guiltily. "Good. It clogs the pores. You have a clean, masculine scent, Joel." He sniffed me once more, then stepped back and eyed the crotch of my briefs, like maybe he was checking for pee stains. "You get dressed, and then we'll get started with your training." He reached out, like maybe he was going to grab me by the shoulders. His hands were so close I could feel his heat, but he didn't touch. He just licked his lips again, turned on his heel and left the room. As I scrambled to get into my uniform, it occurred to me that I wished he *had* put his hands on my shoulders. Weird.

My job at the pharmacy settled into a routine pretty quickly. I spent most of my time stocking shelves, dusting merchandise, washing windows, and cleaning floors. Mr. Jeffers was a stickler for things being clean. That included me, of course. He was always popping in on me when I was getting dressed to inspect my fingernails, or check for wax in my ears or some damned thing. One morning he even rooted around in my navel, looking for lint. He was standing behind me, both hands splayed on my belly as he gently probed the mossy hollow. When he dug out a little wad of white lint and a couple of stray hairs, he didn't seem the least bit disgusted. After he left, I realized I'd sprung a woody. I sure hoped Mr. Jeffers hadn't seen it.

"Are you living a celibate lifestyle, Joel?" Mr. Jeffers sprung that on me one day in the stockroom while I was eating a sandwich. We were closed for our daily lunch break, and he was doing what he usually did—biceps curls. He'd come into the back while the pharmacy was locked down for lunch, strip out of his white tunic, and do about a million curls, pumping these really heavy barbells he kept stashed there.

Mr. Jeffers had a real thing about bodybuilding, and he was in incredible shape. He didn't have a hair on him, so there was no hiding the razor-sharp definition of his muscles. His gut was rippled like a washboard, his pecs were enormous and his biceps were totally awesome. I always made a real effort not to stare at him, but it was tough not to look. Right now, he was pumping those weights, and his biceps looked like they were ready to explode. You could see all the individual muscles that made up the huge flexing knots and all the veins that bulged just beneath his pale skin. The only sign he was making any effort at all was the way his big nipples were all puffed up like pink candy kisses. I had only noticed it because he was back there in the small room with me for an hour every day, pumping away like clockwork. They always went from flat to fat in about two minutes. It must've had something to do with his blood pressure.

"What do you think, Joel?" He had stowed the weights and was standing in front of me, his left arm flexed.

"Looks great, Mr. Jeffers," I said, watching a vein that snaked across the swollen curve of flesh twitch with his pulse.

"You can touch it if you like." Well, I guess I liked, because almost before I knew it, I had both hands pressed against the hard, hot knot of muscle. It was so alive, throbbing with blood beneath my fingers. "Squeeze it," he urged me, his voice almost a whisper. I flexed my fingers against the unyielding mass. "Harder!"

"Like a rock, Mr. Jeffers," I said, aware that my heart was thudding against my ribs for no particular reason. It was like a rock, but it was a rock covered with pale, warm silk. The skin on the inside of his arm was like touching a puppy's belly. No telling how long we stood there, head to head, staring at his biceps. The spell was broken when the clock chimed the hour, signaling the end of lunch break. I let my hands drop, and he slipped back into his snowy-white tunic. He buttoned it and turned to leave the room.

"Mr. Jeffers?" He glanced over his shoulder at me. "You've got something on the back of your pants." He took a swipe at it, but the lint didn't budge. "I'll get it," I offered. He nodded. I touched the full curve of his butt. Damn, it was as hard as his arm! I brushed my palm back and forth across the tautly stretched fabric of his white pants until the offending fibers were gone. I was looking for more lint to brush, when we heard a knock at the front door and Mr. Jeffers had to go.

After the door shut behind him, I looked down and saw that not only did I have a hard-on, but I'd also leaked a quarter-sized spot of cock snot onto my pants. I tried to readjust myself and ended up with a second spot below the first. There was no way I could go out on the floor with a drooling stiffer stuffed down my pants leg. I peeked out and saw that Mr. Jeffers was busy with a customer, then closed the door and unzipped my pants.

My cock jutted up, all red and swollen, the foreskin already drawn back behind the glans. I looked at it, and it flexed, rising high, spitting slime onto the floor at my feet. I grabbed it, closed my eyes and started pumping.

All of a sudden, Mr. Jeffers popped into my mind, grinning at me, his huge arms flexed. I shook my head to clear the image, but he was still there when I shut my eyes again. Well, I didn't have all day, so I just went for it, beating my meat while thinking about Mr. Jeffers' arms.

Inside of five minutes, my balls were fighting for space on top of my cock shaft, and I was leaking like a broken water pipe. I stopped stroking and squeezed. My knob bulged, shading from crimson to purple. My jizz hole gaped wide. I reached out and tickled under the tip, rubbing the mass of nerves where all my sex wiring came together. I grunted with pleasure, and the muscles in my groin started to contract. I just barely had time to grab a wad of paper towels and point my prick at it before I let fly with a huge, gooey load that would've wiped out half the boxes of beauty supplies on the shelves across from me if I hadn't taken precautions. I squirted my last, wiped myself clean, then stuffed my dick back into my trousers. When I went back to work, I found myself thinking about jacking off every time I so much as looked at Mr. Jeffers. Weird.

* * *

"Joel! Just a moment there." I froze. Mr. Jeffers sure had an uncanny knack for knowing when I'd have my pants down around my ankles. This morning I was wearing a jock-strap because all my underwear was dirty. I'd mooned him with my fuzzy butt and was probably going to catch hell for it. He came towards me, staring intently at my left ass cheek. He knelt and touched me. I shuddered, and my hole slammed shut so hard you could practically hear it. Mr. Jeffers chuckled softly but didn't move his hand.

"What is it?" I asked, sparks shooting through me like maybe I'd swallowed a Fourth of July sparkler.

"I thought it might be a boil"—I flinched at that. *A boil? On my ass?*—"but it's just a mosquito bite. I'll take care of it." He rummaged in a drawer, squeezed something out on his finger and smeared it on the bite.

"Thanks, Mr. Jeffers." I started to pull up my pants, but he motioned for me to stop.

"Joel?" I looked at him. It was weird to look down at him, but since he was kneeling and I was standing, I didn't have much choice. "Are you circumcised?" I shook my head warily, hoping he wasn't going to offer to take care of that for me as well. "May I see?" My eyes got wide, and I swallowed noisily. Mr. Jeffers smiled. He had very white teeth.

I was afraid to dump the contents of my jock pouch because I was already getting a hard-on from having him touch my ass. My belly was churning, my balls were tingling and my dick was twitching to life. Still, I didn't like to say no to Mr. Jeffers.

"Hygiene is very important if the foreskin is still intact." Oh, great! Another health lecture. I'd been hoping…well, I don't know exactly what I'd been hoping for, but it wasn't a discussion about taking a bath. My dick began to deflate, and I let it flop out of my jock for him to inspect.

"Very good, Joel. Very impressive." He was staring at my cock like maybe he was looking for printed instructions about what to do with it. He slipped his hand up and under, and my prick was all of a sudden draped across his palm. It wasn't deflating any more, either. We both watched as it stretched to full length and began to levitate.

He wasn't embarrassed or anything like that. He gripped the tip of my prick and peeled my foreskin back, baring the fat pink glans. Blood surged down between my legs, and my prick started pointing at the ceiling. Mr. Jeffers looked at it from all angles, ran his fingertip around the rim that divided head from shaft, then popped his finger into his mouth.

"Very clean, Joel. Excellent." My dick jerked and spit slime against his chin. He wiped it up and licked his finger again. His smile broadened.

"I..." That was as far as I got, because Mr. Jeffers popped the cherry-red head of my pecker into his mouth and started sucking, hard. I grabbed his shoulders to keep from falling and watched his lips massage my bulging shaft. My nuts started to do pull-ups, and a flush of pink began spreading from my groin to my belly and beyond.

"Are you all right, Joel?" Mr. Jeffers was looking up at me, lips glistening, pupils dilated, nostrils flaring. He licked my dick and stood up. A second later, his white tunic was on the floor, and his pants were around his knees. I looked at his stiffer— it was straight as an arrow and tightly clipped. The head tapered to a blunt point. His fat balls hung down low between his sleek thighs. He must've shaved off his pubes, because there wasn't a trace of a hair in sight. It looked sort of cool.

"Oh, man," Mr. Jeffers sighed. He had pulled my over-hang out beyond the tip of my prick and slipped his own cock head inside. I grunted and squirted a shot of lube that oozed out of my skin and ran down his shaft. When it dripped onto his balls, they rose up between his legs, hovered a minute, then sagged back down. He pulled harder on my skin, and I squirted again.

"Put your hand between my legs, Joel," Mr. Jeffers demanded, his voice hoarse. I obeyed, my palm sliding under his silky-soft balls. He spread his legs slightly, and my fingers skidded against the puckered flesh surrounding his hole. No hairs there either, or anywhere on the marble-solid cheeks of his ass.

"Finger me, Joel." I did, mesmerized by the sight of his abs flexing in rhythm with my probing fingers. I was tentative at first, then pressed harder. When my middle finger slid up into him, his eyelids drooped and all his muscles bulged. "Deeper, Joel. Deeper!" My finger went in all the way. He was soft and wet inside, his tight channel squeezing my finger as he started to writhe and twitch.

"More, Joel. Give me more!" I pushed a second finger up into him, then a third. He kept making this soft groaning sound as he pushed his butt against the palm of my right hand. I was using my left hand to explore the rest of his body, touching all those places I'd only looked at before. Mr. Jeffers saw me eyeing his swollen tits, then put his hand against the back of my head and pushed my face into his chest. "Suck it," he cried. "Bite it, chew on it. Yes!" I chewed his tit while his asshole chewed my finger. It was quite a sensation.

He was still jacking me, and I was drooling like crazy. When he let go, my dick started slapping my belly. Mr. Jeffers pulled open a drawer in the counter behind us and got out a box of rubbers. He took one out, tore open the foil, and started to put it on me. He rolled it down all the way, then grabbed my cock and squeezed it till it bulged inside the rubber like a big sausage. Then he spun around and braced his hands on the counter. His butt was thrust towards me, cheeks split, his well-fingered hole blowing little kisses at me.

"Fuck me, Joel. Put your hard cock in me and fuck me. Do it!" The very idea took my breath away. He reached back and grabbed my cock. My knob touched the puckered ring of muscle, then disappeared. Mr. Jeffers grabbed my ass and pulled me forward. I watched, as inch after inch of my hard-on slid up into him. When I was in him up to my balls, he put his hands back on the counter and dropped his head. I grabbed him by the shoulders and let my instincts take over.

"That's it, Joel!" he grunted when my belly smacked his

butt. "Put it in me. Pump it! Drive it in deep. Good man! Yeah!" Nothing in my life so far had prepared me for the feeling of fucking. With Mr. Jeffers, it was like finding a soft spot in a stone wall and putting your dick in it. I pulled out and rammed him again. My balls bounced off of his, and I almost turned inside out.

I started humping, driving in and out of the clutching heat of his bowels. My hands slipped from his shoulders to his arms. He flexed his biceps, and my fingers spread wide apart. I felt him up all over, his chest, his belly, his rigid prick. Whenever I stopped pumping, he'd start smacking his butt against my belly as he bounced up and down on my prong. I pinched his tits, and his hole grabbed me like a wet fist.

"I…I'm gonna…" I groaned, starting to shiver and shake.

"Pull out," he cried, pushing me back. My cock popped out of him, and he spun around and stripped the rubber off my flexing meat. He jacked it a couple of times, and I let fly, shooting long strings of jism up onto his sweat-slick torso. It hit him and he scooped it into his palm and began jacking off with it. I shot another blast up the inside of his right thigh, and his balls jiggled. I pumped a third shot onto his belly, and he blew. Thick ribbons of come spouted out of him, spattering my right forearm and thigh.

"Mr. Jeffers?" He raised his head. His torso was glistening with jism. He reached out and ruffled the line of hairs that split me in half, neck to navel. His fingers continued south, tangling in my pubes, then wrapping around the sticky stalk of my cock. "Uh, could you maybe explain to me how all this fits in with your 'Clean Living' theory?"

"That's easy, Joel." Mr. Jeffers slowly insinuated his thumb up into my overhang. "I signed a pledge that I would abstain from sexual relations with the opposite sex. There was no prohibition against the prevention of a toxic buildup of testosterone."

"Toxic?" I gulped. Mr. Jeffers nodded solemnly. "So that was therapy?" He winked at me, gave my foreskin a pinch, then slipped into his white tunic and buttoned it over the glistening expanse of his chest.

"Our public calls," he quipped, closing the door of the storeroom behind him. As his footsteps receded, I stood there, my pants around my ankles, my cock angled high, thinking that maybe this clean living routine wasn't such a bad deal after all.

The Setup

I downed the last of my coffee, unplugged the pot, grabbed my keys, and bounded out of the house. I got to the car, then almost started back for my briefcase before I realized that I wouldn't be needing it. I backed out of the driveway, cranked the radio up to throb and began singing at the top of my lungs as I headed off to work.

The wind blowing through the open window on the driver's side was warm against my bare skin. Tank top, cutoff jeans, thick white socks, and steel-toed boots—now that was the way to dress for work. No more slacks, ties or sport coats for me. Well, not for three months in any case. I'm a high school teacher by profession, but during the summer months I work for a friend who owns a landscaping business. Planting, pruning, and general maintenance—whatever my friend wants me to do, I do it. The extra money helps out, but the best part is that I get to be outside all day, every day. I get a tan, and I get the chance to mellow out after nine months of corralling adolescents. I also love the manual labor aspect of it. Believe me, a day of digging holes and setting a hedge makes the most strenuous workouts I've ever devised at the gym seem like child's play. I ache for the first week or so, then I'm ready to handle anything Dan can throw my way. Well, almost anything.

When I pulled into the parking lot behind Dan's office, he was supervising the loading of one of the company trucks. I waved at him and took a quick look at his helpers. One was a slender blond, not bad-looking at first glance but not really my type. The other guy was single-handedly lifting a redwood tub that contained a large evergreen tree. This one was tall, built, and definitely caught my interest. When he gripped the edges of the container and hefted it, his biceps bulged and the muscles in his forearms stood out in ridges. He deposited the tree in the truck, then stripped off his T-shirt and wiped his forehead. The guy had obviously sculpted his torso with care. His squared pecs were dusted with silky charcoal fur. A thin line of the same luxuriant growth trailed down the middle of his chiseled belly, fanning out slightly before it disappeared into the waistband of his jeans. It wasn't a bad view to start the day with. Not bad at all.

"Pete!" My friend Dan saw me and jogged over to my car. "Glad to see you." We shook hands, then embraced warmly. "Got a couple of rookies out there, Pete. Would you be willing to ride herd on them, at least until they learn the ropes?"

"Sure, Dan. I guess so." I had always cherished my summer job, because it entailed no responsibilities except getting to work on time and doing what I was told. I really didn't want to be in charge of a crew, but Dan was looking frazzled, and I didn't have the heart to turn him down. I copped another glance at the dark-haired hunk out by the truck. I definitely had no objection to working with him. Actually, I couldn't think of a soul I'd rather flex and sweat beside on a hot day.

"I'll pay you extra, Pete," Dan assured me.

"Tell you what, Dan. Why don't you just whip up a batch of your special barbecue sauce and invite me over to eat ribs till I explode?"

"Sure. Rick would love that."

"What? Watching me explode?"

"No, dope. Having you over for dinner. Maybe we'll even round up a date for you."

"Maybe not, Dan." I shook my head. Those two were always trying to fix me up. I couldn't seem to get the message through to them that I was happy being a bachelor. I had been in a relationship for almost seven years, but things had fallen apart almost a year ago, and I had managed to readjust to life as a single man. I was actually pretty content, although my sex life sucked—or didn't, if you know what I mean. I was cheerful, fit, and self-sufficient. I also had a strong right hand and a raunchy imagination, which kept the old juices flowing if all else failed. None of this kept my happily coupled buddies from worrying about me, however.

"Pete, don't be difficult." Dan was ready to lecture. "Rick and I just hate to see you unsettled."

"Dan, I'm settled. I cook, do laundry, clean house—I even get my bills paid on time. I can take care of myself, you know."

"Fine, Pete." He looked me up and down with a frown. "You're looking a little thin."

"I'm not thin, Dan." I pulled up my shirt and tensed, popping up a perfect six-pack of abs. "I'm just in shape. I've been working on this belly for almost a year."

"Very impressive." Dan didn't sound too impressed. "I still think you should eat more."

"Thanks, Mom," I teased, clapping a hand on his shoulder. "I love you dearly, Dan, but knock off the parental bullshit." Dan snorted. "Now, let's get a move on before these plants die of old age."

Dan gave me the working diagrams for the landscaping project and sent me on my way. I walked back across the parking lot to the truck, arriving just in time to see the dark-haired guy I'd been admiring when I drove up stretch mightily. It was an edifying scene. His lats flared, his pecs bulged, his biceps quivered—and he had muscles in his midsection that I hadn't managed to locate in all my years of working out. When the man caught sight of me, he smiled and extended his hand.

"Leo Hopkins," he said as his big hand enveloped mine. "Glad to meet you."

"Pete Sears. Likewise." I looked at him up close. Leo Hopkins was one very fine fox of a man. He was closer to my age than I'd thought when I first saw him across the lot. He had fine lines around his eyes and flecks of silver at the temples. His chiseled features had been burnished by the sun. His smile broadened, and my heart began to thump. Things were getting more interesting by the minute.

Just as we were ready to head out to the jobsite, Dan waved us down and snagged Ben, the young blond who had been helping to load the truck when I arrived. One of Dan's workers had called in sick, and Ben was needed to fill in on another crew. That meant that Leo and I would be working alone on our project.

"Sorry," Dan had said when he stuck his head through

the passenger window of the truck.

"We'll cope, Dan," I assured him. Dan watched us drive away, a self-satisfied smile plastered across his face.

"So, Pete," Leo asked as he threaded his way through the morning traffic, "have you been doing landscaping work for a long time?" I cleared my throat and gave him the two-minute version of my life story. Leo had one hand on the wheel, the other draped across the back of the seat. He hadn't bothered to put his shirt back on, and the view was magnificent. I scanned along his muscular arm to his shoulder. From that point, after a brief stall in his pale, furry armpit, my eyes wandered across his chest, down his belly, to the denim-clad bulk of his thick thighs.

"How about you?" I asked.

"This is a first for me, Pete. I moved here from Chicago about six months ago for personal reasons. Left my job, the house, friends—everything. A relationship I'd been in for several years went sour, and I had to get away."

"Why Seattle?"

"Because it was a long way from Chicago." Leo laughed wryly. He didn't offer any more information, and I didn't ask. We rode the rest of the way to the jobsite in comfortable silence.

✳ ✳ ✳

I got home that night, suffering from a stiffness in my shoulders and a serious testosterone overload. Leo was not only physically gorgeous, he was witty, articulate, and comfortable to be around. By the end of the day, we had discovered several areas of mutual interest and managed to solve quite a few of the world's most intractable problems.

Unfortunately, Leo had inadvertently made one of my most intractable problems a whole lot worse. Up until about eight hours ago, I had almost convinced myself that I could be content with solitary sex. That lie now lay shattered on the field, laid low by Leo's mere presence. I liked the way he looked, the way he smelled, the way he moved. Most of all, I liked the man who inhabited that perfect physique.

I unlaced my boots, pried them off my tired, sweaty feet, then stripped out of my dirty clothes. I stood in front of the bathroom mirror and surveyed the terrain with satisfaction. I was no Leo, but I was looking damned good. When I stretched and flexed my muscles, my cock followed suit, rising up from between my thighs to point at the mirror.

"Not now, guy," I muttered, hooking my forefinger around the shaft and pushing it down. My cock wasn't having any of that. It flew back up and smacked me in the belly, twitching anxiously. "Can you wait till we get into the shower?" I asked. "That way we can avoid messing up a towel." The head flared and my balls climbed up to hug the shaft. "Fine. We'll go right now."

I turned on the faucets and stepped under the hot pounding spray. When I closed my eyes and collared my cock, my mind's eye was filled with images of Leo gleaned from our day together. I tried briefly—and unsuccessfully— to push them aside. It hardly seemed ethical to make a masturbatory fantasy out of a man I was already beginning to think of as a friend. My resolve was quickly undermined. My hard-on and I had only one thing on our collective mind—Leo.

I leaned forward, slipped my forearm between my legs, and began grinding my hips slow and easy. I fantasized that I was humping Leo's chest, although the downy fuzz on my arm was a poor substitute for the springy, gleaming curls that clustered in the valley between Leo's bulging pecs.

Our bodies had been in contact more than once during the course of the day. Shortly after lunch, I was struggling to move a huge rhododendron that we were going to transplant, when Leo stepped in to help. The location of the shrub made it necessary for him to ease in behind me and slip his arms around my body. His biceps pressed against my sides, and his chest rubbed against my back as he added his muscle to mine. The contact had been brief but electric.

I continued to hump my arm while images of Leo flashed across the screen of my eyelids. I began rubbing my belly, tracing the ridges of my abs, letting my fingers trail down into the tangle of my pubes. I pushed my fingers lower, pressing them tight against the ridge of cock that ran between my legs, back to my tightly puckered asshole. The soft skin on the inside of my biceps rubbed against the tender point of my nipple, jolting me with a little shock of pleasure.

My balls scooted up higher, getting cozy with my cock shaft. My shoulders hunched forward, and I groaned softly as the urgency of orgasm began to overtake me. I knelt in the shower stall, both hands between my legs, my cock pistoning against my tensed forearms. I rocked back and forth, the heft and hardness of my own muscles substituting for what I really desired. Perfect or not, the moment came, freezing me in place, head down, staring into the gaping slit in the end of my meat.

I tickled my balls and poked at my asshole. My glans bulged, and I roared out my relief. A drizzle of white oozed out and dripped onto my thigh, then my muscles knotted and I blasted myself right in the face. I felt the sticky heat on my cheek and chin and lips. I stuck out my tongue, lapped at the reeking goo, groaned, and shot again. Jism gushed out of me, splattering my forearms. I sagged against the side of the tub, panting, my body still shaking with pleasure. Afterward, I pushed myself back to my feet and stood there until the hot water ran out.

＊ ＊ ＊

That pattern became habitual during the course of the next few weeks. Leo and I worked well together, and Dan left us teamed up. We never got around to asking for a third man to fill out the crew, and Dan made no effort to find anyone. My days were filled with sun, hard work, and Leo. My nights were filled with fantasies of sex with Leo and an increasing level of frustration. I thought I sensed that the attraction wasn't all one-way, but I shied away from pursuing it. If I got involved with Leo, I knew I'd want more than a one-night stand. We had both talked about our former relationships and our subsequent fear of commitment. I wasn't quite ready to deal with any of it.

On a fine hot Saturday in late July, I drove over to Dan and Rick's for a barbecue. I saw Leo's car when I pulled into the drive. Dan had mentioned he would be there when he called to invite me that morning. This would be the first time we had gotten together outside of work. I knew I liked Leo, but I hadn't anticipated the almost giddy feeling that assailed me as I walked up to the front door. I berated myself for having the emotional maturity of a horny adolescent, but I could do nothing to stop the butterflies swirling in my gut or the tingling sensation in my groin.

Dan and Rick greeted me, thrust a beer in my hand, and shooed me out to the pool in their backyard. I looked around but saw no one except Leo, who was swimming laps in the pool. When I asked about the rest of the guests—these barbecues tended to be big affairs—Rick muttered something about lots of last-minute cancellations. I shot him a suspicious look, but he just smiled blandly and went back to preparing what appeared to be an elaborate salad.

"Pete!" Leo swam to the edge of the pool and hoisted himself out, rising from the waves like Neptune. Water coursed off him, plastering the short hairs flat against the heroically sculpted curves of his body. He shook his head, flinging glimmering droplets in a wide arc, then shook my hand vigorously. "Looks like we're the only ones who didn't cancel."

"So Rick said."

"We'll manage. Right?" Leo smiled at me, banishing any further concerns about missing guests. "You brought something to swim in, didn't you?"

"Right here under my pants," I assured him.

"Too hot for clothes today, Pete." I started to say something about any day around him being too hot for clothes but decided against it. Instead, I stripped down to my Speedo. It was red, streamlined, and not too subtle. I had almost put it back in the drawer at the last minute but had convinced myself I could get away with it. All that gym time coupled with this landscaping gig had to be good for something. Leo's frankly approving gaze when he saw it made me glad I hadn't chickened out.

"If you'd like, I can put some oil on your back and shoulders, Pete. This sun is brutal."

"Sure, Leo." He was sitting astride a chaise, bottle in hand. I straddled the lounge and presented my back to him. I felt the warm oil drizzle onto my shoulders, then Leo's big, strong hands rubbing it in. He massaged my shoulders, then his hands slipped down onto my back, lower and lower, till his fingertips were nudging the waistband of my swimsuit.

"Lean back, Pete," he murmured, scooting in closer to me. His hairy thighs pressed against mine, and I felt the lump in his crotch against my ass cheeks. I leaned backward, and my shoulders met the unyielding mass of Leo's pecs. My skin was so sensitized by his touch that I could even feel the nubs of his nipples. I sighed softly, and my prick began to stir.

Leo lifted the bottle and squirted a stream of oil across my chest. Then he began smoothing it over the rise of my pecs.

When his fingers trailed down onto my belly, I clamped my hands on his thighs. My cock was hard now, jutting over towards my right hip. If Leo looked down along my torso, there was no way he was going to miss it. I had a feeling he wouldn't mind.

"Hey, guys!" I jumped guiltily at the sound of Rick's voice. Leo still had both arms wrapped around me, rubbing my chest and belly, so I didn't go far. "I forgot to buy a couple of things, so we're going to pop off to the store. We'll be right back. Carry on." He waved and was gone, leaving Leo and me to fend for ourselves.

"This looks like a setup," I chuckled, leaning my head back against Leo's shoulder.

"Do you care?"

"Not at all. How about you?"

"I want you, Pete," he whispered, his breath hot against my ear.

"You got me," I replied, pushing back tighter against him. His fingers brushed against the stiff hot cylinder throbbing in my swimsuit. I turned my head and began nuzzling his neck. While he teased at my hard-on, I eased my oiled hands between his belly and the small of my back, then started working my way down. Leo's dick was rigid, twitching as I explored it from knob to balls and back again. I played with him till my hands were slippery with his cock slime, then twisted around in his grip and looked him in the eyes.

"I think it's about time you handed that oil bottle over to me, Leo." He grinned raunchily and did as I suggested. I stood up, stripped off my trunks, and straddled the chaise again, facing him this time. Leo shed his trunks as well and resumed his seat, his legs draped companionably over mine. I squeezed the bottle and squirted oil across his chest and down over his washboard belly. Then I upended the bottle and let it drizzle onto the swollen dome of his hard-on. The oil ran down the shaft and beaded up in his black pubes.

I began rubbing, savoring his heat and the hardness of his muscles. His eyes fluttered shut, and his mouth opened in a silent groan of pleasure. I touched him everywhere, saving his cock for last. At first, I barely grazed the tip, watching the ruddy glans swell and darken. After I had fingered his knob for several slow, sensual minutes, I gripped the shaft and squeezed it tight. Leo's eyes opened, and he humped my fist. I scooped his fat balls up in my other hand, and his hips pumped again.

Leo latched onto my prick, and we began jacking each other off. I leaned forward and our lips touched, then our tongues. We scooted closer. I tugged on his balls and rubbed them against mine. Leo grunted with pleasure, and his cock jerked against my palm. As we inhaled, our chests touched. I could feel his heart pounding against my ribs. I pumped faster, and the veins in his cock shaft began to swell like tiny cables.

"You close?" he gasped. I nodded. Leo pried my hand away from his hard-on and winked at me. "How's that?" The swollen dome of his knob rubbed up my juice tube to the trigger of nerves that was currently the center of my entire universe. I gasped and nodded again. He clamped his hands on my hips, and I felt all his muscles tense. We both looked down, watching our cocks go head to head, all our energy focused on maintaining and intensifying that single point of contact.

I saw a drop of clear fluid bubble up out of Leo's piss hole, quiver in the sunlight, then ooze out and drip down onto my knob. Both our cocks flexed, moving apart, connected only by a sticky string of lube. They touched again, flexed, then pressed heavily against one another.

"I'm there," I gasped, every nerve in my body screaming for release. Leo twitched his hips slightly, rubbing me just the right way. I let out a low moan and blew a shot of come up the center of his belly. His glans butted against my shaft again, and I shot another geyser that splattered his left pec. Then, barely able to control my muscles, I rubbed the head of my cock against the bloated underside of his shaft. More come flowed out, white drops that slid down his prick and frosted his jiggling balls. The muscles on the tops of his thighs bulged, and I saw him erupt, shooting a streamer of jizz that hit my neck and drizzled down my back. Leo cried out and pushed me back on the chaise. He humped like mad, draining the aching hard-ons trapped between our bellies.

"That was nice," he whispered in my ear after his hips had finally ground to a halt.

"Very," I replied, stroking his broad back.

"I'm not a guy who likes one-night stands," he went on, raising his head and fixing me with his dark eyes. "Or one-afternoon stands, either."

"I'm with you there, Leo," I replied, rubbing sweat and oil into his furry ass cheeks. "My social calendar is empty into the foreseeable future."

"Good. Mine is too." He lay his head on my chest again and his arms tightened around me. We finally motivated ourselves to get up, wipe each other down, and go for a swim. While we were swimming laps side by side, Dan and Rick reappeared.

"What took you so long?" I asked.

"You boys seem to be surviving without us," Rick replied, stifling a smug grin. "We had a hell of a time finding decent tomatoes."

"Right," I snorted. "Like the ones in the garden weren't good enough." I looked pointedly at the vines along the fence, laden with succulent red fruit.

"Oh." Rick shrugged. "I forgot all about those."

"Think you two can survive if we get back inside and finish up making the barbecue sauce?" Dan asked.

"What do you think, Pete?" Leo swam up behind where I was treading water and slipped his arms around my waist. I responded by popping a rod instantly. Leo rubbed his crotch up against my ass, making it clear that he was suffering from the same affliction.

"I think we may just have to send these guys back to the store for a while, Leo."

"Not a problem," Rick assured us. "Come on, Dan. We're going to the store. I just remembered that we're out of...oatmeal. I need some." Dan shrugged and followed Rick back to the house.

"They didn't plan this dinner very carefully, did they, Pete?"

"I don't know, Leo. I've got a strong suspicion that everything is going pretty much according to schedule."

"Well, in that case, let's not mess with the schedule." Leo paddled around in front of me, kissed me, then ducked his head beneath the water, blowing silvery bubbles all the way down to my crotch.

The Wedding Thief

"Jeffrey!" My sister's harsh voice cut through the pleasant daydream I'd been enjoying, shattering it. "Isn't there someplace you need to be? Someplace far away from here?" I looked into the living room. My sister was lurking in a big chair near the fireplace, one foot drawn up under her, the other scuffing the nap off the carpet. It was clear that she wasn't in a good mood. Karen had never liked me, so her crack about me getting lost was no big surprise. Still, all things considered, I couldn't fathom her ill temper. In less than a week, she was going to marry the most eligible bachelor in Harrisburg. The way I saw it, the dumb bitch should've been turning cartwheels on the front lawn. Unfortunately, she never seemed to appreciate her good fortune. Believe me, I would never have made the same mistake.

"I just got back from someplace, Karen. I've been out running."

"Oh. Well, then, go take a shower and clean yourself up. You look terrible, Jeffrey. You're all sweaty and revolting. And you stink."

"Nothing revolting about good, clean sweat, is there, Jeff?" I recognized Dave's voice, and my heart began to beat a little faster. I heard his footsteps as he crossed the entry hall, then he was standing directly behind me. When his big hands touched my shoulders, I could feel the blood rushing to my cheeks. He rubbed my back briefly, then smacked me playfully on the ass. Right then, I could have died a happy man.

"I...I was out in the park, doing wind sprints. A man...a man's got to keep in shape," I stammered, wishing to hell Dave would touch me again. No such luck. Karen had her skinny ass out of the chair in a flash and came mincing across the room like a damned cat in heat. She sidled up next to Dave and smiled, suddenly all sweetness and light. She was so incredibly phony, I couldn't believe Dave actually fell for her bullshit. Then again, he *had* asked her to marry him. Poor suffering bastard.

Dave kissed her on the forehead, then turned his attention back to me. Karen was still smiling, but the strain of keeping up the façade was obvious. Her eyes met mine, and I could feel the ill-will spewing my way like battery acid.

Dave was oblivious to our sibling drama. "Well, whatever you're doing, buddy, it sure is working," he assured me. "I've gotta be careful, or you're gonna leave me in the dust." He reached out and casually ran a finger down the middle of my belly. "Terrific abs, man."

"Thanks, Dave." I stared at his long, thick finger, totally mesmerized. It hovered at the level of the sweat-soaked waistband of my shorts, nudging the fabric down just a fraction. If he maintained contact for another moment, my burgeoning hard-on was going to rip the crotch out of my shorts and thwack his knuckles.

"Jeffrey!" Karen's voice was shrill. She pulled Dave's hand away from my belly. "Nobody really cares about you or your overdeveloped body. Now go away. Dave and I have things to talk about." She glared at me hatefully, then turned to Dave, her features melting into the phony smile again. "Let's talk about the wedding, sweetheart."

I watched Karen herd Dave over to the couch, then left the happy pair and vaulted up the stairs to my bedroom. I unlaced my Nikes, peeled off my sweaty socks and kicked my running shorts over in the general direction of the burgeoning pile of laundry in the corner of my room. I grabbed clean underwear and socks, then dashed across the hall to the bathroom, locking the door behind me. Privacy was always hard to come by in our small, crowded house, and the upcoming wedding had only made things worse. If I hadn't liked Dave so much, my only wish would've been that the whole fiasco be over and done with as soon as possible. As it was, I hated to see Dave take that fatal walk down the aisle with my barracuda of a sister.

I stepped into the shower enclosure, turned on the water full blast, and leaned against the cool tiles. As the water washed away the sweat from my run, I closed my eyes and thought about Dave. Even now, I could feel his touch on my body. My stiff prick obviously remembered it as well. I gripped the swollen, tender stalk in my right hand and gave myself over to daydreaming about the man doomed to be my brother-in-law.

I had known Dave Ryder all my life. We had lived in the same neighborhood, gone to the same schools, even attended the same church where his father was the pastor. He was two years my senior, and I had always been somewhat in awe of him because he was one of the "big guys." He had always been a good-looking kid, and as he grew to manhood, he became devastatingly handsome. I had indulged in a bit of hero worship during high school but had only thought of him in a vague way more or less, until he started seriously dating my sister. It was at that point that my incoherent adolescent sexual fantasies finally led me to the inescapable conclusion that I was gay.

Once I admitted that, I also had to admit that I had a serious crush on Dave Ryder. No, I take that back. It wasn't a crush—I was in love with him. Nothing else could explain the sensations that churned my gut every time I laid eyes on him. Nothing else could explain the raging hard-ons I experienced whenever he touched me, hard-ons that refused to subside until I had jacked off two or three times while thinking about him.

I stroked my dick, letting my fingers curl briefly around my balls. Dave had always been nice to me, and now that he was marrying my sister, he was more attentive to me than ever. He always came up to my room whenever he dropped over, usually with nothing more important on his mind than shooting the shit for a few minutes, man to man. Somehow we always seemed to get into these long, involved conversations that lasted until Karen came upstairs looking for him. A couple of times, I had actually noticed a pained furrow appear between Dave's eyebrows when he heard her voice, demanding that he follow her back downstairs. He would get up like the dutiful fiancé and go with her, but he always made eye contact with me before he disappeared, flashing me a crooked grin that made me melt.

I stroked myself from crotch to neck, wishing that the hand exploring the sculpted contours of my torso belonged to Dave. As I played with myself, I thought back to an afternoon a few weeks earlier. It had started with a discussion about weight training, and next thing I knew, we had stripped out of our shirts and were standing before the mirror in my bedroom, comparing physiques.

"Looking at you makes me feel fat," Dave had groused. He was built bigger than me, his biceps bulbous, his pecs thick and rounded, whereas mine were flatter and more angular. He outweighed me by at least 30 pounds, every ounce of it solid muscle.

"I'm looking, but I'm not seeing any fat," I retorted.

"I can't believe this gut of mine." He prodded his perfectly muscled belly with his forefinger.

"Neither can I," I muttered, my eyes flickering over his midsection.

"Check it out, Jeff." He grabbed me by the wrist and pressed my hand against his belly. The hairs that coated the hot, hard wall of muscle curled around my fingers and tickled my palm. I looked up beyond his massive, hairy chest to his open, handsome face. I saw his Adam's apple, the little cleft in his chin, the shadow of beard stubble on his cheeks, the single blond hair in his dark eyebrows. His dusky red lips were the same color as his nipples. I heard a thumping sound in my ears. It was the frantic pounding of my own heart.

He had smiled at me then, his hand still holding mine tight against his gut. He was just starting to say something when my bitch of a sister called up the stairs, her shrill voice demanding his immediate presence. He had shrugged, tousled my hair, and departed, leaving me standing in my room, my palm pressed against my lips.

I crouched in the shower. The water beat on my shoulders and the top of my head. I pressed my thighs together, trapping my prick between them, then began hunching my hips. The crimson knob that crowned the shaft jutted up briefly, then receded until it almost disappeared. I rubbed the tip of my prick, smearing the lube that had leaked out of me over the swollen shiny dome. My balls rubbed against my ankles as I kept on humping and thinking about Dave.

On another occasion, Dave and I had been up in my bedroom again, standing side by side in front of the mirror mounted on my closet door, comparing the musculature of our legs. I run six miles a day, so I've got excellent definition in my thighs and calves. I beamed with pleasure while he praised me, keeping secret the fact that I would have traded all of my hard-won definition for the chance to rub my hairless body up and down his furry leg.

"I think we'll make pretty good brothers-in-law, Jeff," he had said, draping his arm over my shoulders. The move pulled me against him, foot to hip, making at least a part of my wish about touching him come true. His big hand hung down over my chest, and he began idly tugging on the swollen point of my pale pink nipple. If someone had crammed a high-voltage wire up my ass and thrown the switch, it couldn't have been any more intense.

Still thinking of Dave's electric touch, I twisted my tits hard, and my cock knob bulged. I laid back on the floor of the shower and braced my feet against the wall. I lifted my ass off the floor and spread my legs wider, baring my knotted balls and aching dick to the watery assault. The needles of water sent jolts of raw sensual pleasure radiating through my entire body. I pulled on my tits and rubbed my belly hard, holding my breath as I felt my orgasm starting to build. The pleasure mounted higher and higher, soon becoming almost unbearable.

The muscles in my groin began to contract rhythmically, slowly pumping the jism up along the stalk of my cock. I moaned out loud and grabbed myself with both hands, pumping madly, spraying my jism high in the air. I watched it arc and glitter, then fall back hot on my skin, slowly washed away by the pounding water. In my mind's eye, the thick white come was Dave's, pumped out of him as he stood over me, straddling my prone form. Long after the last of my load had been milked out, I lay there in the shower, daydreaming about Dave.

* * *

"Hey, Jeff! Let's go." I bounded down the stairs and out to the front porch. Dave had invited me to the bachelor party that his friends were throwing for him. It felt like we were going out on a date, and I was totally jacked. It wasn't going to be anything fancy, just an old-fashioned beer bash, held at a cabin out on Lake Calumet.

Even so, I had spent over an hour trying to decide what T-shirt to wear, finally opting for my favorite—the blue one that matched my eyes. It had been washed about a million times and was a little tight, but I knew I looked good in it. The night was hot and muggy, and I was wearing shorts. They were white, darkening my tanned legs almost to the color of mahogany. Dave looked me up and down when I appeared in the doorway and nodded his approval.

"You're damn near prettier than your sister," he teased. He lowered his voice. "You definitely have better legs." I felt a thrill of guilty pleasure at that. My sister's thighs were a little on the heavy side.

"Don't be disgusting, Dave." My sister had appeared out of nowhere. The expression on her face wasn't pretty. "I wish you wouldn't go to this stupid bachelor thing. I think it's very juvenile."

"Sorry, Karen, but my buddies have been planning this bash for a week. Hell, it took them that long to haul all the beer out to the lake." He nudged me in the ribs, and we both broke out laughing. My sister did not join in.

"I don't know why you wanted to invite him." Karen glared daggers my way. I smiled back at her blandly. "He's a 19-year-old baby. He'll just be in the way. He'll probably have one beer, get sick, and pass out."

"He's my buddy, hon. I'll keep a close eye on him, believe me. I won't let anything bad happen to him." He gave my sister a peck on the cheek, then turned to me with a grin. "Let's go, Tiger." I followed him down to the curb where his Fiat Spider was parked. It was a beautiful little automobile, even if Dave did spend more time working on it than driving it. I climbed into the passenger seat and settled back. The car started with a macho roar, and we tore off down the street. When he shifted from third gear to fourth, his knuckles brushed against my thigh. I didn't move my leg away. Dave left his hand on the gear shift.

By the time we got to the lake, Dave's buddies were already about a case of beer ahead of us. I knew most of them, but they had all been upperclassmen when I was a freshman, so we hadn't really socialized much in school. I know that two years doesn't amount to much, but it can seem like a lifetime when you've only just graduated from high school. I grabbed a beer and settled back in the shadows, content to listen to them crack bad jokes and tell tales on Dave all night. It didn't matter, just so long as I could be near him.

By 2 in the morning, I was hearing more snoring than conversation. I watched fireflies flicker down by the shore of the lake as the last voice faded to a slurred murmur then dropped off into silence. I listened to the crickets chirp for a long time after that, then picked my way across the sleeping hulks of Dave's buddies and went to the bathroom.

When I came out, I started looking for Dave. He wasn't among the snoring crew in the cabin. I walked along the edge of the moonlit lake in both directions, but he was nowhere to be found. I decided to have a swim, then resume my search.

I stripped and stood on the dock over the water, watching the moonlight flicker on the surface. Just as I was about to dive in, a pair of arms encircled me, and I was pulled back against something hard, hairy, and naked.

"Hey, Tiger," Dave whispered in my ear. "I've been looking for you." His breath was hot against my neck. His big hands splayed out on my belly, his fingers tangling in the thatch that grew around the base of my cock.

"Please, Dave," I gasped, my body tensing up like a spring.

"Hey, Jeff, I'm sorry." His grip on me slackened, and he began to draw back from me. "I wouldn't ever do anything you didn't want. I thought..."

"You thought right, Dave," I said, turning around, still close, still touching. I could feel his cock rubbing against my belly. I allowed myself the luxury of putting my hands on his thick chest. I could feel his heart pounding against my palms.

I took a deep breath and started spilling my guts. "My feelings for you are so intense that I just don't think I could take being with you once, then losing you forever. I worship the ground you walk on, Dave. When you come into a room, I feel it like a fist in my gut. When I'm around you, it hurts because of what I can't do. Then, when you go, it hurts even more. I..."

He silenced me with a kiss. His lips touched mine, then his tongue snaked between my teeth and pressed against my tongue. I knew in that instant that he felt the same way I did. I trusted him not to fake it to get what he wanted. Secure in that knowledge, I wrapped my arms around him and began rubbing his broad back. I dropped my hands to his bare ass. It was firm and rounded—and furry as hell.

Dave grabbed my ass and began kneading my tightly muscled cheeks. I groaned, and my hips hunched, rubbing my dick up through the silk that swirled from his navel to his bush. He squeezed my ass harder and drove his tongue down my throat. I moved closer, if that was possible, pressing my flesh against his flesh—skin to skin, muscle to muscle, bone to bone. The sweat that beaded the fan of hairs in his armpit dripped onto me and mingled with the salty water that welled up out of my own pores on this humid summer night. I lifted my right foot and rubbed it against the hard curve of muscle in Dave's calf. The hairs on his leg brushed against the tender skin inside my thigh like a faint breath of air, making my hard prick throb.

Dave dropped to his knees, bringing me down with him. He pressed me back onto the soft, cool grass. I lay there, arms and legs flung wide, while he kissed my chin, my neck, my chest, moving down along my belly to my cock. I felt his breath, the stubble on his chin, and the silky softness of his lips against my inflamed and throbbing sex. He licked me, and I groaned, digging my fingers deep into the lush turf.

"I want…" he began.

"Anything," I sighed, approving all his actions in advance. "I've never done anything before, and I want to try it all."

"I'm a virgin too, buddy," Dave whispered, his head raised from my crotch, his eyes glittering in the moonlight. "I never wanted what I could have, and until now I didn't know how to ask for what I craved. Now I know, Jeffrey. I want to fuck your beautiful ass." I nodded, and he rose to a kneeling position. Before he could make another move, I scrambled up onto my hands and knees and jammed his sweaty, sticky prick into my mouth.

I savored the salt taste of piss and sweat, and the texture of the spicy, gooey slime that was oozing out of the slit gouged in the tip. As the musky smell of him began tickling my nostrils, I breathed deep, sucking his essence into my lungs. The texture of dick skin on my lips and tongue dazzled my senses. I cupped his balls in the hollow of my palm, caressed them with my lips and tongue.

Dave's hands were strong and insistent as he touched me, pulled me up, turned my body, pulled me back between his outspread thighs. I felt his chest against my back, the hairs matted flat by sweat now, the wet head of his cock nudging my tailbone, the pressure of his fingers down between my legs. He lifted me, spread my legs, draped them over his own strong thighs. Hands on my hips, he began to pull me towards him. I looked down. His prick jutted out below my balls, the knob crimson, the shaft netted with thick veins. I reached down and stroked it, knob to balls, watching the glans drag across my palm, up my wrist, and onto the pale, tender skin of my forearm.

"OK?" I nodded. Dave put his hands between my legs and lifted me slightly. Out of instinct more than knowledge, I gripped his prick and pushed it up until it lodged in the puckered slit behind my balls. There was an exquisite tingling of nerves at first contact, then a pressure, then a stabbing pain as he bucked up and penetrated me. I sat upright, the movement impaling me on his hard, thick cock.

"I'm sorry," he murmured in response to my muffled cry of pain. "Do you want me to stop?"

"N-n-no. Don't stop. Just…just go easy." My head drooped back against his shoulder, and my fingers curled weakly around his thick forearms. Dave continued to hold me close, whispering unintelligible words, his breath hot on my neck. The initial pain of penetration faded as the most incredible warmth began flooding my bowels. A point of heat bloomed in my belly, growing and spreading until I was tingling from head to toe. I glanced down at my cock. It was enormously swollen, jutting up out of my wispy blond pubes, throbbing parallel to my belly.

Dave was behind me, under me, inside of me, moving

slowly and rhythmically, his muscles swelling and contracting as he fucked my cherry ass. I reached back, frantic to touch him. I raised my arms above my head, locked my hands behind his thick, strong neck.

The fire in my belly roared through me. Dave's breathing became louder, more labored, puffed in my ear like the snorting of a rutting bull. His cock jabbed deep, shooting sparks that set my nerves to tingling, pushing me dangerously close to the edge of what I most desired. I hovered there, tried to pull back, held my breath. Dave felt my body tense and touched me, deciding the issue for me. His big hand engulfed my cock, squeezing it tight while his own prick continued to piston in the slippery sleeve of my chute.

We both began to groan aloud at the same instant, our voices rising in pitch and volume, intertwined just as our bodies were intertwined. I felt a new heat, different from all the others, flood my bowels. Dave's arms squeezed so tight, I couldn't breathe as his seed spewed deep up into me, making our bodies one. I threw back my head and kissed his stubbled chin as my own jism gushed out, spraying my chest and belly, Dave's muscle-corded arms, and the cool green grass beneath us.

Afterwards, when his cock went soft and slipped out of me, there was no need for speech. We both seemed to know what was inevitable—what had to come next in the natural course of things. We left the cabin without awakening anyone, got into the car and drove, heading west, toward the mountains, oceans, and sunsets piled so thickly on that edge of the world.

The highway out of Harrisburg passed my childhood home, so I saw the place one last time, porch light still on, paper uncollected, the window of my sister's room dark in the pre-dawn gloom. I waved silently as we sped on our way, chuckling to think how she would react when she discovered what had occurred. I had stolen her wedding from her and sneaked away with it clutched to my heart like a thief in the night. I didn't feel a moment of guilt, not even one. Dave and I were fated to be together, joined body, mind, and heart. I knew I would cherish this centerpiece to her plans far more than she ever could. I looked across at him and smiled. He was here beside me as we hit the open road, hair blowing, eyes bright, his huge hand warm and comforting on my leg.

Curious Heterosexual Male

I stood in the middle of my bedroom, wondering for about the hundredth time just what the hell I thought I was doing. It was totally crazy even to consider it, but here I was, trying to decide what the fuck to wear. Slacks? Shorts? Tight jeans and a tank top? What did a guy wear when he was going off to meet another guy? I didn't have a clue, and right now I wasn't sure whether I'd ever get up the nerve to find out.

I stepped across to the bureau and picked up the wrinkled scrap of paper. I couldn't imagine what had made me tear it out in the first place, let alone keep it, or follow through with it and all it implied. "I'm anxious to meet a curious hetero-sexual male. Solid, sane, sincere only. Got what it takes to give it a try?" That was it. That, and a post office box number. Hell, I don't even know why the dude had picked me—unless I was the only fool who'd responded to the ad.

Well, I was a heterosexual male, and I'd been curious enough to respond. I'm not even sure why I was curious, except maybe because my sex life had gone to hell since I got divorced last year. I'd tried a couple of singles bars (a big mistake), a dating service (pure misery), and even hung around in the grocery store, where I learned all about pro-duce from women old enough to be my mother. After the first six months, I'd started to worry about myself. At 35, I was way too young to give up sex, but I had definitely lost all interest in women.

That, bottom line, was what really had me freaked. I'd attempted to bed three good-looking women since my wife had left me, but nothing had happened. My cock, which had been in a perpetual state of semiarousal since puberty, just lay there playing dead. No amount of tit-grabbing or pussy-sniffing could wake it up. Then, the minute I was alone, the damned traitor snapped to attention and proceeded to poke me in the navel for the rest of the night. My repeated failures got to be so embarrassing, I gave up trying to get it on with anyone.

And now here I was, getting dressed up for a date with a man, for chrissakes! I had to be out of my frigging mind. Still, I'd answered the ad, and I'd be damned if I was going to chicken out now. That wasn't the way I operated. I pawed through the clothes spread out on the bed, grabbed a pair of jeans and a black T-shirt, and got dressed. You could tell my gut was flat and that my arms were pumped, but I didn't look like a hustler or anything like that.

The place where we'd agreed to meet wasn't too far from

my apartment, so I decided to walk. I was hoping the exercise would calm my stomach. Right now it felt like it was hosting a whole flock of butterflies, all on steroids and all really pissed. I arrived at the bar right on time, took a look around, and went inside.

It took a minute for my eyes to adjust to the gloom. The place looked like your standard working-class bar, nothing out of the ordinary. I'd passed right by it a hundred times over the years but had never been inside. There were a few guys at the bar, none of them even vaguely resembling the description that "Curious" had given me when he responded to my note. Hell, maybe he wasn't even here, which would be great, because then I could go home and forget all about this craziness.

I saw him in a booth near the back, sitting alone. It had to be him—auburn hair, a scattering of freckles across the bridge of his prominent nose, blue eyes. He was better looking than I'd figured—younger too. He was wearing a black T-shirt as well. Hell, maybe that was supposed to be some kind of a sign from the god of weird stuff. The guy had good arms—not as thick as mine but well-defined. He looked up at me and smiled. He had nice teeth, white and even.

"Uh...curious?" The voice was a strong, clear tenor. He didn't sound like a perv, not right off anyway.

"Could be," I replied, using the little code he'd suggested. Shit, I felt like I was in some B-grade spy film. Maybe next we'd be trading briefcases or some damned thing.

"Hi. I'm Gary." He stood up and stuck out his hand, looking really relieved. The way he'd come out with his name gave me the feeling that he hadn't just made it up on the spur of the moment. I came back at him with my real name too, figuring what the hell. "Mike. Good to meet you. Sit down." The waitress came over, and I ordered a beer, then sat back and looked across at the man who'd disrupted my life.

"Why'd you write that ad anyway?" I blurted after I'd taken a sip of my brew. It wasn't what I'd been planning on saying, but I couldn't see much point in talking about the weather, either.

"Why'd you answer it?" he countered, a little gleam of amusement in his eyes. We both laughed, and my stress level slowly started tapering off. Turned out Gary worked with computers, lived in the neighborhood, and had gone to the same high school I went to—only about 10 years after me. The guy was only 24, which threw me for a minute. Then I figured that was the least of my worries under the circumstances.

"You've never…uh, been curious enough to try anything at all, huh?" With that, Gary brought the conversation wheeling around to the reason we were both sitting here, talking to total strangers. "You must've thought about it a lot."

"Nope," I replied. "Not really." Well, that wasn't quite true. I had thought about it a few times. And then there'd been that time with Ray—but that hadn't amounted to anything. Still, I had to admit, it fell under the general heading of "curious." I wasn't planning to tell Gary about that, but it just sort of popped out.

"I'm gonna tell you something I've never told another living soul," I said, lowering my voice. Gary folded his arms on the table and leaned forward expectantly. "This happened to me about four years ago. Hell, I didn't give it much thought at the time, but now…" I shrugged my shoulders.

"Anyhow, I was out with a crew of guys on a job. We were stringing wires out in the middle of nowhere. We ran out of wire, so two guys drove back to the city, leaving Ray and me all alone. After a few minutes of sitting in the heat, Ray told me he was gonna take a swim in this little pond he'd spotted when we drove out to the jobsite.

"Well, after sitting in the cab of that truck for about 15

minutes watching myself sweat, a swim sounded like a damned good idea. When I got over to the pond, I couldn't believe what I was seeing. Ray was sprawled out on the opposite bank, naked as a jaybird, his feet in the water, his cock in his hand.

"The guys all teased Ray because he always showed this huge basket. Well, there was a reason for it—the guy had an enormous prick. Right at that moment, it was towering over him like a big pink club, with a knob about the size and color of a ripe tomato perched on the end. Ray was jacking the thing with both hands, obviously enjoying the hell out of it.

"He looked right over at me when I hit the edge of the water. The pond wasn't much more than 15 feet across—just a big puddle, actually. Hell, I expected him to get pissed or try to hide himself, but he didn't miss a beat. He just nodded and winked and kept right on skinning his big meat.

"I don't know why I didn't just turn and walk back to the truck—but I didn't. Instead, I stood there and watched my buddy work himself over. He milked the stalk, and a big glob of juice oozed out. Then he touched it, and a string of goo stretched from cock tip to fingertip, gleaming in the sun. I watched him while he smeared that cock snot up over his abs." I looked over at Gary. His expression was intense, cheeks flushed, his full lips slightly parted. The tip of his pink tongue flickered along his upper lip. He saw me staring at him and winked.

"Anyhow, Ray told me that I was welcome to join him. Said me having my clothes on made him feel a little nervous."

"What did you do?" Gary licked his lips again and leaned closer to me.

"Hell, I stripped and sprawled out on the opposite bank. It wasn't like I walked over and jumped him. We were separated by that muddy little pond, you know."

"Were you turned on by him?"

"I don't know." I shrugged and felt myself blushing. "I sure as hell was turned on by the situation." Gary ran his fingers through his hair. The action popped his biceps into a knot. A pale blue vein meandered just beneath the surface of his pale skin, branching out as it curved over the lump of muscle in his arm. Little tendrils of damp coppery hair were visible where the rolled up sleeve of his T-shirt gapped open.

"Uh...it sounds kind of hot."

"Does it turn you on, Gary?"

"Yeah. Sure it does, Mike." He took a sip of his beer and leaned forward again. "So then what happened?"

"So then we were both beating off in the same spot at the same time. After I was naked, Ray grinned at me and went back to stroking his meat. I had a hard-on that wouldn't quit by then, so I started jacking off as well. Then Ray started talking, low and dirty, and we both went at it like a couple of horny teenagers."

"So what did he say?" Gary was obviously getting off on my confession. Thinking back on it was getting me revved up as well.

"Oh, just stuff. You know, like 'Hey, you got a nice dick, man'; 'You got a hot bod'; 'Great arms, dude'; 'Big balls'—crap like that."

"He was right about the arms, Mike," Gary said, appraising my assets openly.

"That's what manual labor does for you," I muttered. Gary's eyes were glued to my biceps. I tensed them, showing off a little. Gary wriggled around in the booth like he had ants in his pants.

"So then what happened?" he asked, forcing himself to look me in the eyes again.

"Not a hell of a lot. We both beat off till we came in the pond. Afterwards, we sat there for a few minutes, then got dressed and went back to the truck. Never said a word about it afterwards or did it again. It just happened."

"No thanks," Gary said, waving the waitress away when she came by to ask if we wanted another beer. "I got plenty of beer at my place—if you maybe want to come over and talk some more."

"Sure," I said, draining my beer and sliding out of the booth. "What the hell."

* * *

"Make yourself comfortable. I'll grab us a beer." Gary's place was in the same neighborhood where I lived, about 10 blocks from me. It had the sparse look of a young bachelor's pad—a good sound system, TV, VCR, a row of books on a shelf that ran under the windows. There were a couple of framed posters on the wall, a single chair, and a big pile of cushions in one corner. I stood in the middle of the room, looking around nervously.

"Sorry about the lack of chairs," he said, handing me a cold beer. "I haven't had much need for them. I don't have many people over."

"No problem," I replied, plopping down on one of the cushions. "This is great." Gary circled around the chair a couple of times, then perched on the other end of the nest of pillows. We looked at each other uncomfortably for what seemed like forever, then Gary took off his T-shirt, balled it up and tossed it across the room. He knelt there, arms at his sides, obviously waiting for me to make the next move.

"You got a nice build," I said, my voice sounding a little raspy. It was true. Gary obviously took care of himself. He had broad shoulders and a hairless chest. His squared pecs were capped with prominent pink nipples. His belly was flat, abs clearly etched under the skin. His arms weren't massive, but they looked nice and solid. Those butterflies were coming on strong in my belly again, and I could feel little beads of sweat forming on my forehead. I took another swig of beer, sat forward, and pulled off my own shirt.

"That wasn't so tough, was it?" he teased. I shook my head. "Mind if I touch you?" I nodded, and he moved in on me fast. He was close enough for me to smell him—a combination of soap and sweat, and a raw, animal smell that made my nostrils quiver.

"You're really a hot-looking guy, Mike. You've got a dynamite chest." He pressed his hands against my pecs. They were warm and strong. "All that fur is very sexy," he said, his fingers tangling in the dense curls on my chest. His hands trailed up over my collarbones to my shoulders, then down my arms till he was gripping my biceps.

"Make a muscle, Mike," he whispered, squeezing my arms tightly. I flexed, and my biceps swelled. "Solid as a rock," he muttered, his face so close I could feel the heat of his breath. When he leaned forward and pressed his face into the furry valley between my pecs, I gasped but didn't move away.

No doubt about it, this Gary dude was feeling me up. And I was sitting there, letting him do it. He poked and probed at my biceps, then his hands were everywhere—on my chest, my sides, my belly, even tugging the sweaty curls in my pits. I glared at him when he hauled off and smacked my left pec with his open palm, but then his thumb made contact with the point of my tit and it felt real good. Hell, I didn't even stop him when he stuck his hand between my legs and groped me. That felt real good too.

"Let's get naked," he suggested, planting his hands on my shoulders and pushing himself up off the floor. I stood up, kicked off my shoes, then waited for him. He reached out and started to unbuckle my belt. I let him do it too. Hell, I couldn't remember the last time somebody'd undressed me. He was standing real close, forehead pressed against my chest, his knuckles grazing the skin on my belly as he popped the buttons of my fly. I wasn't wearing any underwear, so when he pulled my pants down around my thighs, there was no disguising my condition. My dick was hard as a rock—a far cry from its recent level of performance when there'd been an audience present.

Gary made this little purring sound and put his hands on my hips. He didn't grab my cock, but he did press his belly forward till my knob touched him. I tensed up, jerking like I'd been goosed. Gary's hands slipped away from my hips, moving back till they were firmly planted on my ass.

"You are a real fox, Mike. I'm glad you answered my ad." I was gonna say something, but then Gary dropped to his knees and started licking a trail along my belly, and I lost my train of thought.

I'd never figured I'd let a guy suck my dick, but all of a sudden it was happening and I wasn't doing anything to stop him. He sniffed at my crotch a little, then stuck out his tongue and licked the shaft of my stiffer. Christ, it felt good! He got my pants off me, then planted his hands on my butt again and slipped his puckered lips over my knob. I grunted and leaned back against the wall, reveling in the feel of his soft, hot mouth against the sensitive skin of my cock.

He was kind of tentative at first, scraping me with his teeth a couple of times. Pretty soon, though, he got into it and started giving me a serious blow job. I'd only had my cock sucked twice before in my life—both times by women who hadn't really been into the idea. Now I understood why guys made such a big deal out of getting good head. It was fucking intense, making the hairs on my balls stand on end.

"Maybe I should take your pants off, Gary," I said after he'd been sucking me till my balls were in a knot. I grabbed him under the arms and pulled him to his feet. His hard body felt real good, his skin like warm silk. I pushed him up against the wall and hunkered down in front of him. I unbuckled his belt and pulled his zipper down. The first thing I saw was his bush. It was redder than his hair, making it look like his cock was on fire. Hell, maybe it was. As his pants slipped down over his lean thighs, my attention was drawn elsewhere.

"Jesus!" I grunted. My curious buddy had an enormous cock. Hell, I had his pants down halfway to his knees before it popped free from the fabric. Once out in the open, it rose up and bounced against my chin. The shaft seemed to go on forever, getting thicker out towards the business end. The fat glans was tucked into a loose hood of skin. Fascinated, I fisted the stalk and shucked back the excess skin. His knob was dusky red and sticky. When I tightened my fist, it swelled, darkening to purple.

"Lick it, Mike," he pleaded. "Please." I hesitated, looking at it appraisingly. I sure as hell hadn't ever figured on doing anything like this. Then again, this wasn't exactly the way I usually spent my Saturdays. I took a deep breath and licked. His piece was hot, and the goo leaking out of him tasted like thick, salty water. Gary moaned happily, and his fat pink nuts started making like a yo-yo. Figuring I might as well go the whole shot, I opened my mouth wide and lunged forward.

I gagged and choked when his knob bounced off my tonsils. I backed off a little and got down to sucking on it, keeping both hands wrapped around the twitching slab of meat sticking out in front of him. I looked up and felt a real shock when I saw his very male body towering over me. If a buddy of mine had told me even the day before that I was ever going to be down on my knees swinging on a dude's cock, I would've punched him out. Now here I was, doing it and definitely getting off on it.

All of a sudden, he leaned down and grabbed my ass. His fingers slipped into my crack, and he started massaging my butt cheeks. Well, that made me nervous. I would've pushed his hands away, but if I let go of his prick, it was likely to get crammed down my throat. His hips were starting to pump, smacking soundly against my clenched fists. Meanwhile, his fingers kept on slipping south, making tracks across my asshole.

"My turn," Gary said. He rubbed my sweaty pucker, then stood up and pulled me to my feet. "Turn around," he growled, tugging the swollen points of my tits. My prick smacked me in the gut, splattering tiny drops of leak on the patch of fine hairs that curled below my navel. I turned around and looked over my shoulder, watching Gary kneel down and burrow his face into my crack. I yelped and started to move away, but he grabbed my dick, pulled it back between my legs, and started licking the tender underbelly. I changed my mind about moving and let him bathe my cock, balls, and asshole with spit.

I couldn't believe how good it felt to have him licking my hole. It seemed like the nerves there all met up in my groin, shooting good feelings from the tip of my cock to the top of my head. He kept pulling my meat back, and I kept leaning forward till I had my hands on my knees and was looking back between my legs at the fat pink tower jutting up between Gary's thighs. Funny, but I got off on watching his foreskin droop over his knob, then snap back when his fist rode down the shaft. Maybe it was because I'd been skinned as a baby and never had the chance to really see one in action.

I was getting used to having Gary's tongue up my ass, but I wasn't quite prepared to have his finger jammed up my chute. What I really wasn't ready for was the way it made me feel. It didn't hurt at all, and when his fingertip punched my prostate, pain was the farthest thing from my mind. I felt that jolt everywhere, especially in my dick. It swelled up like it was going to explode, and the lube I pumped hit me in the chin.

The more he pumped my ass with that damned finger of his, the hornier I got. When he asked me if I could stand another finger, I actually nodded yes, for chrissakes! Then it was three fingers, and I was taking it with ease, feet planted wide, hands braced against the wall, ass wiggling. Gary stood up behind me, still plugging my ass. He put a hand on my shoulder and popped his fingers out of me. Then they were back, only it wasn't his fingers. What he was cramming up my chute was smoother and hotter—and much bigger. His grip on my shoulder tightened, and I felt a moment of sheer panic as the head of his big dick poked through my ass ring and started driving up what had been, until that instant, strictly a one-way street.

I straightened up in a hurry. Gary wrapped his arms around me. He pressed the heel of his hand hard against my lower gut and thrust his cock deep. He hit something up inside of me that damn near turned me inside out. I groaned out loud.

"Found the old prostate, huh, Mike?" He pressed his hand tighter against my gut and jabbed me a second time.

"Yeah, I...I guess so," I wheezed, fighting to catch my breath. His big balls slapped against the backs of my thighs. Shit, his whole damned dick was up inside of me!

"Tell me how it feels," he urged. "Does it feel good?" I didn't say a word, but my cock jerked up and cracked his knuckles, which seemed to give him the answer he wanted. He began pumping, fucking my ass like it was the most natural thing in the world. And I let him do it. It was totally weird, but it felt so good. I really got off on standing there passively, letting him play with my tits, or my cock, or my balls, doing whatever he wanted with me. All of it felt good— his hands, the feel of his skin, the dull ache when his balls slapped up against mine, the incredible feelings that shot through me when his dick slid in and out of me.

It went on for a long time, both of us getting more and more into it. He was pulling my swollen nipples hard, setting more nerve endings on fire. I was moving now, my hands clamped on his ass, my hips grinding around the axis of his overgrown hard-on. He was kissing my shoulders and licking the sweat off my neck, snorting in my ear like a bull in heat.

"I'm there, buddy," Gary announced with a strangled cry. His cock jerked around inside of me, then I felt him shooting his load up into me. I actually felt it, hot little jets of thick juice that set my bowels on fire. Every muscle in my body knotted, as my orgasm began bubbling up from my toes. I squirmed and twitched and started blowing, spouting jism like a fountain. I'd never shot such a load before in my life. It was like a dam had burst and I was going to squirt till my balls were hollow.

After it was all over, neither one of us said a word. We stayed plugged together till his hard-on deflated and slipped out of my ass. Then I wriggled out of his grasp and grabbed my pants.

"Want another beer?" Gary asked, sounding about as nervous as I felt all of a sudden.

"Nah," I muttered, not looking at him. "I gotta go."

"Oh." Gary got dressed and walked me to the door of his place. "Keep in touch," he said.

"Yeah. Sure. See you around." I hurried down the hall to the stairwell, trying to get my thoughts together. I stopped in the lobby and sat down on the bottom step. Hell, I'd run out on him like a total coward. Why? I mean, it wasn't like I hadn't wanted to have sex with him, or that it had felt bad while it was happening. Truth was, it had felt almost too good—which was what really had me freaked. Then it hit me—what was wrong with feeling too good? Didn't that mean that what we'd done was the right thing for me? Hell, I'd had a man's big hard cock up my asshole, fucking me till I shot a no-hands load all over the wall of his living room. It was the most satisfying sex I'd had in my life. I had to face up to it—guys turned me on. Women didn't.

I stood up and took a deep breath, then headed back up to his apartment, taking the stairs two at a time. I knocked on the door and stood there waiting. My heart was pounding, and my cock was growing harder by the second.

"Mike?" Gary looked surprised as hell to see me—pleased but surprised. "Did you forget something?"

"Uh...yeah," I said, shuffling my feet nervously. "I... uh...I forgot to get your phone number." Gary's face broke into a wide grin as he motioned me inside.

"I'll write it down for you, Mike. Sure you won't have another beer?"

"Sure, Gary." I followed him into the kitchen. When he stopped at the counter, I walked right into him. I didn't apologize and I didn't step back. "Uh, Gary?" He turned and our crotches ground together. "I've got a confession to make."

"Such as?" He grinned at me as he started untucking my shirt.

"Such as I'm not exactly sure I qualify any longer according to the terms of the ad in the paper. I mean the hetero part." I slipped my fingers into the waistband of his jeans, my knuckles touching bare, warm flesh.

"That's OK, Mike." He pulled my shirt over my head and tossed it aside. "I don't really think I could handle a hetero on a regular basis. I do, however, have a thing for curious guys."

"Oh, I'm still way curious," I assured him, pushing his jeans down on his thighs and starting a slow, thorough examination of his smooth ass. I started to tell him just how curious, then thought better of it. Better to show him what I meant. Way better.

The Bodyguard

"Jesus Christ! Where do I turn?" I glanced over at Vic. He was studying the map intently, powerful shoulders hunched, brow furrowed in concentration. He poked randomly at the map with a thick digit, then looked at me blankly.

"I...uh...I can't find it."

I slammed on the brakes and pulled over to the curb. "Give me that map." I snatched the creased paper from him, located Fenmore Avenue, then tossed the map into the backseat. "Idiot," I muttered, glaring at Vic balefully. He shrank back against the passenger door as far as his bulk allowed, his cheeks flushing crimson. I popped the clutch and burned rubber as I made a U-turn on the boulevard.

It was an impossible situation. I had been looking forward to college so I could be on my own at last, far away from the oppressive atmosphere of my home. Then, at the last minute, my father had sprung Vic Torres on me. I had sputtered and cursed, but my father's reasoning had been elegantly simple— either Vic went with me, or I stayed at home. I had been venting my frustrations on Vic ever since. He had to put up with it—that was his job.

Vic was my bodyguard—a perfectly natural companion for the son of an organized-crime boss. Father told me that Vic was for my protection, but in fact, he was just covering his own ass. He didn't want a rival family kidnapping me and then using me as a pawn to muscle in on his turf. I had hoped that college would be my chance to experience life on my own terms, but Vic was going to serve as a constant reminder of who I was.

I glanced over at Vic. With his boxy suit, dark shirt, and narrow tie, he definitely looked the part of a hired gun. If only he had been fat and ugly, he would have been easy to hate. He wasn't. He was disturbingly handsome. His eyes were dark, deep-set, and intense. He shaved twice a day, but his strong, squared jaw was always purpled by heavy beard shadow. His prominent nose had obviously been broken at some point, but it didn't detract from the almost classical perfection of his features. Only his full, unsettlingly sensual lips didn't appear to have been carved from some tawny, fine-grained stone. As for the man's body—it remained a tantalizing mystery shrouded under cheap fabric. Although I had seen Vic around over the years, I knew nothing about him, except that he worked for my father. That alone was reason to treat him like the enemy.

I located the house that had been leased for me—a dorm room couldn't be made secure, not to mention the problem of what to do with Vic—and pulled into the drive. While Vic brought in the suitcases, I wandered from room to room. The place was big enough to house a fraternity, its vast lawns surrounded by a high fence topped with wrought-iron spikes. I chose a bedroom that overlooked the rose gardens and directed Vic to the back, as far from me as possible.

"I got everything out of the car, Mr. Grayson," Vic said, stepping into the living room.

"Don't call me that, Vic," I snapped irritably. "I'm not my father. Next thing I know, you'll be calling me boss."

"I'm sorry," Vic mumbled.

"Call me Jeff," I said, softening my tone somewhat. It was the situation I hated, not Vic.

"Jeff." His gravelly baritone caressed the word. He wiped sweat off of his forehead and tugged at the tight collar of his shirt.

"Don't you have any other clothes, Vic?"

"What's the matter, Mr...uh, Jeff? I'm clean." He stood up straight and smoothed the front of his suit jacket.

"I'm not talking about hygiene, Vic. I'm talking about the way you look." He stared at me sullenly. "Vic, this is a college campus, and you look like a gangster. Hell, you are a gangster." I walked around him while he stood uneasily in the center of the room. "In any case, I can't have you following me around dressed like that. I'll look like a bad joke."

"I'm sorry you think I'm nothing but a joke, Mr...uh, sir." He was staring at the carpet now, his face crimson, his hands balling into fists. For all his size and obvious power, he looked like a sad little boy. I started to feel guilty about being such an asshole.

"Tell you what, Vic." I stepped over to him and put a hand on his shoulder. He looked up at me, startled by the contact. "How's about I take you shopping?"

"Shopping?" His tone was guarded, suspicious.

"Sure. You know, check out something a little more collegiate." He shook his head stubbornly. "Vic, it'll make your job easier if you blend in. I'm just asking you to try on a few things. If you don't like them, we don't have to buy them."

"You're not just making fun of me?"

"No, Vic. I promise."

* * *

"Hey, Vic!" I pounded on the door of his bedroom.

"I don't know about these," he rumbled from behind the mahogany panels.

"Come on, guy. I'm already wearing mine. Bet I look better than you do."

"There's not enough room in here for me."

"Braggart." I pounded on the door again. "Come on out." The subject of our exchange was a pair of workout shorts. They were gray jersey with enough spandex mixed in to make them fit like a second skin, only tighter. I had bought them for Vic during our shopping expedition. Once we both got over sulking, we had a great time and managed to turn Vic into a pretty good imitation of a college jock. I had picked up a pair of the shorts for myself, then tossed in a pair for Vic as a horny afterthought. Now, if I could just coax him out of his room, I could finally get a look at the body he kept so carefully hidden. I pounded on the door a third time, fortified by the wine we'd drunk with dinner.

"If you come out, I'll give you some more wine," I teased.

"Wine first." The door opened, and his hand appeared with an empty glass. I filled it, doing my best to see through the crack of the door. Hand and glass disappeared, then the door swung slowly inward, and Vic stepped into the hall.

"Awesome!" I muttered, not talking about the shorts at all. It was Vic. He was drop-dead, hard-on-popping gorgeous, his body conjured out of some impossibly erotic fantasy. Everywhere I looked there was muscle, muscle, and more muscle. His chestnut-furred pecs swelled up like boulders; his abs were cut deep; his biceps and triceps were massive; his long, hairy legs were knotted with muscle at calf and thigh. Dead center, mounded beneath the straining gray jersey, was a bulge that could only be described as monumental.

"I couldn't wear these damned shorts in public, Jeff. I'd feel like a fool."

"You'd start a riot," I replied, licking my lips as I walked slowly around him. His ass pushed back, two lush hillocks of firm flesh that flexed against the jersey as he shifted his weight from one foot to the other. I stopped when I was facing him again, standing close enough to feel the heat radiating from his big body.

"Flex for me, Vic. Show off a little."

"I don't think so, Jeff." He blushed.

"Don't be shy, man. It's easy." I thrust my chest out and struck a pose. Vic barely managed to suppress a chuckle. "No fair laughing, man," I protested.

"You got a nice solid build—for a kid," he replied. He started to reach out and touch me but changed his mind.

"I'm not a kid, Vic. I'll be 19 in a month."

"Right." I thought I detected a flicker of interest in his brown eyes.

"Your turn now, Vic. Make a muscle." He raised his right arm, and his biceps grew to grapefruit size, then got bigger. A vein that snaked over the top of the muscle swelled and began to throb.

"Incredible." I reached out and squeezed. It was like a rock. I ran my hand across his shoulder and onto his chest, leaning forward till my belly brushed the huge knot in his shorts.

"Cut it out!" Vic swatted my hand away and crossed his arms protectively over his chest.

"It feels so good," I leered, stroking the hairs on his thick forearm. They tickled against my palm.

"Stop, Jeff!" He grabbed my hands and held them firmly. His lats flared like wings. "You're drunk."

"I'm not drunk, Vic. I'm horny," I countered.

"Not for me, you're not." A frown creased his brow.

"Come on, Vic. You know I dig guys. Don't act so shocked." I strained to break free from his grasp, but to no avail. "You're into guys, aren't you, Vic?" He bit his lower lip, but he didn't answer me. "I know I used to see you hanging around the pool at home when I was sunbathing. Did you like what you saw, Vic?" His eyes shifted away from me guiltily. "Why don't we mess around, Vic?"

"Go to bed!" he snapped, releasing my hands.

"Aw, Vic." I reached down between his thighs and began rubbing the hot spongy mass of his groin.

"Quit that!" He pushed me away roughly. I hit the opposite wall in the hallway and cracked my head hard enough to see a constellation of stars.

Vic eyes widened in dismay, and he reached out to me, but I knocked his hand aside. "Fuck you!" I screeched. "Just fuck you." I stalked down the hall to my bedroom and slammed the door.

I tossed and turned in my bed, alternately fuming with anger at Vic's rejection and burning with humiliation at the spectacle I had made of myself. Around midnight, I went down to the kitchen for a snack. On my way back, I noticed that a light was still burning in Vic's room. As I paused at the top of the stairs, I heard a soft, whimpering moan.

I crept along the hall to his door. It was ajar, and the mirror on the dressing table reflected the bed. Vic lay naked on the mattress, naked, the lamp on the nightstand washing his body with a golden light. I stopped and stared at him.

Vic was obviously as horny as me. His hard cock rose proudly out of a thicket of silky black pubes. As I watched, his fist climbed the fleshy pole, shucking up skin that gradually hid his gleaming glans from view. His fingers skittered over the hooded knob and pinched the velvety overhang. He tugged the skin beyond the tip, then stuffed his forefinger into the tight sleeve. He pulled his glistening fingertip free, then began the long journey back down the massive shaft. I shoved my hand into the front of my briefs and gripped my own rapidly stiffening prick.

Vic pointed his cock at the ceiling, squeezing it hard, making the knob bulge and blush crimson. Then he let it go, and it smacked down heavily against his concave gut, the head stretching far beyond his navel. I longed to touch it, squeeze it, jack it, wondering how another man's cock would feel in my hand. I had told Vic that I dug guys. That was true, although I had never gotten away from my father's protective net long enough to try meeting anyone. Earlier this evening, I had hoped that Vic would be the first. Now I could only stand and spy on him as he took his solitary pleasure.

He reached between his thighs and scooped his furry balls up in his palm. He rolled them up and down the shaft, the muscles in his arms straining. I saw his toes wiggle, then begin to curl back towards the soles of his feet.

I fisted my own aching dick and rubbed my forefinger over the blunt snout, smearing the tender flesh with sticky juice as I continued to stare at Vic's reflection in the mirror. His fist was in motion, pumping faster and faster as the intensity of his need increased. His left hand hovered over the broad expanse of his furry chest, then dropped down with a loud smack. The point of his right tit rose stiff and hard above the mound of muscle. He smacked it again, then gripped the fleshy nub and twisted it. His hips jerked up off the bed, and a jet of clear lube shot out of him. It sparkled in the hairs on his belly like tiny jewels.

I squeezed my dick hard, holding it tight against my belly, hunching my hips, savoring the orgasm that was beginning to build deep in my gut. I was almost there, and so was Vic. The hairs on his body stood on end like they were full of static electricity, and the veins lacing his prick bulged dangerously. I heard Vic grunt, saw his chest swell, saw the muscles in his jacking arm knot with tension. He pointed his glistening stiffer straight up in the air, pumping it so fast his knuckles were a blur. Then he shook and pressed his head back into the pillows.

I gripped the doorframe and watched, transfixed, as he began to shoot. The first blast arced high in the air and splattered down against his heaving chest. He tensed, his shoulders rising off the bed, his big balls jiggling beneath his fist. Another gusher of come shot high, seemed to hang in the air, then welted on his forearm. I started coming as well. I held my cupped hand above my cock head, catching my spunk as it gushed out of me in a thick hot torrent, smearing it up over my belly and chest.

Vic's hand slowed but didn't stop. It rose up towards his crimson knob, milking out thick jism that drooled down the shaft like cooling wax. He shuddered as yet another dollop bubbled out of his come-hole. Finally drained, he lay there panting, cradling his hard-on in both hands. After he turned off the light, I stayed until I heard the sound of snoring. Only then did I creep back to my solitary bed.

❋ ❋ ❋

In the days and weeks that followed, Vic remained very distant. He followed me to campus every day, waiting patiently until class was over, then escorting me back to the house. His evenings were spent hovering silently in the background while I studied. He took good care of me, but we never recaptured the atmosphere of that day we went shopping together. Those sexy gray shorts I had bought for him never reappeared either.

To add insult to injury, Vic not only froze me out, he kept me from getting close to any other man. Any time I started to talk to anyone about anything but class work, Vic quickly put a damper on things. When I tried to sneak away from him, he always managed to sniff me out like a damned bloodhound. My frustration increased daily, fueled by my isolation from my peers—and by the constant brooding presence of Vic. Being around him made me feel horny all the time—and more alone than ever.

Then, one night about a week before final exams, I snapped. Vic and I were in the student union, grabbing a bite to eat before I went to the library to study. A guy I'd become friendly with in my chemistry class stopped by the table while Vic was on a mission to find mustard. Todd was gay; he was dark and handsome in a way reminiscent of Vic— and he was obviously interested in me. He sat down beside me, and as we began to talk, his knee rubbed intimately against my thigh.

"I know a place where we can be alone," Todd whispered, his fingers hot as they slipped up the leg of my shorts. "You're a sexy guy, Jeff. I've wanted to get it on with you since the first day you walked into class." His fingers encircled my wrist and drew my hand over to the twitching bulge in his pants. My heart began pounding in my chest. Here was my chance to get laid! Todd's approach was far from romantic, but I didn't care. I was too horny to wait for romance. I'd settle for just getting my rocks off with another man.

"I..." I stopped short. Vic was back, looming behind

Todd. He leaned down and whispered something in Todd's ear. Todd stood up abruptly, his face going pale.

"Sorry, Jeff. I…I didn't know." I started to ask him what he didn't know, but I never got the chance. He rushed out of the cafeteria without looking back.

"What did you say to him?" I hissed at Vic.

"I told him we were together," Vic mumbled, staring over my right shoulder, his face grim. "He's not for you, Jeff. I've had my eye on him. He'd fuck any cheap little trick who'd bend over long enough to let him stuff his cock up his ass."

"Screw you, Vic," I snapped, his remark about cheap little tricks bringing the blood to my face. "What the fuck business is it of yours if I want to get laid?"

"I care…uh, I'm responsible for you," he barked back at me, his dark eyes flashing. "I'm not about to let you go down on any hard-on that just happens to point your way."

"You bastard!" I was livid. "Who are you to criticize me, you second-rate petty hood? I want to meet people, real people, not spend all my time with some dimwitted, muscle-bound goon."

"Stop it, Jeff." He reached out and grabbed at my arm.

"Get your filthy hands off me!" I shrieked. Heads turned at the surrounding tables. "I hate you. I hate everything about you and your sorry little life. The very thought of living in the same house with you nauseates me."

"Please." Vic's face was pale, his hand like a steel claw on my arm.

"Let me go!" I grabbed my glass of soda and flung it in his face. He rose from the table, knocking his chair over backwards with a loud crash. The entire cafeteria was silent, like an audience at the climactic moment of some stormy drama. I looked at Vic. The soda was streaming down his face in rivulets, dripping onto his shirt, darkening it like drops of brown blood. A vein in his temple was swollen, throbbing. His expression seemed to show more pain than rage. He turned on his heel and stalked between the tables towards the men's room. I got up and stumbled out into the night, knowing all eyes were on me. As the door closed behind me, a hundred voices rose in an excited buzz.

I walked aimlessly across the deserted campus, trying to sort things out. I was so wrapped up in my thoughts that I didn't see the van, didn't notice the man come up beside me until I felt something sharp poke me in the ribs.

"Get in the car," he growled.

"What?" I glanced at him, recognized only the snub-nosed barrel of the revolver. He led me to the waiting van, tied my hands, pulled a black hood over my head. Once I was trussed securely, he pushed me roughly into the back like a bundle of dirty laundry. The door slammed, the engine roared, and the van lurched forward.

Well, the old man had been right, I thought bleakly as I was bounced from side to side like a loose cannonball. There really were people out there who had been waiting for an opportunity to get to me. Now the negotiations would begin. My mind churned up nightmare scenarios. Maybe they'd cut off my ear, or a finger, and send it to my old man as a warning. Maybe he would decide I wasn't worth saving—he didn't much like me, anyway—and would tell my captors to do what they wanted with me. I'd end up in a ditch somewhere out in the country with a bullet through my head.

My morbid imaginings were interrupted by a loud crash. The van shuddered, bounced over a curb, and sent me flying to the opposite side. I tried—unsuccessfully—to brace my feet against something solid as the van sped up. The driver swore and took a corner on two wheels. I rolled across the floor and cracked my head. I heard the screech of brakes, the scream of metal grinding against metal. The van lurched to a stop, and I was airborne.

I hit the floor of the van facedown, getting the wind knocked out of me. As I gasped for air, I heard the ping of gunshots. Glass shattered, and I heard an anguished scream. There were more sounds—a dull thud, a cracking like bone on bone, a grunt—then silence. I lay motionless, paralyzed by fear, waiting for the end.

Something warm and trembling touched my neck, then my hands were untied and I was pulled into a sitting position. The hood slipped off over my head, and I was eye to eye with Vic. His shirt was ripped open to the waist, and a bruise was rapidly purpling on his cheek, but he was there. I reached out, put my arms around him, and pressed my face against his broad, furry chest. After only a moment's hesitation, his arms closed around me, holding me tight.

"I'm so glad to see you, Vic," I murmured, snuggling into the safety of his strong arms. "I didn't mean any of those ugly things I said earlier. I…I'm sorry, Vic."

"I know," he replied, stroking my neck tenderly. "I know."

❋ ❋ ❋

"You don't have to do it if it hurts."

"I love the way it hurts," I gasped, pushing back, struggling to impale myself on his hard-on. He was beneath me, his hands on my hips, holding me. My hands were splayed out on the swell of his chest, and the strong pounding of his heart vibrated through me.

We were in my bedroom, where Vic had insisted on carrying me after we got home. He had undressed me, then taken off his own clothes and climbed into bed beside me. After I had assured him for about the hundredth time that I wasn't injured—I think my hard-on throbbing against his thigh finally convinced him—he had begun to make love to me, slowly and tenderly, setting me on fire with desire for him.

I had lain there while he kissed me, tantalizing kisses on my neck, my shoulders, my belly, and my feet. He sucked my cock until I pounded his shoulders with my fists to make him stop. Then he had let me wrestle him onto his back and pin his mighty arms to his sides, let me snuggle between his outspread legs and suck his gorgeous cock. I held it in both hands, felt the power pulsing through it as I licked him from his balls to the gleaming, hooded knob on the end. His dick was like heated silk, the goo leaking out of him like honey on my tongue.

I rubbed my body against his until I was ready to explode, then rolled an oversized rubber down the length of his gigantic prick. I knelt over him, my legs spread wide, my own cock arcing towards my belly. He looked up at me, lips parted, his eyes soft and unfocused, stroking my ass as I positioned the head of his prick against my virgin asshole and struggled to pop my cherry.

I felt the head punch through the tight ring of muscle like a huge cork. A sharp pain stabbed through me, but it was a pain I craved. I hung there, poised, my breath a ragged gasp. Then I began to slide down, taking him into me, joining with him in complete intimacy. As he slid deeper and deeper into my straining channel, the pain disappeared, replaced by an almost unbearable pleasure that left my whole body tingling. I rose slightly, felt the jolt of pleasure intensify, then thrust back, engulfing more of his thick length, settling lower and lower until my balls were nestled against the soft hairs that curled on his belly.

I leaned down and kissed him, sucking his tongue out of his mouth and into mine. My chest touched his, the hairs on his pecs tickling my nipples. I humped my cock against him and felt a responding throb deep inside me. He stroked my back, squeezed my butt, trailed his fingers into my crack and around my ass lips. I moaned and squirmed happily on top of him.

"Make love to me, Vic," I sighed, licking the curly hairs away from his left tit so I could suck on the hard, fat point. "Fuck me."

"You're sure?"

"What do you think?" He chuckled, rose up slowly, rolled me back onto my shoulders, braced his mighty arms on either side of my head and started to screw.

I lay beneath him, watching him intently. His body was beautiful as he fucked me. The muscles in his belly contracted into hard ridges as he pumped forward, then smoothed out as he slowly withdrew his prick from me. The hairs on his inner thighs tickled against my sides as he shifted his knees tighter against me. Every time he drove forward, his fat balls smacked hot and heavy against my lower back.

"Oh, yes," I growled when his cock pressed against the inflamed lump of my prostate, shaking me to the core with sensual pleasure. I ran my hands up along his arms, squeezing the hot, hard muscles with all my strength. Vic snorted and twitched his hips from side to side, a move that took my breath away.

"Play with my tits," he urged, opening his eyes and looking down at me. "I like that." I obeyed, latching onto the swollen tabs of flesh, pulling them till his pecs flexed, the muscles beneath the skin as hard as stone. I tugged harder, watched his belly ridge, gasped as his prick plumbed new depths. His balls rolled against my tailbone, and sweat dripped off his forehead onto my cheek.

I wrapped my legs around his narrow hips and raised my head, sinking my teeth into his sex-hard tit. He shuddered and began bucking faster, the friction of his cock almost setting me on fire as he pumped in and out of me. He distended the solid wall of his belly, pressed it against my dick, tortured me with the delicious textures of hair and skin. I put my arms around his neck, pulled him down onto me, pinned myself beneath his sweaty, heaving bulk.

The pressure and friction were more than I could bear. My whole body began contracting as my orgasm shook through me. I bellowed my pleasure, every muscle rigid, tingling with the most exquisite pleasure I had ever imagined. Vic groaned and pumped faster, plunging in and out of my clenched ass channel. He snorted and thrust his hips forward hard. I felt his prick flex, then a ball of heat began swelling in me as he pumped the rubber full of his scorching jism. My body shook, and I squirted hot come between us, gluing us together.

"That was the most amazing thing," I said after I regained the ability to speak. "Thank you."

"For what?" Vic rose up on his elbows and looked down at me. His prick was still in me, still hard, still throbbing.

"For guarding my body so well."

"I damn near lost you tonight, Jeff. Don't you ever pull a damned-fool stunt like again," he said sternly.

"I promise, Vic." I pulled his hand to my mouth and brushed his knuckles across my lips. "You have to promise something too."

"Such as?"

"Such as, you'll keep guarding me just like this." I rubbed the soles of my feet down the backs of his legs. "Up close and personal. I feel very safe."

"I wish I did."

"Meaning?"

"You scare me a little."

"Don't you like being scared, Vic?"

"Maybe." He winked at me.

"Don't worry, Vic. I'll protect you. Just stay close."

"I'm not letting you out of my sight again."

"That's good, Vic. That's real good."

Hot Shots

While I was growing up, I never had a chance to shoot anything more powerful than a wooden pistol that popped a cork out of the end when you pulled the trigger. My mother was terrified of guns and had done her best to instill the same fears in me. I probably would never have gone near the real thing if it hadn't been for the job I landed recently.

I got laid off at Allied Manufacturing back in January. Six months later I was facing the end of my unemployment, so when I got hired by a security company that supplied guards for area banks, I had jumped at the chance, even though you had to carry a firearm. Since most of the other positions advertised in the papers involved flipping burgers, I figured I damn well better learn how to pull a trigger.

Crestwick's Firing Range was housed in what appeared to be a converted bowling alley in a strip mall north of town. The sign claimed I could get excellent marksmanship training at a reasonable rate, so I parked my rig and went inside, ready to take my first step towards becoming a sharpshooter.

Most of the patrons were leaving when I came in. At first I figured maybe they'd been warned I was heading their way, and were making themselves scarce to avoid getting winged. Then I saw the posted hours and my heart sank. I realized that I had less than half an hour to hone my marksmanship skills before my new job started on Monday. The clerk was reluctant to let me in at first, but a little wheedling and my willingness to pay for a full hour of practice soon won him over. I left the desk armed with a paper target, a menacing-looking pistol, and five clips of ammunition.

Attaching the target to the line and sending it to the end of the range was easy. I didn't even have any trouble popping the clip into the gun butt. Where I ran into problems was trying to control the damned gun. Every time I pulled the trigger, my arm jerked up from the recoil, sending the bullet into one of the canvas pads that lined the back of the target area. The more I practiced, the more nervous I got, till I finally imbedded a slug in the ceiling.

I was taking determined aim for about the twentieth time when I felt a hand on my shoulder. I jerked to one side, and my gun discharged, sending a bullet into a target about three lanes over from mine. I spun around to face the man who had suddenly appeared out of nowhere and spoiled my shot. He was dark and handsome with a two-day growth of beard and a thick mustache that drooped to the corners of his chiseled jaw. He wasn't smiling.

"What the hell do you think you're doing?" he thundered. "You can't just come in here and start taking potshots at anything that catches your damned eye. This range is for serious target practice. We're closing up shop anyhow, so why don't you just get out before you do some serious damage?"

"I'm really sorry," I said, blushing furiously. "I'm not doing it on purpose." He was still staring at me stonily, obviously unconvinced. "I have to learn how to use a gun by Monday."

"Monday, huh? I wouldn't count on it, buddy." He still wasn't smiling, but the muscles in his broad shoulders appeared to relax a notch. "What's the big rush?"

"If I can't convince my new boss I'm able to use this damned thing by then, I'm gonna lose the only job I've been able to find in six months. I could really use some help." I shrugged and set the gun down on the counter, figuring I'd better pick up a copy of the paper on the way home so I could start scouting the want ads again.

The man stood there, looking at me like he was trying to decide whether I was sincere or not. I took the opportunity to look right back at him. He was well over six feet tall, and his faded blue T-shirt wasn't doing a damned thing to hide his muscular build. His pecs swelled against the fabric, his swollen nipples clearly visible. Thick veins snaked up along his hairy forearms and across the swell of his biceps. The faded fabric of his jeans cupped his basket, making me think the piece he was packing might have an oversize barrel. I was tempted to ask what caliber it was, but I didn't want to end up at the wrong end of one of his big fists.

"Tell you what, buddy," he said, startling me out of my assessment of his assets. "I'm getting ready to shut up shop for the day, but if you can hang on for about 15 minutes, I'd be happy to give you some pointers." I nodded. "I'm Eric Crestwick. I own this joint."

"Grant Foster," I replied, sticking out my hand to him. "I really appreciate this." His grip was firm, and the contact sent an agreeable tingle up my arm. I watched him as he strode back out to the front. His pants were tight on his thick thighs and hugged his crack, separating the cheeks of his ass like two small, perfectly rounded melons.

He made it back well within his timeframe, carrying another pistol and several ammunition clips. "OK, Grant, let's get down to business. From the looks of things, you've never fired a gun before. Right?"

"Right. I've tried my hand at most sports, but I've never done anything like this."

"First, why don't you take a couple of shots while I watch you? Then maybe I can tell what you're doing wrong." I loaded a clip and took aim. When I pulled the trigger my arm wavered again and the bullet bit a chunk out of the floor, less than halfway to the target. Things were not looking good.

"This isn't as easy as it looks," I admitted, turning around and shaking my head. "Help."

"First of all, your stance is all wrong." He walked over and motioned for me to turn back to the target. "Put your feet wider apart. It improves your balance and helps absorb some of the kick." He put a hand between my thighs and patted my right leg till I got my feet where he wanted them. "That's it. Now, hold the pistol in both hands and sight down along the barrel. Good. OK, Grant, pull the trigger when you've got your target covered." I tried to do everything he said, but the gun still jerked up when I fired. At least this time I nicked the top edge of the white paper.

"Shit," I muttered.

"That's all right," Eric said soothingly. "It can take a while. I think you're tensing up too much when you squeeze the trigger. If you don't mind, I'll try to guide you through a few shots."

"Be my guest," I said. "I'm open to any suggestions you can make."

"Is that so?" he chuckled. While I was digesting that remark, he stepped up close behind me, so close his chest pressed against my back. "Keep your arms straight," he said, running his hands down along my bare arms and grasping my wrists. "That's right. Now, sight right across the top of the barrel."

"Sure," I mumbled. I tried, but my attention wasn't much interested in sighting beyond his muscle-corded, furry fore-arms. They were pressed tight against me, the long, silky hairs tickling my skin. His lips were right beside my ear, and I could feel his mustache brushing my neck. If he kept this up, I was going to be shooting more than just bullets!

"Squeeze the trigger, Grant." I did, and a hole appeared in the outside ring of the target. "That's better," he growled sexily. "Do it again." His hips humped tight in against my ass, mashing the hard lump in his crotch into my crack. I shivered when the stubble on his chin prickled the skin of my shoul-der through my thin T-shirt, but I hit the target again anyway. "Good job," he said, his lips brushing my neck just under my right ear.

"Keep your eye on the target at all times," he ordered. "Don't be distracted, or you'll lose your competitive edge." Easy for him to say! "Keep those arms straight." He pulled his hands back, barely grazing the tender skin on the insides of my arms with his fingertips. "Stay tight through the chest, Grant. Tense those pecs. It'll keep you from jerking up with the kick." He stroked my chest, his palms rubbing against my nipples. They popped up into thick points, sending hot sparks down to my aching groin.

"Good," he said, when my next shot hit an inner ring. "Don't tense your belly too much. You'll draw your arms down." His fingers traced the ridges of my abs, to my belt and beyond. I moaned softly when he finally began stroking the throbbing tube of flesh that was pushing down the left leg of my jeans. "Real nice, Grant," Eric purred. "Real nice."

I got off a few more shots before he tugged my shirt out of my jeans and his hand slipped up onto bare flesh. I ground my butt back against him, getting hotter than the smoking pistol I was holding. When he started pinching my left tit, I put the pistol down on the counter in front of me. I was afraid I might shoot myself in the foot.

If Eric noticed, he didn't seem to care. He was nuzzling my neck now and working the buttons on my fly. I reached back and struggled to unbuckle his belt as he shucked my pants down over my thighs. My cock, freed from captivity, swung up and slapped me in the gut. I could feel the cock honey starting to ooze out of me, warm and sticky against my skin. Eric fisted my meat, milked me till his palm was slippery, then moved down to cup my balls. He pressed them up between my legs, increasing the pressure until my twitching asshole throbbed. He fingered my hole briefly, then his hands slid back up to my chest.

I spun around to face him and worked his pants down over his narrow hips. His hard, fuzzy butt flexed against my palms. I felt something hard and hot pressing down against the inside of my thigh. I dropped to my knees and nuzzled in his crotch, sucking the smell of him into my lungs. His sweaty pubes clustered around the base of his long, vein-laced prick. I lapped along the broad back of it till I got to the snout. It was soft and hot, the springy tissue swelling against my lips as his hot blood pumped into it. I worked my tongue over the mass of nerves tucked just beneath the helmet-shaped knob till every impressive inch was hard as a steel bar.

"Get it wet," he groaned, his hands slipping around to the back of my neck. I wrapped my fingers around the shaft. When I closed my mouth over his sticky knob, his belly tensed, popping his abs into stark relief. I took a deep breath and went down on him, slowly swallowing his thick meat. I didn't stop till his hairy nuts bounced off my chin.

I started pumping up and down on his throbbing hard-on. I swallowed him to the hilt, grinding my forehead against his hard belly, sucking him till he was gasping and I was out of air. I came up off him, and his cock rose high in the air. I dove under it and went for his big, hairy balls. I sucked the fat orbs into my mouth, bathing them with spit. When I finally let go, they snapped up high on either side of his shaft.

"Get up here, buddy." Eric hauled me to my feet and flipped me around, bending me over the shelf of the shooting booth. The howl I let out when his chin raked across my crack dissolved into a series of low, moaning whimpers when his tongue shot up into my manhole.

He tongued my chute and licked my balls, moving from one to the other till I was within a heartbeat of popping my rocks. Just when I thought I couldn't take it any more, he stood up and pulled me back against him.

"Pick up the pistol," he commanded, his hot tongue darting around my earlobe. "Do what I told you. Remember, I'll be right here watching you." I picked up the gun and tried to focus on the target. It wasn't easy because I was so horny I was almost cross-eyed.

I felt his hot cock-knob press against my ass ring, and my trigger finger twitched convulsively. The shot went wild, sending a cloud of dust up out of the canvas barrier below the target.

"You can do better than that," he said, thrusting forward and impaling me on his hot rod. I bucked back and took him to the hilt. "Keep your arms stiff, and I'll take care of the rest." He wrapped his big arms around me, holding me tight.

"Man, that feels good," I sighed, shivering as he started battering my prostate.

"Shoot it, buddy," he cooed, driving his hard-on deep into my ass. I pulled the trigger, and this time I hit the target.

"Good boy. Do it again." I got off another one, the heat in my guts starting to flow through my limbs.

"Every time you squeeze that trigger, your hot hole grabs my dick like a hot, wet fist. Feels good, man. Do it again!" I started firing in rhythm with his thrusts, stopping only long enough to pop out the spent clip and reload. By this time I was squirting clear cock juice up onto the counter every time he rammed it home. His hands were all over me, rubbing my belly, stroking the insides of my thighs and up over my aching prick. I could feel his chest hairs against my shoulders as I writhed against him. The fur on his arms was tickling my sides, driving me wild.

"You're doing real good, Grant. I'm about to get off a shot myself. Fuck, yeah! Squeeze me, baby. Squeeze me!" I sucked my belly back tight and clenched my ass down on him as hard as I could. He drew in his breath sharply and stopped pumping my ass. His body went rigid, the veins in his arms standing out like cords.

Then there was a hand on my cock, pumping frantically. I let fly, blasting high-arcing streams of white jism over the counter. Eric bucked hard, then my well-packed chute was flooded with his steaming load. I felt shot after shot fired deep into my guts. I kept on squeezing the trigger long after the bullets were gone, my hands frozen on the butt of the gun.

When Eric finally stopped humping my ass after the last of my jizz had been drained, I dropped the pistol. I clasped my arms around his neck and craned my head around to kiss him. His chin was like sandpaper, but his lips were soft as silk, a combo that started getting me hot all over again.

By the time Eric was finished with me that night, I'd gotten off over a hundred rounds and my balls were drained as dry as the Mojave Desert. After we got the place all locked up, I got in my car and followed him home. He had offered to give me some more pointers the next morning, bright and early. I figured that by the time Monday rolled around, I'd be able to shoot the wings off a gnat at 150 paces.

On the Road

I remember it was July 24, 1979—a day that will be emblazoned in my memory forever. It was hot and sultry, the temperature already hovering around 90 degrees before the sun had even cleared the tops of the cottonwoods along the eastern edge of my father's cornfields. I hadn't slept much during the long humid night, and as the first glimmers of dawn gave substance to the shadows in my attic room, I quietly climbed out of bed. I crept into the bathroom and pissed, then splashed water on my face. Once back in my room, I slipped into an old pair of cutoffs, laced up my tennis shoes, and grabbed my favorite shirt off the hook on the closet door. I tucked the $200 I'd managed to save up into a back pocket, took one last look around the shabby, low-ceilinged room I'd lived in for the past 18 years, then climbed out the window and shinnied down the drainpipe.

I'd left a short note for my mom on my old desk. There wasn't much to say. She knew all about how my dad and I got along, and she was fully aware of my feelings about taking over the farm now that I was out of school. I'd been a farm-hand for most of my life, and I'd hated every frigging minute of it. I wasn't meant to be tied to the soil. I had an itch in my blood that drew me to the open road. I didn't know what it was I wanted so bad, but I did know that I wasn't likely to find it in Parson's Corner, Illinois.

I'd always been a square peg in a room full of round holes. "Give it time," my old man had said to me. Hell, I'd given it all my life so far and I wasn't any nearer to fitting in than I'd ever been. I couldn't see the point in hitching myself up with some local girl and setting out to raise a pack of kids while trying to eke out a living on the land. I wanted something more, something different, something I didn't even have a name for. Didn't matter, though. I wasn't going to let whatever it was pass me by without making a run for it.

My heart beat faster with every step I took—first on the track that cut through our fields, then crunching on the gravel of the county road that ran along in front of our place, and finally slapping my feet along the hard edge of the pavement. I was looking for a ride out, a ride that would take me on to excitement and adventure and into the great unknown beyond the endless sweep of the rustling corn.

I wasn't just looking for any ride, though. I wasn't going to start my odyssey on the back of a farm truck heading to the county seat. Hell, no. I was going off in style—riding high above it all in the cab of one of the sleek 18-wheelers that rolled along State Highway 18 day and night, winter and summer, going somewhere far beyond this hot, flat, corn-cluttered part of the universe.

I saw my first truck almost immediately. I straightened my shoulders and flexed my toes in my shoes, ready to test my thumb for the first time. The butterflies in my belly churned thick and fast as the rig approached, shimmering in the veil of heat mist that rose off the surrounding fields like a desert mirage. The chrome glistened blindingly in the morning sun as the truck bore down on me.

The blast of the air horn made me jump back as the huge beast streamed by me, throwing up a cloud of dust and gravel off the road that swirled around my bare legs like a dust devil. I saw the trucker's arm sticking out the window of the cab, raised in warning or greeting or defiance—I couldn't really tell. Then I realized that the big rig was slowing down, the gears shifting noisily, bringing it to a stop about a hundred feet down the road. Goddamn! He was stopping for me. All you had to do was stick your thumb out in the air, and the world was yours. I sprinted along the edge of the highway till I came up even with the tall cab.

"Where you headed?" a deep rough voice called out from high above me.

"Don't much matter," I replied, emboldened by my success. "I'm just going."

"Shit!" the trucker spat back at me. "Well, climb on up then. I've already stopped the damned thing. Move your ass!"

I shot around to the passenger side and scrambled up. The man had the rig back on the roadway before I'd even pulled the door shut. He was performing complicated maneuvers with the gears, wrenching the knobs and levers around with authority. The driver was a big, rangy-looking dude, probably in his early 30s. His brown hair was a little long around the ears, shaggy on the neck, falling over his forehead in a straggling V. He looked over at me and gave me a crooked smile and a wink. For some reason, I shivered in spite of the heat.

"Hi. Thanks for stopping, mister. My name's Sam. Sam Davis." I had to shout to be heard above the whining roar of the diesel engine. I stuck out my hand, wondering why I was feeling so flustered. There was no reason for it. None at all.

"Jim Pickett," he replied, reaching over and enveloping my hand in his big, callused paw when he'd gotten the rig back up to cruising speed. "I don't usually stop for hitchers," he said, looking me over appraisingly, "but you looked like a young man with a purpose. You sure you don't know where you're heading?"

"Just as far away from this stretch of road as I can get," I replied. He squeezed my outstretched hand, and his grip made me feel like I'd been jolted with electricity. The jolt was the strongest right in my crotch. It was kind of weird, but I can't honestly say that I didn't like it while it was happening.

"Well, Sam, we're on our way to Tucson, Arizona. You think that'll be far enough for starters?"

"That'll do just great, Jim." I couldn't help grinning back at him like an idiot schoolboy. This was definitely going to be my lucky day! We rode along in silence for a while, Jim whistling tunelessly to himself, me looking out the window as the fields rolled by like an endless bolt of bright green cloth.

The cab was stifling hot. Jim told me that the condenser on the air conditioner had blown out during the night and that it wouldn't be fixed till we hit Kansas City. In the meantime, all we could do was sweat. He asked me to hold the wheel steady for a minute while he peeled out of his T-shirt. He balled it up and tossed it back between the curtains that screened off the sleeping area. My eyes strayed to his naked torso, almost like I didn't have any control over them. I usually made it a point not to pay any attention to other guy's bodies, but I found myself wanting to have a good look at him. His chest was deep in bulging muscle and silky brown fur that was ruffled by the scorching breeze that blew through his open window. His belly cut in sharply just below his rib cage, sporting a thin line of hair that trailed down into the waistband of his pants. I'd been able to see his big arms all along, only now I could see how the muscles of his biceps swelled and flowed into his brawny shoulders. Sweat glistened in the short, coarse hairs that curled in his armpits. Something about the man disturbed me, made my heart race and my skin tingle. I felt an overwhelming urge to reach across the space that separated us and touch the tanned skin of his shoulder. I laced my fingers tightly together and cupped them over the throbbing bulge between my legs.

"Hey, Jim. Where the hell are we, man? This frigging heat is killing me." I jumped guiltily and spun around. A very handsome redhead with intensely blue eyes was looking down at me from the sleeping compartment in the back of the big rig's cab. He smiled at me and winked.

"Hey, Hercules, how's it hanging?"

"Uh...OK, I guess," I stammered, my face flushing deep crimson.

"Damn, I knew they grew them big around here, but you've gotta be way above average." Years of hard labor on the farm had pumped my muscles and burned away all vestiges of fat from my six-foot frame. An interest in high school sports had sculpted my bulk, leaving me looking like the gymnast I had long aspired to become. The redhead's tongue flickered across the curve of his full upper lip as he eyed my bare torso. I squared my shoulders and looked straight ahead, like I'd always done at school when the coach was evaluating my progress on the rings or parallel bars. I got a definite feeling I was being evaluated, but I wasn't yet sure what for.

"Where'd you find this one, Jimmy?"

"Dave, this is Sam." Dave's huge hand engulfed mine. It was warm and dry. He locked eyes with me and I stared at him, powerless to look away.

"Planning to keep this to yourself?" Dave asked, turning to his buddy.

"I forgot all about you being back there, man." Jim looked over at me and grinned conspiratorially. "Sorry I didn't tell you this big ugly galoot was lurking back there in the sleeper, Sam."

"That's OK," I muttered. My skin was tingling again and I shivered in spite of the hot, humid air blasting through the cab of the truck.

"Slide your ass over, Sam. I'm coming on down." Dave motioned me into the middle of the cab and swung his bare legs over the edge of the sleeper area. He slipped down onto the seat, wearing only a skimpy pair of white cotton briefs— the kind I'd seen in catalogs but never at the Sears outlet store in town. He was stocky and freckled all over. His legs and forearms were hairy, but his chest and belly were smooth as a baby's butt.

Three pairs of broad shoulders made for tight quarters in the cab of the truck. I pressed up close against Dave, doing my best not to crowd Jim and interfere with his driving. Dave's sweaty thigh rubbed against mine, skin to skin, and we couldn't seem to find room for our arms. He finally draped his left up across the back of the seat to make more room and my shoulder nestled into his sweaty pit. As his hand slipped back behind me, it grazed the little tail of long hair at the base of my skull. I'd seen someone in a magazine with a similar tail and decided it might make me look less like a hick when I started my journey. My old man had thought it was weird, so I had been encouraged to keep on growing it. I thought it made me look cool. I also liked the way it felt when it tickled the skin between my shoulder blades. Dave wound it around his finger and gave it a tug.

"That's quite the pigtail, Sam. That mean anything?"

"I don't know," I mumbled, suddenly more confused than ever.

"I bet it means you're a little sex pig, doesn't it? I bet no matter how much you get, you just can't get enough. Is that right, Sam?"

I blushed scarlet, and my gaze dropped to the floor of the cab. Dave chuckled and gave my shoulder a friendly squeeze. To my immense relief, he didn't pursue his teasing, and the three of us rode along in companionable silence. After a few miles of rocking back and forth, I started falling asleep. My head would roll forward on my chest, and then I'd sit up with a start. After the third time I'd done this, Dave looked over at me and chuckled. "Why don't you just go on to sleep, dude? There ain't nothing to see for the next 300 miles, except what you've been looking at all your life. Go on and climb up into the sleeper. It's no hotter back there than it is up here. There's even a fan on the wall."

"I'm feeling pretty wrung out myself," Jim said as I was crawling into the back. "How about taking over for a while, Dave?"

"I'll bet that's not all you're feeling," Dave whispered, just loud enough for me to hear him. Jim pulled the truck over onto the shoulder and slowed to a stop. Next thing I knew, the truck was out on the highway again, and Jim was scrambling up into the back with me. He pulled the curtains closed behind him. The place had seemed pretty big when I'd crawled in, but with Jim there, it was really crowded. He pulled off his shoes and started unfastening his belt.

"Might as well get comfortable, Sam. No reason to be shy

on the road." He peeled out of his jeans and shucked his briefs off as well. He was on his knees now, legs spread wide, his cock damn near dragging on the mattress in the sleeper. It was thick and veiny, the bulbous head covered by a full foreskin that dangled down well below the tip. His nuts swung back and forth, heavy in their hairy bag.

"You like the looks of that big old thing?" he whispered, giving me a heavy-lidded grin. "You can do anything you want to with it, Sammy, my man. Just as long as you don't try to yank it out by the roots, it's all yours. I've seen you watching me. I know you want it, only you're too shy to do anything about it. All you have to do is reach out and latch onto it. I'm pretty sure you'll be able to figure out what to do with it after that."

It was too damned hot to think. All I knew was that my prick was screaming to be released from the tight confines of my cutoffs, and my hand was aching to wrap around that long, fat tube of flesh hanging down between Jim's hairy thighs. I fumbled with my belt, but my fingers refused to cooperate. Jim finally took pity on me, leaning over and unbuckling my belt, then unbuttoning the buttons on my fly. I closed my eyes and leaned back on my haunches, my heart pounding in my ears. The head of his prick rubbed against my leg as he pulled my pants down over my hips. My cock slapped against my sweaty belly, a steady stream of juice already leaking out of the distended slit in the big, spongy head.

Jim grabbed my hand and guided it to the shaft of his meat. My fingers closed around the fat column of flesh, and I practically passed out. His dick was hotter than the air around us, twitching and swelling in my grip. A low gurgling moan escaped his throat as my thumb brushed against his fat nuts. His hand was on my cock, milking the ball-juice out of me, collecting it in his rough palm.

Suddenly I knew. This contact, this male flesh, super-heated and pulsing with nerve and blood and sticky come was the object of my quest. It was the reason my life had never come together back at home. This possibility was so far from the reality of Parson's Corner that I'd never even dared to dream it. On those stolen afternoons up in the tall silos, sprawled back on the golden corn, pumping my prick alone, I'd never been able to imagine a partner to share in my private pleasure. However, just one touch of Jim's cock, and I knew that this was the key to the puzzles of my life. I squeezed the bulging shaft again and practically shouted out my joy.

Next thing I knew, I felt something hot and wet close over the head of my dick. I opened my eyes and stared down at the top of Jim's head. I held my breath, watching in amazement as my prick slid into his warm, moist mouth. He sucked and licked and massaged me with his tongue, pressing down till my hard-on was wedged deep in his throat. Then his head was bobbing up and down, his forehead slapping against my belly. He probed my ass crack, his stubby fingers rubbing against my tightly clenched ass pucker. I bucked and gasped, responding to the movements of his tongue. This was what I'd been waiting for all my life—to be naked with a man, to have my hard-on sliding in and out of his tight throat.

Jim must have sensed that I was close to blowing my wad, because all of a sudden he stopped sucking and looked up at me. "How'd you like to work on my prick for a while, buddy?"

"I've never…I mean, I don't…" I stammered to a halt and looked at him wide-eyed.

"Learn by doing, I always say." He grinned at me, squatting back on his haunches, his huge cock jutting out from between his legs like a club. I got on my hands and knees and lowered my head slowly into his crotch. I loved the way he smelled. That was the first thing I noticed. It was a combination of his sweat and a strong, musky male smell that rose from his bush and his huge come-heavy nuts. I stuck out my tongue and licked at the drop of clear juice that was trembling on the end of his cock head. It was salty but sweet at the same time. The taste made my prick jerk up and poke me in the belly.

I opened wide and stretched my lips around the bulbous head. I wrapped both hands around the pulsing shaft and shucked back all the extra skin, leaving me with a mouthful of sticky, naked head. When my tongue dug into the distended come-hole, his knob flared, forcing out a stream of warm, salty cock snot. I was getting off on the tastes and textures of cock. It was like sucking on a big salty pretzel, except when the salt was all licked off, instead of going limp and dissolving, it got fatter and harder in my mouth, not like a pretzel at all.

I leaned into his crotch, pushing inch after inch of his stiff prick into my greedy mouth. When I hit the back of my throat with his cock head, I stopped for a moment, not sure how to continue. Then Jim grabbed the tail of hair at the base of my skull and pulled. I lurched forward till he was buried deep in my throat. When I came up for air, I looked up at him. He grinned, then leaned down and kissed me right on the mouth. Shit! I'd never had a man kiss me before, sticking his tongue in my mouth and all. It felt damn near as good as having his dick in my mouth. I kissed him back hard, my fingers tangling in the luxuriant mat of fur growing on his broad chest.

He pushed me down on my back after we'd kissed for a long time and straddled my hips. I looked at him kind of funny, but I figured I'd let him keep on running the show. Then he grabbed my cock, pressed it up between his legs and sat down on me hard. He grunted, and his prick bounced against my belly as I penetrated deep into his asshole. Holy shit! I never figured a big hulking he-man like this trucker would take another man's cock up his butt. What the hell, I never would've figured he'd suck a dick either.

Once I was planted inside of him up to the bush, Jim started moving up and down, the walls of his asshole caressing my prick like a silk glove. I was gasping and rolling my head from side to side, punching my dick deep into his guts as he writhed around on top of me. I clamped my hands on his narrow waist and started fucking him as hard as I could hump, moaning and groaning as I got closer and closer to spilling the contents of my nuts up his butt.

"Come on, Sam. Dump that hot load up my ass. Pump me full of your man-cream. Stir that stiff prick around inside of me. Let me know you're dicking my ass. That's right, guy. Jab it in deep. Fuck me, dude. Fuck me."

It didn't take much encouragement to get me hot enough to shoot my load. I hollered at the top of my voice and let fly, filling his shitter with my come. Jim took my first two shots up his chute, then pulled off of me and started jacking my cock. Jizz flew everywhere, up onto his sweaty chest, onto the ceiling of the cab, and over my heaving belly in a thick white flood. When I was finally drained dry, I lay panting and wheezing while Jim massaged my cock and balls.

"What's that I smell?" Dave called out from the front.

"Virgin's milk," Jim laughed back at him. "Thick and sweet and creamy. I just took this young bull's cherry load up my ass. Made me horny as a goat." He grinned down at me. "You liked plugging that man-hole, didn't you Sam?"

I nodded vigorously. "Shit, man, I've never felt anything like it."

"How's about you return the favor for me? I can promise you that taking it feels as good as giving it. What do you say?"

What can you say to a man who's just let you shoot a big slimy wad of your spunk up his butt? He hadn't done anything to make me feel less than great up till now, and I was still horny, so I figured what the hell. "Sure, man. Only take it real slow at first. I haven't ever done anything like this."

"I just happen to be an expert at popping cherries, buddy. Just do what I tell you, and you'll be shooting another load before you know it."

He rolled me over on my right side and pulled my left leg up against my chest. I rested my head on the pillow of his biceps and closed my eyes, waiting for the pain to start. There wasn't anything painful about it. I felt this pressure as his cock head pressed against my ass ring, then he pinched one of my swollen nipples and breached me, simple as that. He slid in nice and slow till I felt his scratchy pubes crushed against my ass. My whole body was tingling, and there was something that his prick was mashing in my gut that sent waves of pleasure washing over me. I reached down and grabbed his balls, pulling them up against my cock shaft. He tightened his grip on me and started pumping in and out, in and out.

He went slow at first, then picked up speed as I started gyrating my ass around the axis of the thick stake pounded up into me. Before long, I could feel my balls knotting up, ready to shoot another load. "Jim, I can't help it," I moaned, "I'm gonna shoot it off again. Oh, Jesus!"

"Atta boy, Sammy," Jim whispered in my ear as I spouted out another sticky load into his fist. "I can feel your asshole all up and down my prick. Oh, man, that feels great. Clamp that asshole down on my cock. Squeeze my big cock tight. Fuck, that's sweet."

As he talked, he was pumping faster and faster, his sweaty belly slapping against my lower back as he fucked my cherry into history. I could feel his prick flexing and thrashing around inside of me, the head flaring in my gut till it felt like it would explode. Then he tightened his hold on me and whimpered in my ear. The sensation of his hot juice spouting into my guts and leaking out of my asshole onto my legs and butt was so intense that I shot again, then lay trembling against him in the oppressive heat of the Illinois afternoon. He never loosened his hold on me till we were both fast asleep, lulled by the steady throbbing of the diesel engine that was carrying us westward.

*** *** ***

By the time we pulled into the State Line Truck Stop on the outskirts of Kansas City that night, I'd lost count of the number of times I'd felt that wild tingling sensation in my guts, triggering the spasms that pumped yet another load of spunk out of me. Jim and Dave had taken turns fucking me all afternoon and into the night, and I still couldn't get enough.

"You're cock crazy, buddy," Jim had chuckled the fourth or fifth time his big dick had slipped up my come-slimy chute. "In just one afternoon, you're trying to make up for all those years of fucking you've missed."

"Yeah," I groaned, clamping my asshole down tight and grinding my butt back against his rippling belly. "I always knew something was missing in my life. Now that I know what it is, I can't get enough of it. I want you to fuck me and fuck me and fuck me till my gut stops tingling when I see your cock. It's like there's always been this piece missing, and now I know what it is. It's thick and it's long and it's hard and it grows between a man's legs." He picked up speed and my babbling degenerated into long, low moans of sensual pleasure.

When the truck's engine wheezed to a halt, I reluctantly pulled on my cutoffs and clambered down out of the cab. The heat that radiated up from the asphalt made you think you were jumping down onto a griddle. We'd eaten about 100 miles back down the road—it was the first hamburger

I'd ever downed while I was getting fucked. I'd take a bite, then hold it up over my shoulder for Dave to have a chomp on it. His ass-pumping was in sync with his chewing, and believe me, by the time we were finished with the second burger, he was chewing pretty damned fast. When we were done, we both got to laughing so hard we were practically sick. I wasn't the least bit hungry, but I figured I was in dire need of a shower to wash off the grease and the sweat and the come.

"Just head through those doors over there on the left," Jim said, nodding to a low sprawling addition that stretched off to one side of the greasy-spoon restaurant that was the heart of the truck stop. "There's a shower room about halfway along the corridor. You can't miss it. We'll be on along after we make arrangements to get the air-conditioning on this rig repaired. Otherwise, once we're out in the desert, it'll be too hot to fuck, even for you."

I shook my head in amused disagreement and walked briskly back to the doors Jim had pointed out to me. Sure enough, about halfway down the fluorescent-lit hall, I saw a set of double doors with the word SHOWERS painted in two-inch-high letters. I pushed them open and stepped into a changing room. A bench ran around three sides with a single row of brass hooks spaced evenly above it. I counted about six sets of clothing hanging around at random. I spotted a pile of clean white towels near the door, grabbed one, stripped out of my shorts and shoes, hung them on a hook and stepped across to the shower room. The steam was thick as an autumn fog. I couldn't see a thing, but I heard jets of water splashing against the tile of the floor and the deep rumbling voices of men. Just the sound made my nuts vibrate and got that funny tickling sensation stirring again in my guts. Be careful here, Sam, I told myself as I waded into the wall of steam.

"I am so fucking horny I could punch holes in the walls

of this shower, man. If I don't get it on soon, my nuts are gonna explode," a disembodied voice rumbled out of the densest part of the shower fog. I moved ahead slowly, silently, my hands held out in front of me, searching blindly for a vacant stall. Suddenly, I made contact, but not with a tiled wall. My hand brushed over a soap-slippery belly—rippled with muscle, dense with coarse hair. I started to draw back my hand but was caught in an iron grip, one huge hand grabbing my wrist, the other reaching out to check me out front and rear.

"Who the fuck are you, man?" a voice growled at me. From the way your ass feels, you're nobody I've ever seen around here before."

"Hey, man, I'm sorry," I began. I heard more movement all around me, feet shuffling across the slippery floor, first one, then several hands on my body, groping my chest, my trembling ass, and down between my legs. The tingling was back in my belly now, growing stronger as every second passed. My aching cock, too stupid to know when to stay still, was swelling rapidly, imagining the invisible bodies of the steam-shrouded truckers.

A fan kicked in, rumbling overhead, sucking the steam out into the humid night. Body parts appeared all around me. There was a leg, thick at thigh and calf, peppered with short dark hair. A chest, broad and bulging, hovered only inches from my face. The hand that held my wrist in a handcuff grip, was thick-tendoned and gnarled with pulsing veins that ran up along a bulging hairy forearm. Two, then four, then many eyes appeared, all looking intently at me, waiting for an explanation.

"Name's Sam," I whispered, my voice quavering uncertainly as I tried out my best smile on them. "I came in to take a shower. I've been traveling all day with Jim and Dave, the dudes with the cherry-red Peterbilt. They told me to come on in and take a shower. I hope you guys don't mind."

"Not likely we'd mind much of anything, dude." A tall, tight-muscled blond grinned over at me, his blue eyes openly appraising me. I could feel the blood tingling in the shaft of my cock and my nuts shifting and squirming in my low-hanging sack.

"What're you into, Sam?" This voice came from behind me. I spun around and my cheek brushed against a chestnut-furred chest. I looked up into brown eyes twinkling with mischief, above a pair of full red lips half-hidden by a bushy moustache.

"Look at the cock on him," the blond chuckled, his hand cupping my left ass-cheek, "I figure it's pointing right at what he wants to be into, or rather wants to have into him." I looked down and saw that my prick was jutting out in front of me, pointing directly at the thick, uncut sausage hanging between the strong thighs of the dude with the moustache. I started to say something, then just grinned and reached out for the object of my desire. They knew what I wanted, and there was no need to put any of it into words.

Next thing I knew, there were hands all over me, massaging, pinching, rubbing, stroking all over my tingling body. The big man with the sausage cock and the perfect chest reached out, grabbed me by the waist and flipped me upside down, holding me tight against him, my cock in the furrow between his bulging pecs. His tongue slithered over my balls, then dug deep into my tight pink asshole, making me squeal with lustful surprise. Other hands grabbed at my legs, pulling them wide apart, exposing my quivering ass lips to view.

After a few ecstatic minutes of the first tongue job I'd ever experienced, I felt a stubby finger digging into me beside the wriggling tongue. Another hard-cocked trucker was down on his knees, feeding me all the dick I could eat. I swallowed him greedily, determined to feel his springy black pubes against my chin. My hands groped blindly out at my sides, grasping at the steamy air, desperate for contact with other male flesh.

Again, success! Two veiny, throbbing, jutting pricks bounced eagerly against my palms. I was complete, every surface of my sweaty body in contact with another man. I don't know how many of them there were that night, maybe five, maybe a hundred. It didn't matter who or how many. The brotherhood was all, the feeling of total abandon as we laughed and played out every fantasy that shot across our brains.

After what seemed a long, long time, the hot man who'd been rimming me set me down. He pushed his big hard-on up against my ass-lips, then suddenly jammed it in me up to the ass-stretching hilt. I bellowed like a gored bull, my eyes popping open wide as my cock spit out a shot of spunk halfway across the room. Another dude, redheaded above and below, grabbed my prong and started jacking me like mad. By the time I'd finished squirting my load, the man fucking me was scratching yet again at that itch deep in my gut that couldn't ever seem to get enough attention paid to it.

Other hands found my tits, and soon I had new sparks arcing through my body, buckling my knees and making me suck even harder to get the juice out of the cocks that kept pummeling at my swollen lips. I heard a grunt behind me and felt my gut flooded with hot juice. Then there was a change of rhythm, length, and thickness that signaled a new cock up my hungry ass pipe. Moments later, a load of jism flooded my mouth, salty, strong, almost choking me with its force and volume. It didn't matter. I took it all, making myself a glutton for come and cock as I received tribute from every man who walked into the shower room that evening.

When it finally ended, we all washed each other's backs and balls and asses in a laughing, panting chain of brotherhood. I walked back to the bunkroom with them, talked, drank, then finally settled in to sleep with chest hair tickling against my shoulders, and a warm, moist cock nestled in the crack of my aching ass.

***

The next morning, we all went off to breakfast together in the truck stop cafe. We sat around the long formica counter, drinking coffee, flirting with the waitresses and trading news about road conditions and speed traps. I felt like I belonged, like I was finally in the right place—a square peg in a whole fucking box of them.

"Still coming along to Tucson, Sam?" Dave asked as he leaned across the counter to grab the sugar bowl.

"I'm off to Baton Rouge," one of the guys from the previous night offered. "Truth is, you can get damned near anyplace from here, dude. Just say the word."

I looked around at them all, not sure what to do next, where to go. It was true then, the open road was there, waiting for me, ready to take me on forever to any destination or to none. All I needed to do was choose, and the choice was never final, and the road flowed on from sun to sun, leading me out of the infinity of cornfields to the wide world beyond.

The First Time

"Hey, Jay! Great day for a barbecue."

"Brett. Glad you could make it. You're looking fit, buddy."

"Thanks, Jay." Brett shrugged his broad shoulders. "Got to give you a run for your money." We both chuckled. We'd been competing with each other physically—and sexually—for more years than I cared to count, and there had always been an edge to our friendship. Brett was extremely competitive, and he did his damndest to bag any man I showed an interest in. It irritated the hell out of me, but whenever I mentioned it, he had always blown it off. I had finally gotten fed up with the situation and, for the past few years, had done my best to confine our competition to the gym.

"Go on around back, Brett. You know everybody." I was throwing a barbecue to celebrate the completion of the swimming pool I'd been working on for three years. By the second year it had become a standing joke among my friends, so I couldn't pass up the chance to vindicate myself by showing off the finished product.

I started to follow Brett, but I was stopped in my tracks when my neighbor suddenly materialized on the other side of the fence.

"Tad? Uh...hi. I thought you'd already packed up and gone off to college." Tad was the boy next door. When I had moved in 16 years previously, he had toddled across the drive, arms outstretched, demanding to be picked up. We had bonded instantly. After his parents got divorced, I had assumed the role of surrogate father, taking him on camping trips and helping him with his homework as I watched him grow up.

Looking at the superbly muscled young man in front of me was something of a shock. It seemed only yesterday that he had been a gawky adolescent, all skinny arms and legs that weren't always entirely under his control. Then he got interested in gymnastics, and during his senior year in high school, he had been asked to become a member of the U.S. gymnastics team for the upcoming Olympics. At 18, he was handsome, smart, and built like a young Greek god.

"What's up?" Tad brushed his thick blond hair back from his broad forehead and smiled at me, his azure eyes twinkling.

"I just invited a few friends over to initiate the pool," I muttered noncommittally. I'd never made a secret of my sexual orientation, but I wasn't sure I wanted Tad involved in that aspect of my life. He was so young and innocent—

and so irresistible—that I was worried about what might happen to him.

"Well, hello." Brett materialized beside me, eyeing Tad wolfishly.

"Hi. I'm Tad. I live next door." He stuck his hand over the fence. Brett grasped it and didn't let go.

"I'm Brett. Glad to meet you. Why don't you join us for a swim?"

"You don't mind, do you, Jay?" Tad asked eagerly. I nodded, and he dashed off to change into his swimsuit. I had a feeling I was going to have my hands full, running interference between Tad and some of my more aggressive buddies.

About 15 minutes later, all conversation in the yard suddenly ground to a halt. I glanced over my shoulder and saw that Tad had arrived, resplendent in a black Speedo and a baseball cap turned back to front. He was heart-stoppingly perfect—his biceps pumped, his concave belly tightly ridged, his ass inviting hackneyed comparisons to ripe melons.

"Welcome!" Brett draped a brawny arm around Tad's shoulders and began introducing him to the crew. My stomach started to hurt, gripped by the green fist of jealousy. I jabbed irritably at the coals and slammed the lid of the grill down hard enough to turn several heads.

After the party, Tad offered to help me clean up. Once we had carried the last of the picnic supplies back into the kitchen and loaded the dishwasher, we sat down at the kitchen table for a soda. Tad sipped, set the bottle down and looked across at me, his expression solemn. "Can I talk to you, Jay? About something really serious?"

"Anything, Tad. You know that."

"I'm gay." He took a deep breath and plunged on. "I've thought about it and read about it and I know it's true. I haven't told anyone else, Jay. I knew you'd understand."

"If you're sure, of course I understand. Have you met anyone?"

"Yes. Someone very special. Someone I've known for a long time." He reached across the table and grasped my hand. I felt my heart begin to accelerate. "Someone I respect and admire—and love a great deal. I haven't had sex with anyone yet. I...I want the first time to be really special, Jay."

"Oh." I sat back in my chair, trying to take it all in. "Tad. I'm flattered, believe me. But I can't."

"Why not? I trust you, Jay. I know you'd never do anything to hurt me. Don't you think I'm sexy?"

"Come on, Tad. You know the answer to that one." He smiled with pleasure. "It just wouldn't be right."

"Would it be better with a stranger? I could call your friend Brett. He gave me his telephone number."

"No!" I snapped, pounding my fist on the table.

"I didn't mean that." He looked stricken. "I want you." We looked at one another in silence for a long time, then Tad began to speak. "Well, I guess it's my move. I've got nothing to lose, Jay." He stood, slipped his thumbs into the waistband of his Speedo and wriggled out of them. I swallowed noisily, unable to take my eyes off of him. He walked around the table, straddled me, and sat on my lap, arms around my shoulders, dick and balls hot against my bare belly.

"Make love to me, Jay." He stroked my neck, sending shivers down my spine. I shook my head. "Are you going to send me home?" Before I could speak, he kissed me, and my self-control dissolved. I clamped my hands around his narrow waist, fingers splayed over the lush curve of his butt, and began kissing him back. His lips parted and our tongues touched. I felt his hard-on scooting up my belly. Tad's hands strayed down to my chest.

"That feels sexy," he murmured as he stroked the long hairs that feathered up over my collarbones. "I always wanted hair on my chest. I don't think it's going to happen."

"I don't think it matters," I assured him, my hands slipping up his sides. When my thumbs grazed his plump nipples, his fingers curled against my pecs and his eyelids fluttered. I lowered my head and lapped at the succulent flesh, then pressed my lips against the full curve of muscle and began to suck. The nipple stiffened instantly, poking against my tongue. Tad arched his back, and his tight ass muscles flexed against my bare thighs.

I lifted him from my lap, set him on the edge of the table, licked down his torso to his crotch. I nuzzled his hairless balls, then began kissing the shaft of his dick, moving up, inch by inch to his helmet-shaped glans.

When I capped his tightly clipped meat, I felt a bare foot rubbing against the inside of my thigh. His toes curled around the ridge my dick had formed in the leg of my shorts, the contact shooting intense jolts of pleasure along the shaft and up my spine.

"I do turn you on, don't I?" he asked, a hint of triumph in his tone.

"You have a great future as a psychic," I teased, mumbling around the sweet obstruction of his dick.

"Let me see you," he demanded, wiggling his toes against the cloth. I stood up and dropped my shorts. My dick rose up between us, rock-hard and throbbing. Tad fisted it and pulled gently, bunching my foreskin up beyond the tip. He fingered the crinkled skin, stretched it, then pushed his thumb up into the moist little sleeve.

"Want to try it on?" I asked, my voice thick with passion. His eyes widened and he nodded eagerly. "Stand up." He slipped off the table and stood in front of me, forehead pressed to mine as we both looked down. I pressed our knobs together, then shucked my foreskin up and covered him.

"Oh, man," he sighed. He tilted his head to one side and

kissed me again, his hips rocking tentatively as he humped my foreskin. I cupped his balls and rubbed them back along the swollen ridge between his legs. When my fingertip grazed his ass pucker, his tongue drove deep into my mouth.

"I want to suck you," Tad whispered, his lips brushing my ear. His dick slipped out of my skin and snapped up against his belly. He kissed my neck and began a slow, delicious slide down my front. He knelt at my feet and looked up at me. "It's big," he said matter-of-factly. "I always thought it would be." He grinned disarmingly and began to inspect my dick.

"First things first," I said, pulling a rubber out of a drawer beside the refrigerator. I tore open the packet and dropped it into his palm. He gripped the rigid shaft and looked up at me. "Pull back the skin and bag it, buddy," I said, winking at him. He bared my purple knob and began rolling the lubed latex down the veiny shaft.

I rested my hands on his shoulders, watching him. At first his tongue barely made contact, flickering tentatively. Then he began licking, the pressure increasing, making me harder, setting every nerve to tingling. I gasped when he went down on me, tongue pressed against the tender underbelly of my meat, lips tight around the shaft. He looked up at me then and smiled, an angel with a hard-on in his mouth.

"Can I make another request?" he asked, looking up at me, lips glistening. I nodded, stroking his thick hair. "Will you fuck me, Jay? I want you to be the first."

"You're sure?"

"I'm sure." I pulled him to his feet and led him into the bedroom. He jumped into the middle of the bed and held out his arms to me. I climbed in and knelt beside him.

"Come here, guy." I rolled him onto his belly and pulled him back onto my lap, legs spread out on either side of me, his cock and balls wedged between my thighs, my thick hard-on pointed at his asshole. When I smacked his ass cheeks, he flexed, and the muscles in his broad back shifted enticingly. I began to stroke the backs of his thighs, fingertips curving up over the firm mounds of his glutes. My thumbs slipped up along his crack, grazing the tender lips puckered around his hole. I squirted a few drops of lubricant on the target area and began to massage the moist little opening with my fingertips.

When a digit finally popped up inside him, Tad didn't move or say a word. I stroked the silky walls of his channel, gradually screwing my finger in up to the webbing. I stirred it around, relaxing his sphincter till I managed to insert a second finger, then a third.

"I think you're ready," I said, keeping the plug of fingers firmly inside him. "If you change your mind at any point, Tad, you just tell me and I'll stop."

"I won't change my mind, Jay," he replied, reaching back and tugging the hair on my belly. "I know I won't." I slipped out from under him and reached for the lube again. I started to roll him onto his right side, but he turned the other way. "I want to watch," Tad grinned, pointing at the mirrors that sheathed the closet doors on that side of the room. I chuckled and hooked my hand behind his right knee, pulling his leg up towards his chest.

His asshole was pale pink, hairless, quivering. I bent my head and kissed it, then pressed the long applicator against his virgin ass ring. At the first touch, the little mouth gaped, and I slipped the tube into him. I gave the bottle a squeeze and Tad pressed his hand against his lower gut.

"Man, I felt that," he sighed. "Nice and cool." I squeezed the bottle again, then set it on the floor beside the bed.

"If this hurts, you tell me," I instructed. Tad nodded, his eyes already focused intently on our reflection, watching the point where our bodies were about to connect. I planted my knees on either side of his left thigh, braced one hand on the bed near his shoulders, and gripped my sheathed dick with the other. I made contact, then pressed gently. His ring opened slightly, then clenched shut. I applied more pressure, and my knob popped up into his hot channel.

"You OK?" Tad looked up at me and nodded. He raised his hand and pressed it to my chest.

"Please put it in me, Jay. I want it." I pumped my hips and watched another two inches of my dick slide into his clutching heat. Tad's hard-on jerked and shot a little streamer of clear juice up onto his belly. I pumped again, and his fingers dug into my pectoral muscles. I eased back out, then pushed, burying more of my rigid dick.

I continued my slow progress until I was buried to the hilt. I didn't move for a long time after that, except to run my hands over his sleekly muscled perfection, memorizing the contours of his body with my hands. As I did so, Tad was getting used to the sensation of having a man's hard-on throbbing inside him. He lay still at first, breathing deeply. Then he began to twist and writhe, tentatively grinding his ass around the axis of my stiffer. When he looked up at me the next time, his gaze was dreamy, his blue eyes misty with lust.

"Can I be on top?" he asked, his voice thick. I nodded, pulled out of my slot, and lay back on the bed. Tad straddled me, grabbed my dick, and pointed it straight up. Then, with one hand planted firmly in the middle of my chest, he sat down, engulfing me completely in his silken heat.

"I like this," he announced, flexing his ass muscles and squeezing my dick tight.

"You're dangerous," I groaned, rubbing the insides of his thighs. He smiled angelically and began to ride my dick like a rodeo cowboy on a bucking bronco. I let him have at it for a while, then grabbed him and held him tight as I rolled on top. I pinned his knees to his chest and started fucking him, easy at first, then harder and deeper as I saw how he responded to my increasingly frantic thrusts.

"Oh, God, Jay. This is so good. I'm starting to tingle all over. I feel like I'm going to explode."

"I can guarantee it," I gasped, rising up, then slamming into him, smacking my heavy balls against his ass. He grunted and flexed, his channel squeezing my dick spasmodically. Tad's eyes were wide as he reached between us to get at his flexing rod. I grabbed his wrists and pinned them above his head, determined to fuck the come out of him without any manual assistance. He frowned briefly, but I speared him several times in rapid succession, and his expression changed to one of purest bliss.

"I'm...I'm gonna...ai-i-i-e-e-e!" Tad twitched convulsively, snapping his head from side to side among the pillows of the bed as he began to shoot. His asshole spasmed and a gusher of jizz pumped up along my torso, scoring the flesh with a white, sticky line. I pounded harder, fucking three more creamy streamers out of him, bringing myself up to the critical point.

He felt my dick flex, and his eyes flew open. "Let me see you shoot!" I pulled out and stripped off the latex sheathing. I grabbed my balls in one hand, my cock shaft in the other, and jerked off frantically. Tad propped himself on his elbows, eyes fixed on me hungrily. I let fly, my first shot arcing high above my head, then splashing down all over both of us like hot rain. Another blast followed, then there were a couple of dribblers that hung off my knob like candle wax. A final wave of pleasure built as I continued to pump my fist. My balls rolled onto the top of my shaft, and every muscle in my body knotted. Jism spewed out of my gaping come-hole, shot over Tad's blond head, and hit the wall. I sank back onto my haunches, gasping for breath.

"Wow!" Tad exclaimed, scrambling up and throwing his arms around my neck. "That was incredible." He groped for my dick, squeezed it. "Let's do it again, OK?"

"Give me a minute to catch my breath, guy. What are you, anyway. Some kind of a sex maniac?"

"Yeah. I think so," he grinned, still playing with my dick. "What about you, Jay?" He squeezed me, and my meat flexed against his palm.

"Maybe so," I groaned, kneading his sweaty ass cheeks with my fingers. "Maybe so."

"We've got three whole days to find out. I don't leave for school until Tuesday afternoon. Cool, huh?"

"Way cool," I replied, wondering what my chances were of surviving that long. On the other hand, if a man had to go, what a hell of an exit.

Jimmie Ray Hicks Versus
the Ingrates

First off, I just want to say that I had no intention of walking out of the Piggly Wiggly without paying for that damned ham. It was just that when I saw Rafe Cates and Sammy Lee Dubermann trailing along through the meat department with Joe Bob Jeeter, that slutty, double-dealing ex-roommate of mine, something snapped.

Joe Bob just stood there and glared at me across a big display of hickory-smoked pigs feet. I smiled real sincerely and said "Hey" just to be polite, you know. Joe Bob didn't say a damned word in reply, not that I cared one way or the other.

Then he turned and whispered something to Rafe and Sammy Lee, and they both stared over at me like I was something they'd found stuck to the bottom of their shoe after a stroll through the chicken house. I was so upset I grabbed that ham without thinking about it and stormed right out of the store. I was just about to take the damned thing back when Orville Saunders, the butcher, came running out to the parking lot, carrying on like I was trying to abduct his firstborn child.

The thing I hated most about the whole ordeal—I mean, even worse than the fact that my mother first heard about it when they interrupted *Oprah* with that totally unnecessary news bulletin—was knowing that Joe Bob Jeeter had him a ringside seat for the whole thing. The little turd stood there, flanked by Rafe and Sammy Lee, watching the police haul me off in a squad car, all the while pretending like it all hadn't been his fault, totally.

Truth be told, Joe Bob managed to ruin my life and reputation in less than a month's time. I wouldn't even have met him if I hadn't been so dedicated to getting in shape. With that in mind—and nothing else, thank you very much—I had driven out to the new fitness center at the mall south of town. Well, when I walked into the gym, there was Joe Bob, spread out all over this bench, showing off.

After he finished doing about a thousand reps with this huge barbell, he commenced talking to me. I've always told anybody who'd listen that Joe Bob was the one who picked me up. If he hadn't been so pushy, I wouldn't have given him a second look. Well, he did look cute—in a cheap sort of way—in his skin-tight red shorts and a black tank top that scooped down to his belly button, baring his pink tits. He obviously tried real hard to look good, poor thing, but his proportions weren't quite right, you know? In my personal opinion, he'd gone completely overboard with his pecs and biceps, not to mention the fact that his ass was just a teensy bit too big to be mistaken for anything but a target for any heat-seeking missile in the vicinity.

Well, now, when we got down to the locker room after a very strenuous workout, you could tell that Joe Bob was real excited. He had a stiffer when he pulled off his shorts, and he didn't care who knew it. I could tell he was doing it for my benefit, you know, but I didn't do anything about it, because I've always thought locker-room sex was so tacky. Joe Bob obviously didn't agree with me. There was this guy with lots of muscles and a hairy chest in the shower, and when Joe Bob got a look at him, he jumped into the stall with him so fast you'd have thought he saw a quarter on the floor or something.

There wasn't a curtain or anything, so I couldn't help but see what happened next. The guy flexed a couple of times, then grabbed Joe Bob by the waist, hoisted him up and started sucking his cock. Next thing I knew, Joe Bob had been flipped around and was hanging there, head down like a damned bat, slurping on the muscular dude's hard-on. It was a big one, but Joe Bob managed to swallow the whole thing without choking. I should've known all I needed to know just seeing that, but I've always been too good-natured for my own good.

Well, after a couple of minutes, the guy put Joe Bob down. They stood there, flexing at each other like a couple of damned peacocks for a while, then the man with the hairy chest spun Joe Bob around and rammed his huge dick into him, right up to the balls. I winced, but Joe Bob didn't bat an eye. The guy laid into him for a good 20 minutes, balls swinging, muscles bulging, chanting "fuck, fuck, fuck" till my ears were ringing. Finally, Joe Bob's stiffer exploded in a spurting gusher of jism. The dude with the hairy chest pulled his cock out of Joe Bob and pumped about a quart of hot cream, frosting Joe Bob like the twinkie he was.

Afterward, Joe Bob told me he would've introduced me but that he'd forgotten the guy's name. I mean, come on, do you even believe that?

While he was drying off, Joe Bob told me all about himself. Well, naturally, when I found out that he'd been thrown out of his apartment, I immediately asked him to come and stay with me. In spite of what you may hear to the contrary, I did it to be nice and wasn't even thinking about getting a piece of his big ass or anything like that. Well, Joe Bob jumped at the chance to live with me, and you could just tell from the way he was looking at me in the car on the way home that he thought I was pretty hot stuff.

I loaned Joe Bob a set of my best sheets, some towels, and one of the brand-new feather pillows off my bed. While he was getting settled in the spare room, I went to the store and bought a couple of steaks, then came back home and cooked supper. After he was done eating, Joe Bob sat down and started watching the TV, leaving me with the dishes to wash. I didn't mind, because I figured he was just resting up for later, not that I was expecting him to put out or anything. It was just that he had been traipsing around in a skimpy pair of drawers that wasn't doing much to hide any of his talents, constantly telling me how horny he was and how he needed to get his rocks off before he could sleep.

Right when I was ready to settle down beside him on the couch, the doorbell rang. On my way to answer it, I suggested to Joe Bob that he might want to go and put on some clothes, but he just stared at me like I was speaking Chinese and didn't move a muscle.

"Hey, Jimmie Ray."

"Hey, Rafe." Rafe Cates worked at the factory with me, and he was this total hunk. I mean, he was tall and lean with big shoulders, gorgeous arms, and all his own teeth. I'd been angling for a date with him for months, and I figured that since he'd showed up on my doorstep he'd finally gotten the hint.

"Gosh, Jimmie Ray, I hate to bother you, but do you think I could borrow 20 bucks? I'm flat broke till payday."

"Sure, Rafe." It meant dipping into my emergency fund, but Rafe was special and I didn't mind loaning it to him. "Rafe, this here's Joe Bob Jeeter. He's my new roommate."

"Hey, Rafe," Joe Bob said, getting up and prancing right over to my buddy. "How's it hanging, dude?" Honestly, if Joe Bob could've only known how cheap that kind of talk made him sound.

"Long and loose," Rafe retorted, shaking Joe Bob's hand. Joe Bob held on like he thought Rafe was the door prize. It was sad. "Could I buy you a beer, Joe Bob?"

"Sure." Joe Bob scooted out of the room and was back in a flash, crammed into a tight pair of jeans and a blue T-shirt that made his curly blond hair look kind of brassy.

"I don't think I'll join you," I said, fighting to keep the smile from sliding right off my face. "I'm real busy."

"Oh, did Rafe ask you to come too?" Joe Bob said, flashing this phony grin. "See you later, Jimmie Ray. Maybe you should spend some time doing a few sit-ups. Be better for you than those chocolate chip cookies you were pigging out on earlier."

"I had a couple for dessert," I retorted.

"Couple of dozen," Joe Bob shot back at me. "Don't wait up." They left and I heard them laughing as they drove off in Rafe's pickup. Once the truck was out of sight, I found that bag of cookies and grabbed me a double handful.

✳ ✳ ✳

It was well after midnight when they returned. My bedroom door just happened to be open a crack, so I saw them when they came staggering in, both drunk as skunks on my $20. Joe Bob, that cheap slut, was through the door first, his shirt pushed up into his armpits, his pants riding on his thighs. Rafe was right on his heels, his shirt completely missing, a hard-on the size of a grain silo sticking out of his fly. I'd always known that Rafe had an impressive basket, but I never would've dreamed he was hung that big. It was all red and shiny with spit, so I figured Joe Bob had been performing a skin flute recital on the way back from the bar. I've always thought car sex was so tacky. Obviously, Rafe knew better than to pull a stunt like that on me, so he'd settled for Joe Bob.

The front door wasn't even closed before Rafe was pawing Joe Bob's big old butt. He pulled Joe Bob's rosy cheeks apart and started fingering his asshole. Joe Bob spread his legs and took a whole handful without even blinking. After about 10 minutes, when Rafe had managed to retrieve his hand, he started getting ready for the main event. Joe Bob braced his hands on the arm of my couch and watched over his shoulder while Rafe spit in his palm, lubed his piece, then began shoving it up Joe Bob's asshole.

"Put it in me, Rafe. That's it. Fuck that ass."

"Nice tight hole, Joe Bob. Fuckin' hot." Well, I would've shut my door and gone back to bed, but I didn't want to draw attention to myself. Rafe sank in up to the hilt, groaned, then started to hump, his hairy butt flexing as he pumped his big prick in and out of Joe Bob.

Joe Bob was hanging onto the arm of the couch for dear life, sweat beading on his back. I was close enough to take in the whole scene. There was the glistening shaft of Rafe's dick as it pistoned in and out between Joe Bob's cheeks. And there was the little triangle of dark hairs at the base of Rafe's spine that pointed down into his furry crack. And, of course, there was the way Rafe's thick brown nipples poked up out of the forest of hair on his chest. Looking at Rafe made me horny. Looking at Job Bob made me mad. I got a grip on myself and started to jerk off.

Every once in a while, Rafe would yank his horn out of Joe Bob and rub it up and down his spine. Every time he did it, the damned thing got bigger and redder, the veins more swollen, the enormous knob a deeper shade of purple. Of course, you could also see Joe Bob's hole, gaping like the mouth of a big old cave. It was sort of pathetic, really.

By about the fifth time Rafe had removed his dick to check on it, you could tell everybody was getting close. My toes were digging deep in the pile of the carpet, Joe Bob was slobbering on the couch cushions, and Rafe's hard-on was flopping around like a fish out of water. Rafe grunted and grabbed his horn with both hands. His biceps flexed and his belly sucked back, making his chest look even bigger than normal. He threw his head back, pumped his prick a couple of times and shot a ribbon of jism that flew over Joe Bob's head and hit the opposite wall.

Well, that impressed me, I'll tell you. I popped my own wad while I watched a couple more big gushers blast out of Rafe. Hell, I'd probably have to repaint, but it sure was hot to watch. About the time I had myself all composed again, Joe Bob started screaming and jumping around, spitting little white slime balls all over my damned couch cushions. Looked like I'd be spending my morning with a bottle of spot remover. I could've killed him.

✳ ✳ ✳

"Come right in this house, Sammy Lee," I said, holding the screen door open for my date. Sammy Lee Dubermann wasn't much of a talker, but he had a nice build on him and had been voted handsomest guy in the sophomore class. I always said he should've been a movie star, but it never worked out for him. Matter of fact, Sammy Lee had been pumping gas since he dropped out of high school. "You know Rafe Cates, don't you?" The two men shook hands. "That's Joe Bob Jeeter," I mumbled, pointing vaguely in the direction of my roommate. "You want a beer, Sammy Lee?" He nodded. "I'll be right back."

I hoofed it out to the kitchen and stuck my head in the fridge. Damn it! I told Joe Bob to pick up some beer on my way out of the house this morning. He still didn't have a job, so why the hell couldn't he manage a trip to the store? I popped the top on the single remaining bottle and marched back to the living room.

"I forgot all about it, Jimmie Ray. I was really into it at the gym today. I just pumped and pumped." He crooked his right arm and made a fist. "My biceps got so big they practically scare me." He flexed, and everything from the waist up began to swell.

"Oh, get over yourself, Joe Bob," I snapped, trying not to let on how pissed I was about the beer. "I'm sure Sammy Lee isn't the least bit interested in your damned muscles. Are you, Sammy Lee?"

"Huh?" Sammy Lee looked over at me and licked his lips. "Is that my beer?" I gave him the bottle and he chugged a fair portion of it in one gulp. "Nice pump on those pecs, Joe Bob," he said, his huge paw obscuring almost half my roommate's torso.

"I just tend to muscle up, I guess," Joe Bob simpered. "Better than running to fat, like some." He glanced at me hatefully.

"I'm going to the store so we'll all have something to drink tonight. You want to ride with me, Sammy Lee?" He belched noisily and shook his head. Probably too tired after a day at work.

The line was long at the Piggly Wiggly, so it was almost an hour before I got back. I was walking up to the front porch when I happened to look at the picture window. The blind was pulled down and you could see three shadows—two standing, one kneeling. The two standing shadows either had hard-ons or they were holding their beer bottles at about crotch level, which made me real suspicious.

Well, I sneaked around back and came in through the kitchen. I crept over to the living room door and, sure enough, Joe Bob was down on his knees, doing what he did best. The daily special was obviously a knob job, and Joe Bob was handing them out left and right. He had Rafe in one hand, Sammy Lee in the other, his tongue darting back and forth like a snake's. Both men were gaping at their crotches, just like neither one of 'em had ever seen a blow job before.

All of a sudden, Rafe and Sammy Lee got Joe Bob by the ears and really laid into him. Rafe went at it for a minute, then Sammy Lee took over, then it was back to Rafe. Once, when Rafe was only about halfway out, Sammy Lee started packing his pecker back in, stretching Joe Bob's mouth till he looked like a gargoyle. The two of them got a rhythm going, and it wasn't long till Joe Bob's head looked like one of them two-cylinder engines.

"Jesus Christ!" Joe Bob gasped, falling back on his butt with a splat. "You boys gotta let me breathe once in a while. You wait here for a minute. I got something even better in mind." The guys nodded, their spit-slicked hard-ons bobbing up and down like a couple of them redheaded birds you get at the circus and put on the edge of a glass of water. Joe Bob dashed into the toilet.

I ducked out of the kitchen and ran around to the other side of the house, hoping Joe Bob'd be in the can long enough to do what I planned to do. I pried the screen off his window and climbed through. I removed the items I'd pocketed in the kitchen and got to work. I was just putting the lid back on when I heard footsteps in the hallway. I slipped into the closet and pulled the door closed almost all the way. Joe Bob waltzed in, rummaged around under the bed for a trick towel and his super-jumbo-sized tub of lube, then sashayed out.

"I got you guys a real hot surprise," Joe Bob announced, reappearing in the living room. "You lube me up good, and I'll get those dipsticks of yours all primed and ready to go. We're about to do us some fancy fucking." He scooped out two big handfuls of lube and started slicking down their poles. The two men began packing their well-greased fingers up Joe Bob's asshole. I popped a beer and settled in to watch the fun.

The two men lined up behind Joe Bob, Rafe first, Sammy Lee close behind. Rafe mounted and slid in to the balls on the first try. Joe Bob groaned but held his ground. After Rafe had pumped a few times, Sammy Lee stepped up to fill the breach. He fisted his piece, squeezing till his knob swelled up big as a baseball. He thrust it at Joe Bob like a deadly weapon. He butted at Joe Bob's hole a few times, then drove it in deep.

"Fuckin' lube is all runny," Rafe groused, dipping into the tub and smearing more on his hard-on, working it in across the blunt dome of his knob.

"Yeah," Sammy Lee agreed, riding Joe Bob hard. "Shit's dripping off my balls."

"You boys are just such hot fucks the stuff's melting," Joe Bob gasped. "Ready for some real fun?" The men nodded. "Rafe, you sit down on the couch." Rafe did. Joe Bob straddled him and mounted his towering erection. "Sammy Lee, kneel down behind me and ease on in. I'm gonna take you both on. Grab some more of that slick stuff, guy. That's a lot of cock to be packing up my tight hole."

Sammy Lee coated his cock with a new layer of lube and started wedging up into Joe Bob. I watched in amazement as his huge knob disappeared. The muscles in Joe Bob's shoulders popped up into big knots, and his mouth gaped wider than his asshole. Sammy Lee clamped his hands on Joe Bob's shoulders and started driving it home.

"Damn, my balls are burning," Rafe groused, still humping Joe Bob.

"Mine too," Sammy Lee agreed. "My dick's getting hot too. Real hot."

"That's because my hole's so tight," Joe Bob groaned, squirming around between them. He'd been fucked so much his butt hole was probably numb.

"I don't think so," Sammy Lee said, standing up and grabbing at his pecker. "Jesus! What have you done to my damn dick?" Poor bastard. His cock was scarlet. His balls too. He touched the tip of his meat and squealed in anguish. I felt my groin muscles tighten in sympathy. "Man, I'm really hurting." He pumped his prick a few times and came. It didn't seem to make him feel better, but he shot an impressive load all up and down Joe Bob's back. "Ow!"

"Hey!" Joe Bob protested when Rafe pushed him off on the floor and staggered to his feet. Rafe's big prick looked like it was on fire. Even the thick blue veins that wrapped around the shaft looked sore and swollen. The strings of jism clinging around the tip looked like snow on a fire hydrant. Both men reached for their pants and shoes.

"I don't know what...A-a-ai-e-e-e!" Joe Bob finally got it, and when he did, you could tell he'd got it bad. He started hopping around, fanning his asshole. "I'm on fire!" he wailed. "Help me."

"I'm out of here," Rafe gasped, running for the door without even bothering to pick his shirt up off the floor. Sammy Lee was right on his heels, and you could hear both trucks firing up and the spatter of gravel as they tore off down the road.

"Wait for me!" Joe Bob cried in a panic. He busted through the screen door, buck-naked. "Help!" he cried out, running down the middle of the road, both hands clamped to his scorched asshole. I watched till he was out of sight, then stepped into the kitchen. I took the hot pepper flakes and the tabasco sauce out of my pockets and put them away, then opened me another beer.

* * *

Joe Bob didn't even knock on the door the next day. He just picked his belongings up off the lawn where I'd thrown them, stuffed them into a plastic sack, and left. Sammy Lee was decidedly cool when I ran into him down at the gas station the following Monday, and Rafe never did pay me back that $20 he'd borrowed, but I could live with that. What I couldn't get around was the trash those three started talking around town about me. You would've thought Joe Bob would be recognized as the villain, but...oh, no...I ended up being the heavy. I'm convinced that's why everything went against me in court when I got hauled in about that damned ham.

The good news is that I've met somebody special, right here at the Drucker County Correctional Facility. I've knocked off 22 pounds and my pal Vern has become my weightlifting coach. When I get out of here, that Joe Bob Jeeter better hope he sees me before I see him. For that matter, Rafe and Sammy Lee better give me a pretty wide berth as well. Damned ingrates! Fuck 'em. Fuck 'em all.

On the Midway

Hot outside. Hotter inside. The fan, its bent blades pinging against the wire cage, just barely moved the heat. My old dog Jake lay curled up under the bed, tongue hanging out, slobbering a puddle on the bare floorboards. I was laying naked on my bed, hotter than the weather. Sweat glistened on my chest and belly, pooling in my navel, beading on the shaft of my hard cock and tickling my balls as it slithered down between my legs.

Supposed to rain soon, bring relief. Relief! Man, I needed some of that. Eighteen, horny, confused as hell about everything except the feeling I got when I put my hand on my cock. I kept my hand there a lot. Had it there right now, down around the base, my pubes twining round my fingers. I squeezed, pushed down, pointed the bullet-shaped head up at the ceiling. It grew, swelling all the tiny wrinkles out, flaring around the rim so it looked like some kind of gigantic pink mushroom.

I pumped my fist up, let it sink back down. I was big, big enough to get teased about it by the guys at school. "Hung like a donkey and strictly handmade," they'd shout in the showers, knowing I was a virgin. Always egging me on to fuck some girl, any girl, just get fucked. Drove them crazy, me with a big dick like I had and still a virgin. Only reason the teasing didn't get ugly was because I could've knocked the living shit out of any one of 'em, and they knew it.

I rubbed the ball of my thumb over the tip of my dick and shuddered. My belly muscles tightened, my shoulders hunched, my big balls pulled up between my legs, then sank back down again. I let out a moan. Old Jake whimpered but didn't move from under the bed. I squeezed my dick harder, and a big drop of clear goo oozed out of my piss slit, quivered there for a second, then rolled down slow over my knuckles. I squeezed again and got more.

I closed my eyes tight and started cranking. Everything was totally black at first, but then, as my skin started to tingle and I got that funny feeling deep in my gut, I started seeing guys in my head. Nobody in particular, just guys. Tall guys, hairy guys, guys with big hard muscles. Never any girls, just guys. All the guys had big hard-ons and fat balls dangling between their legs. All of them had these sexy, shit-eating grins on their faces, and all of them were watching me watching them. It was weird, but it was hot. Real hot.

I was pumping like crazy now, beating my meat, pounding my belly with my fist. My balls were in a knot, my toes were curling, my skin was on fire, my heart was slamming against my ribs. It was coming, it was coming. It was there. My hips jerked up off the mattress, and my eyes flew open. I flexed my fingers around the rigid stalk of my cock, saw my come-hole gape wide, watched as the first big drop forced its way out and drooled down onto my belly. I flexed my fingers again, and a thick streamer of white shot out. It flew up in an arc over my torso and splattered down on my face. I jerked again, and more jism scalded my skin. I kept pumping, watching the white drops spatter my belly and my chest. As I lay there panting, rubbing come into my skin, I thought I heard thunder rumbling in the distance.

* * *

When I went downstairs about 7 that evening, my father glanced at me disapprovingly over the top of his newspaper and snorted. He didn't say anything—he rarely did—but I knew he disapproved. Hell, he disapproved of almost everything, especially me.

"There's a storm coming, son." My mother stood in the doorway to the kitchen, rocking back and forth on the balls of her feet. Mom always looked like she was on the verge of bolting—you know, running off down the road and not coming back. I wouldn't have blamed her. My father didn't approve of her, either. She had, after all, given birth to me.

"I'll be fine," I replied, turning to leave.

"Shouldn't you wear something, son? I mean…"

"I'm wearing something," I retorted, cutting her off. I knew what she meant—my old jeans had been washed so often, they had faded out as pale as the white athletic undershirt I was wearing. They were my favorite jeans, and I liked the fact that they fit me like a second skin. The old undershirt was damn near transparent, except for the narrow straps, which were almost Day-Glo against my tanned skin. "G'night." I stalked out of the room, letting the screen door slam behind me.

I walked across town through air thick with moisture. There wasn't a breeze anywhere, and leaves hung on the trees like limp green hankies. Folks were sitting on their porches, drinking iced drinks, and fanning themselves. Some spoke or waved. Most didn't. Every small town needs somebody to disapprove of, I guess. Besides, they were just following my old man's lead. Hell, I didn't care. I straightened my shoulders and stuffed my hands into my pant pockets to emphasize the lump of cock and balls tucked down along my right thigh. Give 'em something to talk about—what the hell.

Fairgrounds were crawling with people—rugrats running around all over the place, hollering and squealing. The parents of the screaming rugrats were my old pals—guys and gals I'd known at school but hadn't kept up with since graduation— all looking beaten down now, like they'd just bet the whole works on a losing hand of poker. I wandered along the midway, ignoring them, just looking and waiting.

It was a pissant fair, just a few rides and a long row of booths hung with stuffed toys and other crap you wouldn't have stopped to pick up off the street any other time of the year. Still, folks were lined up three deep, waiting to pay good money to take a chance to win some of that crap. Go figure.

I walked the midway from end to end twice and was thinking of leaving. The weather hadn't let up any, and it was hotter 'n' hell. Besides, some of the gals in the midway crowd were starting to give me looks, hungry looks. Scared the shit out of me.

On the way out, I threaded my way through the bumper cars, the merry-go-round and the tilt-a-whirl, dodging kids and thick power cables that lay in the sawdust like long black snakes. Way back by the stock barns, there was a Ferris wheel. It was by far the biggest of the rides, its slender steel frame outlined in multicolored neon. It was spinning slow, lazy circles, every car full of laughing people.

As I stood and watched, the wind started to blow, and lightning began to lick the night sky. I took a deep breath and smelled rain. Maybe it would cool things off. Might even cool me off, my skin at least. I needed something else to cool the other fire that licked down in my belly, making my cock tingle and my balls ache.

While I was watching the Ferris wheel, I got a feeling that somebody was watching me. I looked left, then right. Then I saw them. There were two, one blond, the other dark. Carny guys. Leastwise not from around this hick town. They were both tall and filled out their jeans real nice. The dark one's chest was bare, showing plenty of muscle and hair. He had a band around his left wrist with numbers on it. Both of them kept looking over to where I was standing. They'd look at me, then look at each other. I saw their lips moving and their heads nodding, but I couldn't hear what they were saying. The blond one winked at me and licked his lips.

The wind was starting to blow good now, and a clap of thunder followed close behind the next lightning flash. Storm was moving in fast. Parents were starting to gather their kids up off the rides, and the dust was swirling. The carny guys stopped the Ferris wheel and emptied the first seat. They cranked it around to the next one, then the next. Before they were halfway done, the rain started.

It came down in big fat drops that exploded against the ground and the rides and the tents and people's bodies. It felt cool, plastering my hair against my scalp. The carny guys kept on letting people off the ride, pushing them down the ramp as the lightning flashed brighter and the rain fell harder. When they were done, the rain was falling in sheets like transparent curtains. They were soaked with it, and their clothes were plastered against their bodies, making them look almost naked.

I looked at myself. I looked naked too, nipples dark beneath the thin fabric of my shirt, my dick outlined like a cylinder under the sopping denim. The carny guys were looking at me again, staring at my tits and my crotch and my arms and at the curve of my thick thighs. I was feeling hot, a kind of hot that all the rain in the world couldn't quench. I looked back at them, looked at their big arms and at the hunger in their eyes. The dark one curled his fingers around the lump between his legs and squeezed. I felt the pressure on my own balls. The blond took a step forward, like he was going to walk off the platform and come over to me.

I felt this rush between my legs and then—then I felt nothing. Or it was more like I felt everything. The loudest noise in the universe deafened me, just as a bright flash lit up the area around me and erased it, leaving me in total darkness. I didn't feel anything for a moment, then I felt my skin tingling, like it was crawling with something. But instead of being creepy, the pleasure took my breath away. I opened my eyes and looked down. I was laying flat on my back in the sawdust, naked, my stiff cock levitating about an inch above my belly. All my muscles were flexed and my tits were jutting up from the curve of my pecs like little fingertips. Pale blue flames curled above the surface of my skin.

I looked beyond my bare feet and saw two pairs of shoes. I looked up along jean-clad legs to two enormous hard-ons, drops of rain exploding in silver fountains off their broad backs. I looked up further, through tangled pubic hair and over washboard bellies. It was the carnies—or maybe not. These men had neon pulsing in their eyes, blue for the blond, acid green for the dark one. They looked like the carnys, a little. Only they changed every time I looked, their faces and bodies melting and swelling and regrouping until I couldn't tell who they were.

They both leaned forward, their swollen cocks bobbing, laced with thick purple veins. They stretched forefingers towards me, towards my chest. I saw sparks arc from their fingertips to my nipples, felt a pressure like we were attached by tiny chains. I felt my body rising from the ground, pulled upright by the force of them. The dark one grabbed my cock, the blond my balls. They pulled me up onto the platform, into one of the rocking Ferris wheel seats.

They got on after me. The blond kicked a lever and the wheel rocked to life, rising up into the howling storm. Rain lashed my hot, throbbing body, beat against my aching prick, streamed down over my chest and thighs. The dark one sank to his knees, began licking my thighs, teasing me, his tongue coming closer and closer to my balls, never touching them.

The blond was touching everything. He stood behind me, making the car rock dangerously. I felt his hands up my naked sides, his fingers against my belly, his cock pressed tight against my ass. Thunder rumbled, lightning flashed. The dark one looked up, his eyes pinwheels of green and yellow neon. I looked over my shoulder at the blond. His forehead beetled above his neon eyes, his chin tapered to a fine point. He smiled, and needle teeth glittered in the silvery lightning light.

Both men moved in on me, the dark one in front, the blond behind. I felt lips against my cock snout, a cock against the tender, quivering lips of my virgin asshole. The dark one lunged forward, the blond did the same. I was impaled, fore and aft. I howled my pain and ecstasy as the wind howled the rain around us, rocking the Ferris wheel like a doll's cradle.

The car swept up to the pinnacle as the blond thrust his cock deep into me. I reached back and grabbed at him, pushing the waterlogged denim down his strong lean thighs. His cock knob pumped up into my body, stretching my bowels, stoking the inferno in my belly. The dark one burrowed in my groin, swallowing all my cock, pressing his hot lips into my pubes. His tongue shot out of his mouth and slithered across my balls.

The Ferris wheel car swept down in a wide arc, slashing neon bands into the storm. Rain exploded against the dark one's shoulders, slid down his bare back in rivers of red, green, purple, and blue. I pressed my hand against the back of his skull, and tendrils of his thick hair curled around my fingers. The muscles in his neck and shoulders swelled and shifted beneath his swarthy, rain-mottled skin.

I raised my arms high and threw back my head as the car began to arc up into the sky again. The blond man was fucking me, pumping his cock in and out of me, his forehead against my neck as he nibbled my shoulders. "Eat you up," he growled, his powerful hands squeezing my arms till my fingers tingled. "Eat you all up."

We all three shifted as the car thrust up into the swirling sky. I sat, impaled on the blond. The dark one gripped the front of the car and, muscles bulging, hoisted himself up into a handstand. I gasped to see him teetering so high above the sparkling ground. He fell back against me, his cock filling my mouth, flexing as it slid down my throat. I reached for him, gripped his waist, felt his fuzzy ass, hard as rock. I sucked the cold rain off his cock, tasted the salt sweat, the musk of him, felt the heat of him trickling down into my belly.

The wheel spun faster and faster, rocking the car. We all groaned and snorted, blood racing as we got ready to shoot. I was trembling on the verge, ass battered by the blond's enormous cock, prick caressed by the dark one's supple tongue, my own tongue curling around the surging hardness in my throat. The car soared up, reached the peak, shuddered, broke free and began to fall, end over end through the crystal rain.

I held out my arms, soared up, howling my pleasure,

shooting come like bolts of lightning along my cock. The blond and the dark one soared with me, pricks jutting, shooting enormous explosions of thick white through the air. Our spunk began to spiral, three streams becoming one, the white now streaked with gold and lavender and scarlet. The stream swirled around my torso, brushing my nipples, arcing sparks. I screamed in ecstasy, raised my voice to the sky. I screamed and screamed and...

"It's OK, buddy." I heard a voice, felt a hand on my chest, felt my heart pounding against a man's hot palm. "I think he's coming around, guys." I looked up into a shadowy, unfamiliar face. "Hey, fella. Can you hear me?"

"I...I..." I opened my eyes. "What?"

"Lightning, son," the man replied. "You got struck. Lucky for you, you grounded out on this old Ferris wheel. Must've been something, though. Burned all your clothes away but didn't even singe the fuzz on your balls." I sat up and cupped my hands over my groin, struggling to hide my hard-on. It was all sticky with jism. "Never heard of a dude shooting a load after getting hit by lightning. Must've been a hell of an orgasm." The man chuckled and closed the black bag on the ground beside him.

"Thanks for the help," I mumbled, wondering what to do about being naked.

"Glad I was here. You're OK, son. I'll leave you with your buddies. They told me they'd take care of you." I looked up. Two guys, one blond, the other dark, stood behind the man. They reached for me. I gripped their big hands and rose to my feet.

The dark one's gaze flickered down to my rigid cock, his pinwheel eyes flashing. "Don't worry," he whispered, his voice low and rough. "I'm a real meat-eater, baby. I'll gobble you all up." The blond one smiled, his sharp teeth glittering in the light. I smiled back and let them lead me away.

Arnie

"Here, let me help you with that."

"Thanks," I gasped, grateful for the extra pair of hands that had just slipped under the opposite edge of the cabinet I'd been trying to wrestle single-handed off the back of my pickup.

"No problem, guy. Shit, this sucker's heavy. Let's get a move on." My unseen savior panted and cursed right along with me as we maneuvered the bulky piece of furniture through the front door and into my new living room.

"I'm Arnie Williams," the man said, wiping the sweat off

his forehead. "I live in the next house over." He jerked his thumb over his shoulder. "We share the driveway. Welcome to the neighborhood."

"Pete Richmond." We shook hands. "I appreciate the help, Arnie. A couple of my buddies are supposedly on the way to help out, but they haven't showed up yet."

"I was taking out the garbage when I saw you struggling. I figured there was no use letting you throw your back out— not that you look like the kind of guy who'd throw his back out just by picking up stuff. You're in pretty awesome shape, Pete."

I glanced down briefly at the sculpted planes of my sweat-slick torso. "I do my best, Arnie. No use letting…" I was cut off by a shrill screech that came from somewhere nearby. Arnie winced. I looked at him questioningly.

"Jill," he said by way of explanation. "She gets meaner than a junkyard dog if I'm not right there when she gets to looking for me." The screech ripped the peace again, and Arnie began to retreat. "Nice to meet you, Pete. See you around."

He rushed out the door just as the unearthly screech was repeated for the third time. Jill apparently needed an attitude adjustment—or a muzzle. At that moment, a blue pickup truck came barreling up the drive, and my buddies Jack and Dave jumped out.

"Sorry we're late, Pete. Got stuck on the Bay Bridge." Jack loped over to the porch and threw a brawny arm across my shoulder. "Who's the dude?" he whispered, jerking his head towards Arnie's retreating form.

"That's my next-door neighbor Jack."

"He's got a nice ass. Single?"

"Straight and married, Jack. At least he's living with a woman."

"Maybe he's a switch-hitter."

"Forget it, Jack. He isn't my type." Jack was untiring, some-times even obnoxious, in his efforts to get me settled down.

"Hey, Pete."

"Good to see you, Dave." Dave was Jack's partner. "Thanks for taking the time off to come and help me."

"So, who was that dude?" He nudged me in the ribs. "He sure as hell didn't waste any time coming over here and checking you out."

"Jesus! Who hired you two guys to be my surrogate mother? He lives next door. He helped me move a cabinet. He's straight. Drop it."

"Touchy, ain't he, Jack?" Dave shook his head, punched me playfully on the shoulder, then began unloading my pickup. Neither of them mentioned my new neighbor again that night, although they both made it abundantly clear that they didn't approve of my single state of existence.

* * *

I'm not sure exactly when I fell for Arnie. I'm not even sure why I fell for him. He was just a regular guy, easy enough to look at, but certainly no knockout. His front teeth were a little crooked, and his ears stuck out from his head too much for him to be mistaken for a model. On the other hand, his eyes were beautiful—a tawny gold color flecked with green. He also had this sexy little cleft in his chin and a grin that made me weak in the knees.

Arnie didn't have a perfect body, although he did have a tight, well-rounded butt that filled out the seat of his pants quite nicely. His upper body could maybe have benefited from a regimen of arm curls and bench presses, but Arnie wasn't the least bit self-conscious about taking off his shirt, even in the presence of serious muscle hulks like my buddies Jack and Dave. His chest was actually pretty sexy, dusted with a silky chestnut floss that curled in the valley between his pecs and feathered up over his collar bones. Arnie's belly curved out slightly, sporting a little diamond of fur that sprouted around his navel, then trailed in a narrow line down to the waistband of his pants.

Shortly after I moved in, the irritable Jill had packed up her stuff while Arnie was at work and moved out, leaving him a one-line note of explanation. Arnie had taken the news in stride. After her departure, we started hanging out with each other almost every day. Dinner with Arnie was definitely more fun than dinner alone. Ditto for watching television, doing yard work, washing the car—you name it. Bottom line, I enjoyed Arnie's company

The only problem I had with Arnie was of my own making. The truth was, an evening with him invariably got my libido all stirred up and left me with a raging hard-on. The two of us were always horsing around, getting physical with each other. I'd always been a pretty demonstrative guy, and so was Arnie. Neither of us thought anything about draping an arm over the other guy's shoulders if we were standing next to each other, or grabbing the other guy by the arm to get his attention. Arnie had even fallen into the habit of smacking me on the butt after scoring on me when we shot hoops in the driveway between our houses.

And then there was the matter of Arnie as masseur. His massages were the worst—and the best. He was a genius at working the stress-induced kinks out of the muscles in my neck and shoulders, but his ministrations left me stiff in other places lower down on my anatomy. It all started when I had come home after work one day complaining about a knot in my shoulder. Arnie had offered to help.

"Take off your shirt and relax, Pete. I'll be right back." I stripped out of my shirt and settled down on a stool at the snack bar in his kitchen. He returned a couple of minutes later, stripped down to his boxers and armed with a towel and a bottle of massage oil. "No use getting this stuff all over my clothes," he explained, setting the bottle on the counter. "That just means more laundry, and we both know that's not good." I laughed. We shared an aversion to washing machines because they always seemed to be shrinking things or turning white clothes pink.

I planted my elbows on my knees, closed my eyes, and let my hands hang limp between my legs. I heard Arnie take a deep breath, then sensed his body heat against my skin. A few seconds later he made contact. He ran his fingertips down my neck and across my shoulders. After repeating the motion several times, he laid his hands on me. I shrugged, pushing up against his callused palms. His grip increased, thumbs against my back, his long, thick fingers curving down over my collarbones to the rise of my pecs.

"Tender?" he asked solicitously. I had moaned when he hit a particularly sore spot in my neck. I nodded. He bent forward and slipped his arm around me till it was pressed diagonally across my torso. "Relax," he whispered, pulling my head down until my cheek pressed against his shoulder. As he gently kneaded my neck, a healing warmth flowed from his fingers, dissolving the knot and banishing the discomfort. I could feel his warm breath on my skin. His furry chest tickled against my back. He pressed his thumb beneath my ear, then drew it down along my neck and across my shoulder. If I'd been a cat, I would've started to purr.

As he continued, the warmth that flowed from his hands began to seep lower, down to my groin. My cock began to tingle, then stiffen. Soon, I was squirming around on the stool, trying to readjust my prick in my pants. No sooner had I managed that than I started to leak. By the time he had finished with me, the slippery fluid had soaked through my shorts and my trousers, making me look like I'd pissed on myself. If Arnie noticed, it didn't faze him. After that first time, he offered to rub my neck almost every night. I never seemed able to turn him down.

It was starting to look like I was doomed to exist in a terminal state of horniness. I tried going out to the bars a couple of times, but nobody I met could make me laugh the way Arnie could. Nobody could give me a hard-on the way Arnie could, either. All it took from him was a simple touch of the hand, and my temperature would start to rise. I was a man in dire straits.

＊ ＊ ＊

"Hey, Pete."

"Arnie." I wouldn't have answered the door, but the knocking had persisted, so I wrapped a towel around my hips and went to check it out. I had just embarked on a leisurely Friday night JO session, and having Arnie there in person—as opposed to having him there in my fantasy—was somewhat disconcerting, to say the least. "What can I do for you, buddy?"

He locked eyes with me but didn't speak as he stepped into the house and pushed the door shut behind him. He was still wearing his work clothes, and his gray coveralls reeked of sweat and motor oil. The smell of him made my nostrils quiver. There was a smudge of grease on his right cheek, and a few flecks of unidentifiable debris were caught in his thick, curly hair. He licked his lips nervously and swallowed hard.

"Arnie? Is something wrong?"

"Kiss me." His voice was so soft that I figured I hadn't heard him right. But if he hadn't said that, what had he said? In the course of the next three seconds, I discovered that there was nothing wrong with my hearing. He put his oil-stained hands on my waist, gently but firmly, and drew me towards him. My groin pressed into his, my torso rubbed the coarse fabric of his coveralls, and his warm mouth touched mine.

Damn, for a straight guy, Arnie was a good kisser. Make that a great kisser. He rubbed his lips against mine, then his tongue. By the time he began to insinuate the quivering tip of it between my teeth, I was responding, giving in to the urge to explore his body with my hands.

Arnie was doing some exploring of his own. From my waist, his huge, sexy hands had slipped briefly up to my shoulders, then back down to my ass. He tugged at the damp towel that separated us and tossed it aside. My dick pressed against his leg. I could feel his body heat. I worked my left hand between us and tugged at the zipper of his coveralls, inching it down, baring a line of flesh from his throat to his pubes.

Instead of hauling his cock into the open, I tucked mine into the humid confines of the coveralls. It rubbed against his, and we both shook like we'd had live electrodes clipped to our balls. His tongue hit the back of my throat, and he began fondling my ass more insistently. Both of us were hard in a couple of heartbeats, stabbing our stiffers at each other's groins like blunted daggers.

Arnie broke the kiss and looked at me intently, as though making a fateful decision. Then he sank to his knees, licking all the way. He lashed briefly at my nipples, continued down over my belly and through my pubes, moving right along to the bloated shaft of my hard-on. He licked around the hairy hilt, kissed my jiggling balls, then licked a trail out to the tip. He kissed that part of me as well, looked up at me from under lust-droopy eyelids and began to swallow. I reached back and braced my hands on the cabinet, still struggling to take in what was happening.

Arnie gave good head—a little toothy at first, but he compensated by his obvious enthusiasm. He alternated between sucking my knob like a vacuum cleaner and going down on me so hard that I grunted when he butted me with his head. Through it all, he kept right on playing with my ass. After fondling and probing every inch of my hard cheeks and sweaty crack, he zeroed in on my butt pucker. He prodded it gently at first, then more vigorously, persisting until my sphincter gaped and his finger slid in deep. I shifted my feet wider apart, and Arnie started playing tag with my prostate while he continued trying to suck my brains out through the end of my cock.

I took it till I was in danger of ripping the top off the cabinet, then reached out to him. "My turn," I growled, slipping my hands under his arms and hauling him forcibly to his feet. He stood up, took a swipe at the string of drool hanging from his chin, and grinned at me like a shy schoolboy. I felt something poke my thigh and looked down. There was nothing shy about what was thrusting up from between his legs. I knelt to get a better look.

Arnie had a terrific hard-on: long, straight, and thick, capped with a scarlet helmet and bound by a network of pale blue veins. I rubbed my lips along the hot stalk. It swelled and rose towards his belly. The head flared, and a quivering drop of crystal-clear fluid filled the gaping come hole. I licked it away, and Arnie's rod rose even higher.

I looked along the underside of his piece, down to his balls. They were doing pull-ups on their cords, fighting to climb up and hug his cock. I hooked a finger around them, pulled down, then popped them into my mouth. Arnie shivered like someone had stuck an ice cube up his ass. I felt his thigh muscles tense against my chest, and his fingers dug into my deltoids. I swirled my tongue around the plump globes, and my buddy moaned softly.

I played with his balls till he was practically dancing around in front of me, then spit them out and started working my way back up to his knob. It was a long trip, but worth the journey. I nibbled at the flexing shaft while lashing my tongue against the tender, nerve-laced flesh. By the time I was ready to cap his throbbing glans, it looked about ready to explode.

I leaned into him, letting the proud flesh part my lips. I felt the hot tip against the roof of my mouth, moving back, plugging my throat, sliding down it and cutting off my air. I pushed on, jamming more of him down my gullet till my forehead was pressed tight against his gut. I wrapped my arms around his waist, and began sucking him, pulling back to knob him, then pounding my face against his belly, plunging his cock down my throat like a sword swallower plying his trade.

"Stand up, man," he said, pulling my head away from his crotch. "Turn around." I faced the counter and leaned forward. I felt his breath ruffle the hairs as he tenderly kissed my ass. He stood and pressed against me, wrapping his arms around my chest. I felt his hard-on slide between my thighs and press up against my balls. I reached back and grabbed it. It oozed hot drool on my wrist as I massaged it. I pushed back, lined it up with my asshole, then let go and nodded slightly, my ear rubbing against his cheek. He gripped me tighter and began to push it home, going slow, easing into me sweet and gentle, like a longtime lover.

I felt his balls bump up against mine, then he began pulling back, drawing out till his knob was kissing my pucker again. I wiggled my ass, and he spiked me deep, his warm belly smacking against the small of my back. The fur around his navel tickled. I leaned against him, licked the curve of his jaw, slipped my hands into the back pockets of his coveralls, and fondled his bubble butt.

Arnie fucked like a man possessed, his cock plunging in and out of my clutching bowels. He was pawing frantically at my body, rubbing my belly and chest, fingering the ridges of my abs, tracing my lats from waist to armpit. When his hands slid down over the tops of my thighs, then up to my crotch, I lost it. He cupped my cock and balls in his callused hands, and I came all over them, spewing jism out through his laced fingers over the top of the counter, streaking the toaster in front of me. My asshole grabbed at his prong, and Arnie gave it up as well. His rhythm broke down into a series of stabbing thrusts, and he dumped his thick hot load in me while he whimpered softly in my ear.

"That was incredible, Arnie." We were leaning against the same counter we had just fucked against. I had my arm around his waist. His hand was planted on my bare butt. "I've secretly been hoping something like this might happen. Not that I ever expected it."

"Me too...I guess."

"Ever do it with a guy before?"

"Never did, Pete. Never even thought about it—until I met you." He was looking down at the floor, his face scarlet.

"I'm flattered, buddy. I really mean it." It was true—the thought that I was the first man he'd ever been with turned me on in a big way. I reached over and pinched his tit. "How'd you get so good, so fast?"

"I...uh...I rented a video and watched it to find out... you know, Pete." His voice had dropped to a whisper, like he was ashamed. I was touched.

"Were you surprised that watching guys getting it on got you turned on?" I nudged him in the ribs.

"Hell, I never even got hard," he admitted quietly. "It was just so I'd know what to do." I looked at him. He obviously wasn't kidding.

"How'd you get hard tonight?" I rubbed his belly, and his

pecker started to rise. "How come you're getting hard again?"

"Hell, Pete, you're the only guy who ever gave me a hard-on. I don't know why." I sank to my haunches and began lapping at the inside of his furry thigh. I puzzled for a moment over the unknown reasons behind my success, then put it aside. Some questions are better left unanswered—at least for the time being.